MW00979867

JOURNEY OF A
THOUSAND STEPS

MADONA SKAFF-KOREN

Renaissance

This is a work of fiction. Any similarity to any events, institutions, or persons, living or dead, is purely coincidental and unintentional.

JOURNEY OF A THOUSAND STEPS ©2015 by Madona Skaff-Koren. All rights reserved. No part of this book may be used or reproduced in any manner whatsoever without written permission except in the case of brief quotations in critical articles and reviews. For more information, contact Renaissance Press. First edition.

Cover art and design by Caroline Fréchette. Interior design by Caroline Fréchette. Edited by L.P. Vallée, Evelyn Cimesa, and Marjolaine Lafrenière. Model on cover photo Dana Fradkin.

Legal deposit, Library and Archives Canada, October 2015.

Paperback ISBN 978-1-987963-02-1
Ebook ISBN 978-1-987963-03-8

Renaissance Press
http://renaissancebookpress.com
info@renaissancebookpress.com

For David and your unwavering love and support when I needed it most

For Sarah, thank you for patiently waiting to tell me about your day while I finished "just one more scene"

CHAPTER ONE

Naya approached her nemesis with caution. This was where pain and exhaustion became unbearable. The place where she began to doubt herself, her ability and if she could continue.

She checked the pulse monitor on her wrist. In the target range. Glanced at her watch. A new personal best. Full of confidence, she pushed on.

And passed the 30K mark. Only twelve kilometres to go.

Easy route from here.

She'd run her first full marathon at eighteen and had immediately fallen in love with the sport. It wasn't about the race. She only ever competed against herself. It was about the unequalled joy she felt as the road challenged her physical limits. Then with a general pig-headedness, she'd always ignored those limits and continued to glide across the terrain to the finish line.

She called on that familiar stubbornness to maintain her steady pace.

The sun peeked from behind the high, scattered clouds as she left the New Edinburgh neighbourhood and turned onto Sussex Drive that tracked the Ottawa River. Her feet pounded in a comfortable rhythm. She came up to a water station with its long line of volunteers holding small paper cups in outstretched hands. Without slowing she grabbed a cup to pour on her head, then threw the empty cup off to the side. She poured another on the back of her neck. Drank a third.

At the beginning of the race when the starting pistol had gone off, Naya had fallen in step amidst other runners of equal calibre. As the kilometres fell away, a few runners had passed her, many had fallen behind. Only a twenty-something man wearing funny red shorts had remained with her. Sometimes he was ahead. Sometimes she was.

At twenty-nine, though in excellent shape, she accepted the fact that she wasn't a teenager with boundless energy anymore. It must be the sun beating down on her that had transformed her easy stride to one of slogging through knee-deep water. The cool breeze that wafted across the river refused to cool her. She never wore a hat while running, but now with the sun heating up her auburn hair she decided to consider one for the next race. Or maybe cut her hair very short. The strands were coming loose from the braid and falling in sweaty, distracting locks before her eyes. Also, next time she'd wear darker sunglasses. Unlike most people with light coloured eyes, her hazel eyes had never been sensitive to the sun. Until today.

The course now followed the Rideau Canal. As she passed the National Arts Centre across the water she envied the people on the outdoor patio and longed to rest in the shade with a tall glass of ice tea. *Concentrate!* Soon she passed her old alma mater, the University of Ottawa. The large eyes painted on the side of the biology building had always watched over her when she'd studied here. Even now they watched, encouraging her to keep going. Within moments the Queensway overpass came into view and she knew that the 40K marker was close. She'd cross over the Pretoria Bridge, then two kilometres to the finish.

A check of her watch reassured her that she'd definitely finish in under four hours. A quick glance over the shoulder confirmed that Red Shorts was out of sight. She could afford to slow to a walk briefly to re-energize.

But when she increased her pace again, the rhythmic footfalls that were as natural to her as walking eluded her. A little more than three kilometres to the finish line. For the first time, Naya noticed that several runners were zipping past. Then Red Shorts came up beside her, slowed long enough to acknowledge her with a look of concern, then sped up and faded into the distance.

She reached another line of volunteers, but this time she had to slow to be able to grab a cup. She threw the water on her face. Two more cups poured on the back of her neck. She barely held onto another to drink. As the moisture touched her lips, the sky darkened. She tilted her head to search for the storm clouds when a wave of vertigo, like a slap on the back of her head, knocked her down. She hit the pavement skinning her hands and knees. Water splashed up her nose with a burning sensation reminding her of the time she was learning to dive and hit the water wrong.

Sputtering, she fought to stand but hands held her down. Between short gasps, she told them she was okay. They weren't listening. She slapped their hands off of her legs. Barely three kilometres left. When the fog thinned she saw that no one was holding her down. Her heart thudded in panic as she discovered that only a single volunteer was dabbing her forehead with a wet towel. He spoke in a consoling voice, saying things like, "Don't worry. I've got you. You'll be okay. Just relax. It's over."

Over? What? The race? She wasn't giving up. She fought to sit. Had to stand. She had to reach that finish line. One last effort and the darkness swallowed her whole.

Naya felt a cool breeze on her face. Distant murmuring voices mingled with the buzzing in her ears.

An IV bag materialized above her head. She watched the silent drip, drip, drip. She needed to get someone to remove the line and discharge her from the First Aid tent so that she could get back to the course.

She heard soft footfalls and strained to turn her head. A nurse, dressed in a pastel blue uniform with tiny yellow ducks, floated into view. Damn! They'd moved her to a hospital. Robbed her of the chance to finish. Unless...

It wasn't her fault that she'd left the route. If she could get back now — maybe they'd let her rejoin. She only had three kilometres left! Sure, any hopes of beating her own record were gone, but at least she'd *have* a finish time. She'd always completed a marathon. No way was she going to let a little dehydration stop her now.

Naya demanded that the nurse release her. The garbled sounds that left her lips terrified her. The nurse turned from the IV bag to look down at her with eyes that were both cold and comforting.

"Well, my dear, you're finally awake," the nurse said, her voice sounding artificially gentle. "Do you remember what happened?"

Naya opened her mouth to answer. This time a croak assaulted her ears. Trembling with rising fear, she tried to nod and with great effort her head moved.

The nurse's eyes widened with shock for a quick second. The smile flickered, then reappeared looking strangely plastic. "I'd like you to squeeze my fingers. As hard as you can. Okay? Whenever you're ready."

Naya felt the nurse's clammy fingers slip into her hand. She squeezed but the nurse just repeated, "Whenever you're ready." After a moment the nurse pulled the sheet up to uncover Naya's feet. Those icy fingers made her gasp. "Tell me when you feel this. Blink your eyes."

Naya blinked as fast as she could hoping the nurse would release her cadaverous cold grip. She sighed with relief when the nurse replaced the sheet and leaned over her. Then the nurse spoke slowly, deliberately, like she was talking to a child with developmental issues.

"Just relax, Ms. Assad. I'll be back in a minute."

The nurse vanished from Naya's line of sight before she could stop her. She tried to wait for the nurse to return, to find out what paralysing drugs they'd given her. The drugs seemed to reach into her brain making the effort of forming a simple thought a monumental task. She closed her eyes and let the outside world trickle in.

Sensing someone nearby, Naya opened her eyes to see a man with a fatherly smile leaning over her. From his tone she knew he'd been trying to wake her for a while.

"Hi, Naya, I'm Dr. Montgomery." He patted her arm. "I know you're tired but try to stay with me, okay?"

She blinked once. He nodded and continued talking.

"You collapsed during the marathon."

She blinked once.

"Good, you remember. We thought it might be dehydration. It was very hot that day."

Blink.

"Good. I know you're having some trouble moving and talking. Like you've been drugged. But we haven't given you anything other than fluids." He tapped the IV bag. "We thought it could have been a stroke ... No, no, relax. It wasn't a stroke."

He left his hand on her shoulder. Its warmth quelled her growing fear as well as her impatience with his agonizingly slow explanation.

"We've already run several tests. They've all come back negative. I'm sending you for an MRI now. I don't believe the paralysis is permanent. There's been some improvement after three days..."

She blinked quickly, repeatedly, fighting to speak.

"Naya, it's all right. Breathe slowly."

Three days? No, it couldn't have been that long. She'd just left the race.

"Naya, I'm sorry, I know this is very upsetting. But I promise we'll find out what's wrong and I promise you, we'll do our best to fix it."

He beckoned to someone out of her line of vision then returned his attention to her. He patted her shoulder again and she forced herself to calm down.

"I'll see you when you get back," the doctor said. He vanished from view and a porter loomed over her head. He unlocked the wheels of the bed with a slight jerk, then pushed her through the cubicle curtains and out of ICU. She rolled in an uncannily smooth motion down the hall as ceiling tiles and fluorescent lights zipped by with dizzying speed. Finally, he parked her against a beige wall below a flickering light. He leaned over her with a smile, patted her shoulder.

"Just relax. Won't be long," he said and left.

For a long time no one came to tell her what was going on, or even to check if she was okay. She waited, enshrouded within her own body.

She was startled awake by a touch on her shoulder and startled again by the sight of a young woman with frizzy orange hair, heavy green eye makeup and three eyebrow rings. Great. In a hospital full of medical professionals she had to get stuck with a wannabe rock star.

"Ms. Assad, we'll be taking you into the MRI chamber now," the woman said. "We'll do all the work, so just relax."

The word of the day must be relax. She couldn't move. She couldn't speak. No one knew why. And they wanted her to relax?

Orange Hair pushed her through a thick metal door into a dimly lit room with a high ceiling. Out of nowhere, a male attendant appeared and helped transfer her onto a narrow table. She felt the edge under her hip and was sure she was slipping off the table. She tried to call out but only managed unintelligible noises.

"It's okay, I won't let you fall." Orange Hair came into view. She slipped a foam wedge under Naya's knees and instantly the unbalanced sensation left. Naya realized that it had been the edge of the cushion that she'd felt, not the edge of the table. The nurse secured straps across Naya's chest and waist, further making her feel stable and safe.

"Ms. Assad," Orange Hair said, "just to let you know that an MRI is painless, but very noisy, so I'll be putting some headphones with music on you. It'll help. I'll tell you each time I start a scan. You'll feel some vibrations at some of the lower frequencies. I noticed you're able to move your fingers, so I'm going to put a call button in your hand. Give it a try now. Good. If you feel sick or just can't take it anymore, push the button and I'll pull you out right away. The scan should last about 45 minutes. Over before you know it. Okay?"

Naya gave her a single, slow blink of gratitude and a tiny smile, regretting her earlier thoughts. What's a few facial piercings and orange hair between friends? She was the first person here to actually speak to her like she still had a working brain.

Through the headphones, Orange Hair said, "I'm going to move you into the chamber now."

Slowly, the table slid into the long narrow tube, her face a few inches away from the top. Light came in from outside. Good thing she wasn't claustrophobic. She slid past a thin blue line, then stopped. Cold air blew on the left side of her face, refreshing at first, until her cheek started to go numb.

Orange Hair announced, "I'm starting the first scan. It'll last ninety seconds. Just breathe normally."

Naya heard the distant sound of eight taps followed by eight louder taps of a different frequency. A few minutes after the first scan was over, the next one began. This one sounded like a series of electric guitar strums. Later, one series sounded like a jackhammer. Another consisted of a distant eight taps, followed by eight deep strums, so low in frequency that the whole chamber vibrated. Others made the fillings in her teeth tingle.

Cocooned in the chamber, with soft rock playing through the headphones, she allowed her eyelids to close.

Naya woke up in her hospital bed. Again, she watched the drip, drip of the IV bag for entertainment. This was certainly boring. Was this how she was going to spend her life, lying around watching dripping IV bags? She sighed and shifted her shoulders. They were incredibly stiff. She reached up with her right hand to rub her shoulder, eyes closing with relief as the knots gradually loosened. What she'd give for a full body massage from that really cute male nurse. She laughed aloud.

Her eyes snapped open at the sound. Laughter. And not that pathetic gurgling sound.

She stopped rubbing her shoulder and watched her right hand as she opened and closed her fingers. She lifted her head from the pillow and concentrated on the other hand. It moved too, but not the arm. Not yet. Wait. She was lifting her head! She laughed as tears filled her eyes.

Searching, she found the call button clipped on the top edge of her pillow. She strained to lift her right arm above her head and after three tries she snagged the cord with her fingertips. An extra yank and she had the call button in her hand. She pushed it and heard the duty nurse answer over the intercom, "Yes?"

"I..." Naya's voice cracked. She swallowed several times. Finally, she said, "I. Can. Move. Now."

CHAPTER TWO

Getting out of the front seat of the '98 Mustang felt like trying to climb uphill while lying down. Naya took a firm grip of Travis's hands and, after a lot of grunting and pulling, she stood on her own driveway. She gazed lovingly at her house with the bright sunlight glinting off the second floor windows and trim that matched the clear, blue sky. She could have stood for hours admiring her home that she hadn't seen in three months. But the muggy July day was draining the last of her strength. As soon as Travis pulled out the walker from the back seat, she pushed it at a sloth's top speed towards her front door. In part to get out of the brutal heat but mostly to get inside before any of her neighbours saw her.

She rolled it onto the cobblestone path and cursed when the wheels caught on the edge, then again as she tripped on every second stone. First thing she planned to do — replace the intricate pattern of reddish brown and beige stones with smooth, practical cement. She paused to catch her breath and watched Travis open the trunk. His dark hair and eyes went perfectly with the brooding expression he wore when concentrating. Which was most of the time. But when he smiled, his face became carefree.

They'd met at the University of Ottawa while they were working on their Masters degrees; hers in software engineering; his in physics. They graduated and both went to work at a mega-corporation. After barely a year they realized that life as anonymous bricks in a corporate building wasn't for them. Over a beer (more like several) their own company was born. She'd insisted that they'd get more business with the name, *Ethical Hackers R Us*, but had agreed to the more mature sounding *Assad and Bloom, Security Analysts*. Despite the conventional name their company grew quickly.

Travis began to empty gift bags from the trunk looking a lot like that joke where an endless string of clowns get out of a tiny car. Why hadn't she left the gifts behind? How many potted plants, stuffed animals, magazines and general knick-knacks did she need? When word had spread through the running community that she was in the hospital, many people, some she didn't even know, had dropped by. Through each awkward visit she'd kept to the cover story that she was recovering from the back injury she'd suffered when she'd fallen during the race. She couldn't bear the idea of everyone knowing what her life had become when she had enough trouble accepting it herself. The last thing she needed now was pity.

Only Travis and their two employees knew the truth.

After the MRI scan at the hospital, her mobility had continued to improve. By the end of the day she'd been able to move both arms. Though her legs were taking longer to recover, she'd planned for her next marathon. Until Dr. Montgomery had visited her. No fatherly smile or comforting touch could soften the blow of his diagnosis.

Multiple Sclerosis.

She didn't know anything about the disease other than there was no cure. She did give the occasional donation to help those unfortunate people trapped in wheelchairs.

She glared at the walker and plodded on towards the two steps leading up to the front door without falling. Wow, what an accomplishment.

Maybe Travis could help her? A quick check over her shoulder found him now arranging the gift bags on the ground by size, for some reason known only to him. Nope, she was on her own. She took a deep breath, bent her knees slightly like a weight lifter ready for the 'clean and jerk' and heaved her walker onto the landing. She held the brakes, stepped up, unlocked the front door, then lifted the walker in ahead of her. She clutched both sides of the door frame and pulled herself inside.

Lightheaded, she staggered to the bottom of the spiral staircase where she sat with an undignified thump on the second step. It felt as if she'd just finished a marathon but without the benefit of an endorphin high.

Eyes closed, she sucked in several deep breaths and revelled in the ability to rest. Eventually she looked up at the high ceiling and the sweeping staircase. The open, bright entrance had been a major reason she'd bought this house.

Off to the right were three doors. One led to the laundry room, one to the bathroom and the last to the garage where her BMW sat, neglected.

After years of barely affording used cars, she could finally splurge on the convertible. The first time she'd driven it with the roof down and felt the warmth of the sun on her shoulders almost competed with the sense of freedom she had when running.

She missed that feeling.

She frowned at the walker.

Travis's comical appearance at the door interrupted her sullen mood. Only he could carry everything in one trip. He wore the large backpack — her luggage — on his back. He'd strung the gift bags all along his left arm by size, with the larger ones at his wrist, smaller ones at his shoulder. He hugged three potted plants in the crook of his arm. Two large fruit baskets dangled from his other arm. His teeth clenched a plastic bag with two more plants.

"But you didn't arrange the gift bags by colour," she said, with a laugh.

"Hmm," he muttered. He went to the small dining area in the foyer. There was a mahogany cabinet that displayed the china dishes that she'd bought when she'd first moved in. She watched, amazed at how he managed to put things down. The booty hugged in his arms was placed on the mahogany table. Then the gift bags slid off landing in a neat row next to the pots. Impressive.

He took the bag from his teeth and said, "That's funny." He shut the front door and added, "How about moving somewhere more comfortable?"

She accepted his hand, grasped the railing with the other and stood, feeling so short next to his six foot lean frame. Usually her eyes came to shoulder level. She pushed the walker from the entrance, to the hallway under the stairs which led to the family room. She reached the sofa exhausted and flopped onto it like a drunk. When she straightened up Travis was offering her a glass of water filled with tinkling ice cubes. How slow had she been walking? A small sip and she felt better.

"We set up the sofa bed for you," Travis said, as he took the backpack off and placed it on the floor near her.

"Oh, I didn't even see it," she said. She put the glass on the coffee table beside the sofa. "Thanks. Wait, did you say, 'we'?"

"Yeah, I came by yesterday with Mackay and Taylor," he said. "We opened up the sofa bed and moved some of your clothes down here." He gestured at the suitcase in the corner.

"You brought my clothes down?" She asked, embarrassed at the thought of him rummaging through her underwear drawer.

"Don't worry, I assigned your clothes to Taylor. Though our goth princess did say you own way too much pink." He laughed. "Mackay and I moved some of your computer stuff down to the kitchen table."

"So you're finally going to give me some work," she said with a pleased chuckle.

"All I ask is that you don't push yourself."

"I promise."

"We also bought a few groceries and tossed anything with the potential to start evolving."

"Thanks. Again." She stifled a yawn.

"I'll get going to let you settle in."

"Travis..."

"What're friends for?" He stood and bent to give her a light kiss on the forehead. "Good to see you back home. I'll lock up on my way out."

She heard him move bags around in the foyer, guessing he was taking the plants out of the bags. Then he was gone.

She stretched her hand and caught the cushion with her fingernails, dragged it close and lay down.

As she drifted off to sleep, she remembered the night nurse at the rehab centre who only ever used her 'outside voice' and thought about how much she wouldn't be missed.

❖ ❖ ❖

Once Naya got over the initial shock of her diagnosis, she'd expected to be up and walking around in no time. Unfortunately, her progress was excruciatingly slow. She had so many questions about Multiple Sclerosis. How did she get it? What treatments were there? She used the hospital's limited internet to find out if a wheelchair was all she could expect in her future.

Even though MS had been discovered in the mid-nineteenth century, scientists were still debating its cause. Most believed it was an autoimmune disease, possibly caused by a virus. Some found genetic markers and blamed heredity. And for a little extra excitement, an old but still controversial theory resurfaced, blaming the old iron-build-up-in-the-brain cause. Even vitamin D deficiency was a possible culprit. Considering that Canada, with its long winters had one of the highest rates, that last theory made some sense to her.

Whatever the cause, it usually struck young adults in the most active time of their lives between fifteen to forty years old, affecting three times as many women as men. The protective layer of the nerve cells periodically become inflamed, leaving behind scars, or sclerosis, which disrupt communication between nerves and muscles. The location of the lesions produce different symptoms making MS an unpredictable disease. She stared at the screen as her research found one fact that she already knew and that all doctors agreed on.

There was no cure.

❖ ❖ ❖

Naya woke in her family room as the sun's red glow came across her face. She'd forgotten what a good night's sleep felt like. Still tired from yesterday's homecoming, she remained in the sofa bed and reached for the TV remote. Catching up on the world's current events should help the transition from the rehabilitation centre back to the real world.

But after not listening for the second time to the update on new hostilities in the Middle East, she shut off the TV. She dressed in jeans and a green t-shirt, made up the bed, put her laptop on the walker and headed to the kitchen. Her world also included cyberspace. She needed to get back to work and immerse herself in writing code and watching programs be born so that she could feel normal again.

Travis had brought down her laptop and printer as well as a variety of office supplies and put them on the kitchen table. She had all the basic tools, but missed the luxury of her two, twenty-four inch monitors still upstairs. She debated asking someone to bring one down for her, but it would take up too much space. Part of her return to a normal routine also meant eating at the kitchen table.

She made toast and marmalade, then sat down to enjoy the happy gurgle and drip of the coffee maker.

She poured a large mug of coffee, tasted it and closed her eyes in near ecstasy. Strong and black. The only way to drink it. At the hospital, once she'd graduated to solid food, she'd horrified the other patients by heartily eating anything the cafeteria served. But once her taste buds had regained their sensibility, she recognized that the only spice used to season the overcooked, nauseatingly predictable menu was salt. Though she could never confirm her suspicions, she was positive the coffee was made from twice filtered grains.

Scanning the emails, she found that practically all were from people asking how she was doing. Even a message from Red Shorts from the race whose real name was Ed. As she read through them she realized that they were all casual acquaintances; from the gym, running mates, or other computer people. No one close enough she could confide in. Was she really that friendless? No, Travis was a good and trusted friend. And, in their own odd way, so were their two employees. Of course she had one more addition to that list.

One of her own steadfast rules had always been to avoid all those time-wasting social networks. Her only contact to Facebook was through Travis who used it to promote their company. But after enduring a week of monotony at the Ottawa Hospital Rehabilitation Centre, she'd succumbed and got a personal account.

It was amazing how many people from her running world she found there. The last thing she wanted to do was to answer a bunch of dumb questions about her injuries, or to even discuss running. And when they discovered her presence on-line that's all she'd hear about.

She modified her profile removing all mention of marathons or any sport, but left in the computer info. This time when she read the list of "people you may know" they were mostly computer types, many of whom she did know. One unexpected name stood out from the crowd. Valerie Peters.

Could it be the same Valerie? Checking out the profile photo, there was no doubt. It was a picture of the Muppet, Cookie Monster sitting at a computer.

'Bestest' friends since Junior Kindergarten, they'd lost touch in high school when Naya's parents moved out of town. She had expected that her friend would follow a different path into adulthood, but after reading her profile, she discovered that their lives had developed in parallel. At twenty-nine, both were still single, basically loners and worked in computers.

When they'd spoken on the phone at the rehab centre, Naya had been amazed at how familiar her friend's voice sounded. They'd chatted for an hour, reliving their childhood adventures. Naya had carefully steered the conversation away from anything current, finding any talk of running or marathons to be too painful. Since Valerie worked from home, she'd left it up to Naya to call when she had time, at any time during day or evening. As much as she loved rekindling their friendship, Naya didn't want to intrude too much, so hadn't called each night. But when she didn't, Valerie would text to remind her to phone.

Without their daily chats, Naya wasn't sure that she could have made it through the long three months of therapy without going insane.

Now, relaxing in her own kitchen, drinking her own coffee, she sent Valerie an email stating simply, "I'm home!" After a few minutes of plodding through the rest of the messages, Valerie replied. Naya enthusiastically set up her computer to talk to her through Skype.

Her cheeks tingled with excitement when Valerie's face appeared on the screen, seeing her for the first time in fifteen years. Her face had transformed from round chubby teen cheeks to lean adulthood. She had the same short, unruly blond curls and memorable dark eyes that still twinkled with youthful mischievousness.

"You look great," Valerie said, her voice clear through the speakers.

"What's great is being able to actually *see* you," Naya said. "When I saw your Facebook photo, I laughed so hard. Good old Cookie Monster. I can't believe you still have him after all these years." An eighteen inch high, stuffed, blue Cookie Monster sat on the bookshelf behind Valerie. Naya's gift for her eleventh birthday.

"How could I get rid of my first true love?" Valerie laughed, sounding exactly like that little girl from long ago. She broke off. "Just a sec, I just got an urgent email message from work." She rolled her eyes and looked back at Naya. "It's just Victor from accounting. He's so needy, always emailing with the stupidest questions."

"Maybe he likes you."

"Oh, please don't even joke about that. Besides he's got a crush on one of my co-workers. Always bringing her coffee, donuts. Never mind him. How about you, do you still have Grover?"

"Of course." Her heart sank as she remembered her abandoned Muppet. "He's upstairs in my office." She wanted to add, out of reach. Brightening again, she said, "Now that I'm home, how about coming over and we can really talk."

"Oh," Valerie began. Her smile flickered and faded. "I'd love to, but I'm really swamped right now. You know how it is. Deadlines."

"Oh, I *know* deadlines. What're you working on?"

"Nothing really exciting just some GUI code for a new gaming system how about you what're you doing these days?"

Naya didn't miss the run-on sentence spoken without a breath. A sure sign that her friend was lying. Evading, might be more accurate.

She suspected the work was more interesting than coding a GUI — a graphical user interface for some game. It was probably some top-secret project for a high tech company. Maybe even military work. A couple of years ago, Naya's company had taken on a military contract to update a public communications satellite. Despite the fact that the satellite had no military strategic links, Naya and her group still had to go through security screenings and sign non-disclosure agreements. And they all gave similar non-answers when someone asked what they were working on.

"Travis is supposed to email something," Naya said. "It'll probably just be some make-work stuff to keep me quiet. I'll eventually get him to give me a portion of this huge cell phone project we just got."

"I doubt it'll be that hard to talk him into *anything* you want."

"What's that little smirk supposed to mean?"

"Nothing..."

❖ ❖ ❖

The next three weeks passed quickly. Travis had finally understood that she needed real work to make her feel useful and had given her a tiny part of the cell phone contract: creating an app for music video downloads. Naya had settled into a routine of work, brief naps and exercise. She'd even managed to read a couple of mysteries.

Her only regret had been not camping during the long August weekend two weeks ago, something she'd done since she was twelve. Despite the disappointment of breaking with tradition, Naya embraced this new, comfortable lifestyle. Her favourite part was the daily talk with Valerie.

Not long after they'd reconnected at the rehab centre, she found herself telling Valerie everything about her diagnosis, how she'd felt that she'd lost so much and several other self-pitying lines. It had been such a relief to have one less person to lie to.

"I really wish..." Naya had started to say, only to have Valerie interrupt.

"Well, you do all the wishing that you want. Just make sure you back it up with a little patience and a lot of hard work. Got it?"

As kids they'd taken turns using the 'stop belly aching and get to work' attitude. Seemed like it still worked. However, these days, Valerie was doing all the work.

When the phone rang, Naya rushed to answer it, expecting it to be her friend. She was deflated to hear the receptionist's voice from the neurologist's office calling to remind her of an appointment next Monday.

"Uh, I'm sorry, I should have called you," Naya stuttered trying to come up with an excuse. Finally she simply said, "I have a prior commitment that I forgot about."

"Ms. Assad," the secretary said, her voice straining with forced patience, "This is the fourth time in three weeks that you've rescheduled your appointment. Perhaps you can suggest a time?"

"Oh, uh, okay," Naya said, not expecting that. "How about next month? Towards the end?'

"Fine." She paused. "You're booked in for September 23rd." She paused again then added, "Dr. Montgomery really would like to see you and check on your progress. Please let me know if you need to change the date again."

"Of course." Naya hung up. She just didn't feel ready to have her progress checked. It felt like she should be cramming for a test, but didn't know what to study. At least now she had a month to come up with a new excuse.

The truth was she didn't want to go outside in case someone she knew saw her. She hadn't even gone out into her backyard despite the beautiful, tempting weather. She couldn't risk being seen by one of her backyard neighbours who would assail her with prying questions. She didn't mind before, but now...

By the time she had her daily video call with Valerie, any trace of guilt she felt over constantly changing her appointment was gone.

"You're looking like your old self today," Valerie said, as she adjusted the camera on her computer.

"I feel like my old self. Do you realize that I've been home for three weeks? We need to celebrate. How about you come over."

"I, uh, I'm sorry, but it's still pretty hectic."

"It's Friday night. You've been working non-stop since we reconnected. I know you have a thing about hospitals and didn't visit there. But I'm home now."

"Uh, I have a deadline that's uh close."

"What's really going on?" Naya asked. She felt hurt and betrayed. "If you don't want to be friends..."

"It's not that!" Valerie snapped. She covered her face with her hands. When she removed her hands, her eyes were moist. "I haven't been completely honest with you." The tensing of chin, the darting eyes, made the inner debate very obvious. After a moment, she spoke.

"Sure I have a great job. I make a phenomenal salary. I have everything I could possibly want. Except one." Exhaling slowly, she added, "I haven't been able to leave this apartment in four years. I'm agoraphobic."

"What?" Naya sat back in her chair. "Why didn't you just tell me instead of making so many excuses?"

"Why haven't you told people that you have MS? Because you're worried they'll think less of you?"

"You're right." Naya nodded. It was ironic that they met again when both were in prisons of their own making. Naya hadn't gone out in case she met someone she knew. She didn't want to look like all those old people with walkers at the mall that she'd seen but pretended weren't there. She wanted to ask Valerie what had happened to make her afraid of the world. A world that had once held endless adventures. She knew from painful personal experience that Valerie would tell her in her own time.

If only they'd met when Naya was still healthy. Then she could have gone over and maybe helped her get outside — if only to the street. To hell with the if only's. Even at an early age, they'd done their best to overcome a bad situation. The first time happened when their grade two teacher had left to have a baby and Mr. Goat-guy (what *was* his real name?) took over. Everyone adjusted to his endless list of pointless rules, until he'd insisted that the class line up by height. That only called attention to the fact that Nelly Swanson was taller than most fourth graders. It didn't take long before Nelly became quieter and more withdrawn than before.

Naya and Valerie persuaded the entire second grade to overcome their fear of Mr. Goat-guy and rebel against his latest rule. They lined up randomly, making their teacher stomp over to his desk. From there he delivered a ten minute tirade on how he was going to enter each and every name into his infamous book. When he opened the desk drawer to retrieve "The Book," three frogs jumped out at him. He would have moved out of the way, but by this time the Super Glue had set and his shoes weren't going anywhere. Crimson faced, he'd tripped out of his shoes and screeched into the class phone for the principal. A new substitute teacher arrived the next day. Naya's lips curved up at the memory.

"Are you laughing at me?" Valerie asked, looking like she was about to sever the connection.

"No, I was just wondering if you have wine at your place?"

"Uh, yes?"

"So, let's each fill a glass and toast my three week anniversary," Naya said, glad to see the look of gratitude on her friend's face.

❖ ❖ ❖

Saturday morning, Naya's phone rang at 7:30. She rolled over to the edge of the sofa bed to answer and mumbled "Hello?"

"Remember when we were in grade seven and all the girls banded together to stop the big kids from picking on the smaller kids?" Valerie asked.

"Sure," Naya said coming fully awake. Her friend's trips down memory lane usually started abruptly as though she was continuing a conversation that had started in her head.

"We cornered the bullies in the school yard. Then Marcus took a swing at you — I'm sure he was just trying to scare you — but you blocked his punch and kicked him."

"Honestly," Naya said, with a sleepy laugh, "I really was aiming for his stomach. It's not my fault he jumped up at the last second."

"Man, that high-pitched screech was annoying," Valerie said. "But they did back off."

"Good thing they didn't call our bluff," Naya added.

"It's a shame that we live in the same city, forty minutes apart and we haven't seen each other in fifteen years."

"We see each other," she said through a yawn.

"On a computer screen. Not good enough. So," Valerie paused. Naya could hear her take a deep breath and let it out slowly. "Is your invitation to visit still open?"

"Yes, of course!" She sat up fully awake. "Are you sure?"

"I think it's time, don't you? Be there at lunch."

Naya got dressed, ate breakfast then inspected the house. She used to be a bit of a neat freak and was disappointed to see that she'd let the place go. She'd even ignored the empty gift bags on the dining room table. She tidied up, taking frequent breaks, then sat on the sofa to rest and wait for her best friend's arrival.

Unable to stare at the clock anymore as it crept through each minute, she turned on the TV and flipped through channels until she got to the CBC news network. She vaguely listened to a report of a gas station robbery in the south end of the city, but the next story caught her attention.

"A thirty-nine year old man fell to his death from the fifteenth floor of a downtown hotel early this morning. Preliminary reports say that Devlin Craig had been drinking, but the police report that his blood alcohol level was so high that they have listed the death as suspicious. A police spokesman..."

Naya clicked the TV off shaking her head at some poor schmuck who didn't know when to stop partying had a nasty end to his vacation. Maybe she'd try reading instead.

Naya was startled awake by the phone. Heart racing, she reached for it and saw the time read 6:27 pm. There was quiet sobbing on the other end.

"Valerie?" she asked.

"I'm so sorry," Valerie cried. "It took me all day — I was shaking and sweating and I had this constant dread that something bad was going to happen — but I got into the elevator. When the doors opened on the ground floor, every sound was excruciatingly magnified and I thought my head was going to explode. I just couldn't get out. I really tried."

"Look, I'm not a psychologist and honestly I don't mean to pry," Naya began, wishing they were on Skype so that she could see her. "But what if you tell me what happened. What changed you. You were always outgoing, never leaving a rock unclimbed." Only silence answered. She quickly added, "I'm sorry. I just thought talking about it might help."

"It's all right." Valerie exhaled a long, heavy breath. After a few more seconds she began to speak, her voice small as though afraid of the waking memories.

"I was engaged to the greatest man I'd ever known — for such an awfully short time." She cleared her throat. She was silent for so long that Naya wasn't sure she'd be able to continue. But she did.

"We'd been hiking all morning and reached a large lake by noon where we stopped for lunch. Even after five years, the image is still vivid. I remember looking up at the sky, blue and clear, imagining that I could see into space itself. At that moment he took my hand and slipped a ring onto my finger.

"We spent the rest of the day just holding hands and looking at the water. The lake was so large you could barely see the other shore." Her voice sounded like she was smiling. "I wanted to stay there forever." She paused. When she did continue, her voice was flat and mechanical.

"We were ten minutes from our home when a drunk driver ran a red light and t-boned us in the middle on the intersection. He hit the passenger side." Her voice faltered. "I was driving. I watched him close his eyes for the last time."

"I'm sorry," Naya said wiping tears away.

"Life went on only because it had to. Then on the anniversary of his death I narrowly missed being hit by someone running a red light. After that, it became harder and harder to get into my car. One day I couldn't even put the key in the ignition. I managed to overcome my fears enough to push away the intense feeling of foreboding and take a cab to work. The next day I tried the cab again but this time I had such a severe panic attack that the cabbie had to call 911. My world shrank fast after that. I sold our house and moved into the apartment. That was four years ago."

"Oh, Valerie, I'm so sorry."

"You don't have anything to apologize for." She sniffed loudly, her voice determined. "I'll be there tomorrow, really." And she hung up before Naya could say anything else.

Sunday went pretty well the way Saturday had gone. Even the phone call in the early evening.

"Valerie, please don't cry," Naya begged. She couldn't bear to hear the pain in her friend's voice. "Skype is perfect for people like us. We can see each other and talk. You don't have to come."

"No! I said I'd come and I will!" She took a slow, deep breath and added, her voice sounding determined. "I'll call a friend."

"No, wait. Valerie, I'm being selfish. Please, don't try anymore."

"Alice will help get me there. Besides, she won't mind being late for work. It'll be a break from love sick Victor from accounting. Tomorrow. Two o'clock. I'll be there, I promise. Can't talk anymore. Need to go throw up."

Naya felt guilty at putting her friend through this emotional turmoil, wishing that she could go over instead. At the same time she felt happy about being the one to provide the incentive for Valerie to finally face her fears. Naya would congratulate her when she arrived. Or support the effort over the phone.

Unable to sleep in on Monday, Naya woke early and made sure the house was tidy. Two days of getting ready for her guest meant there was little left to clean. After a quick lunch she relaxed on the sofa to wait for her friend and not watch the time crawl by.

By 2:30, unable to sit still anymore, she dusted, watered the plants, moved knick-knacks around. She tried reading. Even lay down for a nap, though her eyes refused to close.

Her eyes opened at 5:42.

"Damn it, Valerie," she muttered. Immediately a wave of guilt slapped her. She couldn't imagine how hard it was to leave a place you'd been trapped in for years. She was sure that once Valerie got into her friend's car she'd be okay.

It was just taking her three hours and forty-two minutes to reach the car.

The doorbell rang at 6:10. Using the sofa, walls, then dining room table for balance, she rushed to answer. She thought she might yank the door off its hinges when she opened it.

"Valerie, you made it!" she exclaimed. Then her wide smile faded. She'd forgotten that Taylor and Mackay were bringing groceries. Deflated, she said, "Come in."

"We coming at a bad time?" Mackay asked, hesitating.

"Mac, she told us to come in," Taylor snapped. She elbowed him out of the way and entered, carrying a green plastic grocery bin. She was in her early twenties. This week, her shoulder length, jet black hair sported a purple stripe which radiated from her left temple. It softened the severity of her pale makeup and heavy black eyeliner that tried but failed to subdue her aquamarine eyes. She wore the usual black jeans shorts, black leggings and black high-tops.

"Come in, please," Naya forced a smile. "I was doing some work and I guess I was distracted."

"Working on anything interesting?" Mackay asked, balancing the grocery bin under his arm as he locked the door behind him. Sandy-haired and stocky, he'd always reminded her of a hobbit. Also in his early twenties, he wore jeans and one of his usual t-shirts with a scientific slogan. This one started out with "And God said.." followed by several formulae, ending with, "...and then there was light." She smiled at the joke only physicists would get. Annoyingly conceited, he believed he was smarter than most people. Ironically, he was.

"Not too interesting." She followed them into the kitchen. "I finished the app program two days ago. I could really use some more work."

"Travis wants to make sure you don't overdo it too soon," Mackay said as he put the bin on the counter next to the other. "You want help putting the stuff away?"

"No, thanks, I can manage," Naya said. "Would you like some coffee?"

"We should go," Taylor said.

"Sure, I'm always in the mood for coffee," he said and eagerly plopped himself in front of her computer to check out the open file. As usual it never occurred to him to ask first.

Taylor slumped in the chair across from him as Naya brought three mugs and joined them at the table.

"And thank you again for doing the grocery shopping for me," Naya said.

"Travis said we need to be helpful," Mackay said as he leaned forward to study the computer screen.

Great, Naya thought, it wasn't bad enough she was upset about not being able to do the simple things people took for granted, now she had to feel guilty about imposing on others.

"I like what you've done with your hair," she said to Taylor, in an attempt to change her mood.

"Yeah, it's for my grandmother. Here too." Taylor wiggled the purple nails of her right hand. The nails on her left hand were still black. "When I went to visit her at the Home earlier this week, she thought I was a TV show and kept calling the nurse to come adjust the colour."

"You mean, once you added the purple, she recognized you?"

"Yeah, now that I look like a rainbow," she said, staring at her nails.

"That's a nice thing for you to do," Naya said. Taylor had sworn to avoid any colour until the human race stopped damaging the environment.

"Yeah, well." She shrugged. "She's my grandmother."

Taylor was a genius when it came to building any kind of hardware with a soldering iron and a few microchips. She knew the specs of practically every type of technology invented, top secret and otherwise. But she had little time for people, not even her family, with the exception of her grandmother. She tolerated Naya and the others, but she suspected that was only because they worked together.

Naya remembered the few times that they'd been to Taylor's home, a narrow three-story duplex in a poor area of town off of Rideau Street. The backyard had been paved over, but Taylor slowly chipped away at it, planting wild flowers where she exposed the land. With her tendency to leave the back door open, cats freely wandered in and out. Some were hers, some were strays and some were neighbourhood moochers. Naya had always wondered why Taylor didn't move to a better neighbourhood. She could certainly afford it. The best theory was that she couldn't leave the cats and she had to finish rescuing nature from under its asphalt blanket.

Taylor took her attention from her nails and studied Naya for a moment. "You look good. Healthy."

"Thanks," Naya said, "I feel pretty good."

"Yeah, so, what are you worried about?"

Naya gaped at her for a moment. She prided herself on having a great poker face, it was unsettling to be easily read.

"It's just that, well," Naya said, "I have this friend I haven't seen for a while. She was supposed to come over this afternoon."

"Maybe something came up?"

"She's already tried twice before to get here. She's always phoned to apologize for not making it. Except for today."

"What do you mean — tried?"

"She's agoraphobic." Naya said and clamped her hand over her mouth. How could she blurt it out like that?

"You feel guilty 'cause you didn't go to visit her instead of making her come here. And you think something's happened to her."

A pretty accurate analysis from someone who normally avoided contact with people. Naya played with her sleeve then said, "I was thinking about calling the police."

"Yeah, but I don't know if they'll do anything unless the person's been missing a while," Taylor said. "Unless there's a medical reason. Agoraphobia counts."

Naya glanced at the wall phone.

"Yeah, well, we'll get out of here so you can call. Mac, let's go. Now!"

Mackay looked up from the computer and only now Naya realized that he'd been typing. He stared at them blankly for a second, then hit a few more keys and stood saying, "I tweaked it a bit for you."

"Mac, you didn't," Naya said.

"You're welcome." He angled the computer for Naya to see. She shook her head at all the changes he'd made, glad she'd backed up the original. She repeated her silent mantra, "He means no harm."

"We'll lock up," Taylor said, grabbed Mackay's shoulder to pull him with her.

Alone in the silence, Naya first phoned Valerie, leaving a message asking her to call. Naya doubted that she'd be too embarrassed to

22

answer. Something had to be wrong. What if she was stuck in some alley, all alone? Or had panicked in the car and caused an accident. There were some pretty dark, isolated areas along the route here where a car that had crashed off the road wouldn't easily be seen.

She called 911.

The call started out fine. The male operator suggested that she try phoning her friends, relatives and check the places that she frequents, first, and then call back. Oh, she's agoraphobic, that's different.

"And, you said she had a friend that was helping her get out of the apartment?" he said. She imagined him taking notes, getting ready to call out the troops. "And, what's their name?"

"Alice."

"And her last name?"

"Oh, uh, I don't know. She just said Alice would help."

"And, have you called any other friends?"

"Umm, well, you see, I don't know any of her friends."

"You don't?" The sympathetic tone switched instantly to interrogation mode. "Didn't you say you've been friends since grade school?"

"Uh, we lost touch in high school."

"When *was* the last time you saw her?"

"Just through Skype." When she heard him sigh, she realized her mistake. She really had to work on honesty not being her first response.

"That's a computer thing isn't it?" His voice took on a dismissive tone. "When was the last time you did see her *in person?*"

"Uh," she really didn't want to answer, but didn't dare lie. She practically whispered, "Fifteen years."

She swore she could hear him roll his eyes. "Ma'am, fifteen years is a long time. I'm sure she's gone off with her other friends. The ones she actually sees. In person."

"But something could be wrong. She's agoraphobic, remember?" She heard the whine in her voice too late to stop it. "Couldn't you please check on her?"

"I'll send a car to check her place. I'm sure she'll call you in a few days when she gets back."

She didn't want to say that he hung up on her, but damn it, that's what it felt like.

He *was* right though. She knew nothing about Valerie's life now. Their conversations revolved around the old days or tech talk. They rarely talked about their present lives, as though there was nothing of value to discuss.

After three weeks at home, other than work, what had Naya done that was worthy of a conversation? She'd refused to go out, even to her own backyard, meaning no adventures to report. She was hardly going to reminisce about races gone by. She had no excuse for not learning more about Valerie's life. Some 'bestest' friend she was.

Talk about selfish. And lazy. It wasn't that hard to take the elevator up to Valerie's apartment. Naya's heart broke at the thought of how her friend had begged for forgiveness. Apologizing for having an illness that had imprisoned her for years. What was Naya's excuse? She scowled at the walker in the corner. A little embarrassment never killed anyone.

She phoned for a cab.

CHAPTER THREE

At 7:05 pm, Naya leaned on her walker in front of Valerie's condominium building. The modern building nestled among an eclectic collection of shops and cafes in the Glebe. People dotted the streets, enjoying the warm evening. She could see several people in the cafes and restaurants enjoying conversation, food and wine. Naya had always preferred living in the suburbs, but looking around she reconsidered. After she found Valerie, she might check if there were any units available. It could be fun living in the middle of the action.

From the covered doorway, she called Valerie's unit. No answer. She pushed a few other buttons to ask if one of the neighbours had seen her and was a little dismayed to get buzzed in with no questions asked. Maybe she'd choose a building with better security.

Very spacious lobby, she thought as she headed to the elevators. About to push the up button, she stopped and frowned at the 'OUT OF ORDER' sign on the single elevator. A few months ago she wouldn't have thought twice about simply jogging up the stairs. Now, her life was filled with obstacles. No way could she make it up four flights to Valerie's condo. With an angry grunt she turned her walker around to go home.

As kids, she and Valerie had always been there for each other. Now, as adults that hadn't changed. Without Valerie's encouragement Naya doubted that she would have completed her rehabilitation.

Half way through the treatment a stinging memory came to mind.

"How was your physiotherapy session today?" Valerie asked on the phone.

"Remember I told you I couldn't lift the outer edge of my left foot? This morning I actually lifted it slightly off the floor. Not much, but..."

"It's a great start!" Valerie said, her excitement transmitting through the phone. "Guess those exercises weren't so lame, after all. Aren't you glad you stuck with them?"

"Thanks to all your nagging," Naya said, laughing. "I can't wait to show off to the doctor this afternoon."

That afternoon, Naya waited in the doctor's office, feeling happy and optimistic for the first time since arriving. Within minutes Dr.

Samantha Gregory stormed into the exam room. She sat at her desk with a loud huff, then slapped open the file to read it, not once looking at her.

Naya fidgeted in her chair for a moment then decided to break the awkward silence. She smiled and said, "The physiotherapist gave me some exercises and I wanted to show you how I can move my foot…"

"That's just a waste of time!" The doctor snapped, still not looking her in the face. Gesturing up and down at Naya's leg as though it was insignificant, she added, "It's like flogging a dead horse. The nerve is dead! No amount of exercise is going to change that."

Naya stared at the doctor. Was she wasting her time? Was the physiotherapist?

"Where's your wheelchair? A walker isn't safe!" the doctor demanded.

Taken aback, Naya just stared at her. Didn't she know that Naya had graduated out of the wheelchair two weeks ago? The appointment really went downhill with the doctor asking questions and Naya giving one word answers through clenched teeth. She didn't trust herself to say more.

Naya left the office furious. No way was she putting up with this kind of abuse. She was already half packed ready to leave when Valerie phoned to see how the appointment had gone.

As usual, Valerie put things into perspective.

"Continue with your exercises. When your strength improves find that doctor and kick her butt with the outer edge of your left foot."

They hadn't stopped laughing until their ribs ached.

And Naya had unpacked.

She wouldn't be walking now without Valerie's morale boosting talks. Naya went into the stairwell to park her walker in the corner. She took out the folding cane from her backpack and paused at the bottom of the stairs looking up.

What made her think she could make it up four flights here when she couldn't get up one flight at home? She couldn't answer because she'd never tried. She'd even had a portable shower installed in the laundry room, which removed a major incentive to climb her stairs.

When Naya had first started running, she couldn't make it once around the block. She'd refused to give up, worked hard and crossed all those finish lines.

One step at a time, just like once around the block.

She started to climb.

After five minutes Naya stopped to rest and sip some water. She'd climbed one flight, which meant it would take fifteen minutes to get to the fourth floor. She resumed the slow journey upwards. But instead of the estimated fifteen minutes, it took her forty. Prickly sweat ran down her back and dripped into her eyes. The salty taste brought back wonderful memories of races. She called on them to help her find the strength to reach the hall.

With her legs growing heavier, she limped towards the finish line. She reached apartment 4C wheezing, her vision blurring. She managed a feeble knock that no one could have heard. Painfully, she lifted her cane and gave two hard bangs with its handle.

No answer.

She tried the door and was surprised to find it unlocked. She opened it and called out, "Valerie? It's Naya."

Silence.

Naya entered and shut the door. She squinted at the dim living room. The only light came from a room down the hall. She was halfway to the sofa when she realized that she'd locked the door. Hopefully Valerie wasn't in the laundry room and was now locked out. But with barely enough strength left to stand, she continued forward instead. She dove the last step to miraculously land on the sofa. She desperately tried to get up to search for her friend but her legs wouldn't hold her. Fatigue insisted that she rest. She let her eyes close and her breathing deepen.

Her head still spinning with exhaustion, Naya gradually drifted out of the deep sleep. Why wasn't this her bed? As the last trace of dreams left her brain she remembered being so exhausted that she'd fallen asleep on the sofa. Terrific. Nothing like wasting time she didn't have.

She heard a shuffle. A footstep. She fully opened her eyes expecting to see her friend.

A man was searching the dark room with a flashlight. A nauseating, twisting feeling unravelled in her stomach and before she could stop herself she gasped. The stranger froze and shoved the flashlight into his jacket, his back to her.

Maybe he hadn't realized she was there? Should she try to outrun him. What if he had a gun? She could just see the headlines: ex-marathon runner loses race with bullet. Her mind filled with whirling thoughts of alternate solutions. Only one choice. Fake him out.

She exhaled loudly with a slight moan, then continued to breathe deeply and slowly hoping he'd believe she was still asleep. The ploy worked. In the dark she could just see the outline of his shoulders relax from their ear-hugging position. Now all she had to do was not move and let the burglar finish searching. Steal what he wanted and leave.

Instead, he headed towards her.

It took every shred of self-control and discipline to shut her eyes and remain absolutely still. Surely he could hear her heart try to pound its way out of her chest.

She could feel that he was near her feet and risked a peek through her lashes. He had fuzzy, short hair and a goatee. She had the impression that the hair was light. Musky, burnt wood aftershave assaulted her nostrils and a cough caught in her throat. He crouched on the floor, his back to her. What was he doing? She risked lifting her head to see. He was searching her backpack! She heard the familiar tinkling of keys, then he dropped them into her pack. He flinched and froze at the clink.

In one smooth motion, he clicked the flashlight off, got up from the floor and left.

She scrambled to lock and bolt the door after him. She shoved her weight against it as though that would help keep him out. Then she remembered to breathe.

"Oh, great," she muttered. She'd left her cane by the sofa. Cautiously, she edged her way around the room from the wall, to the arm chair, to the corner coffee table, like a baby learning to walk and finally landed back on the sofa.

She thought about calling the police. And say what? "Excuse me, officer. I broke into this apartment, then someone else broke in after me." Considering her last 911 call she could only imagine how bad this one would be. The only way she'd get the police to take her seriously was to get proof that something was wrong. Proof that Valerie was definitely missing.

She clicked on the lamp on the corner table and quickly inspected her backpack. She sighed with relief when she found her wallet and ID still there. Her keys seemed to be all there; house, car, work; plus a few she couldn't remember what they opened.

She checked her watch — it was 9:43. Hell of a rescue. Break in and have a nap.

She pushed herself to her feet to check the kitchen just off of the living room. No one lying unconscious on the floor. She moved down the hall to the bedroom. The bed was neatly made. A quick peek in the bathroom — no one.

Next she checked out the larger bedroom which had been converted to an office. Obviously Valerie spent a lot of time in here and decided to convert the master bedroom to a very pleasant work area. Under a large window was a low book case where African Violets and Dieffenbachia flourished on top. A computer desk against the wall to the right of the window. The opposite wall had a custom made floor-to-ceiling bookcase home to books, DVD's and, of course, Cookie Monster. She checked outside the window to see the view of the street below and discovered a small two-drawer file cabinet concealed behind the bookcase.

She pulled on the top drawer — locked. The bottom drawer was unlocked but sadly only contained blank notepads and packages of printer paper. Scrambling back to her feet, she thought of how strange it was to lock the cabinet when Valerie never left the apartment and her only visitors would be people she knew and trusted.

She sat at the desk and searched through a stack of papers on the corner. Checking the drawers she found that they were methodically organized with one drawer devoted to receipts, bills, tax papers. She turned to the monitor and that's when she noticed that there was no computer. It could be in the repair shop. She checked the receipts for a claim ticket. Nothing.

On the desk corner sat an open daily planner filled with project deadlines identified by shorthand codes and acronyms.

After a quick look in the bathroom she returned to the bedroom to search for signs that Valerie had gone on a trip. There were no empty hangars in the closet. Dresser drawers were full. Everything was in its place.

Except Valerie.

As Naya circled the bed, her toe caught on the area rug and she fell, her cane sliding under the bed. With a quiet "Damn!" she reached for her cane and spotted a laptop under the night table. Why hadn't she thought of this before? Naya frequently worked in bed, then put her laptop under the bed so she wouldn't step on it in the morning. Something she only did once.

She hadn't found an address book anywhere in the apartment so perhaps it was on the computer. Naya took the laptop to the living room sofa.

The computer booted up and, after several seconds, the black screen displayed a rectangular box above the words 'PASSWORD REQUIRED'.

The last thing she wanted to do was type random passwords and trigger a security program that could destroy the hard drive. This computer might be the only way to find Valerie's friends and hope that one of them knew where she'd gone. With a silent apology to her absent friend she shut it down and slipped it into her backpack. Naya had all kinds of hacking software at home that would help. She turned off all the lights.

She inspected the hall through the peep hole. Not that the burglar would still be lurking around, but why take chances? She double checked that the door was locked behind her then plodded down the hall dreading the long trek down the stairs. She gave a small giggle when she found that the 'OUT OF ORDER' sign was gone. Guess it paid to live in a posh building in the Glebe.

❖ ❖ ❖

At home, Naya fought the urge to look at Valerie's laptop for just 'a few minutes,' and lay down to sleep. Without rest she'd be too tired to remember her own name, never mind hack into the computer. Despite her excitement, she fell asleep quickly.

In the morning she woke refreshed. She left her walker in the corner, slipped her backpack over one shoulder and used the cane to get to the kitchen.

After flicking on the coffee maker, which was always ready to go, she turned on Valerie's computer.

Valerie's security skills were good but Naya's were better. She bypassed the password within minutes. Before doing anything however, she cloned her friend's hard drive onto her home network drive. A habit she'd adopted after a six month contract with Ottawa police computer forensics department. That ensured the data was backed up, unchanged and safe in case her tinkering damaged it.

Not much on the computer except a few encrypted files which would take more work to open. Naya was ecstatic when the email opened easily. Then her anticipation of finding useful information faded. The inbox contained messages from only three people. What was worse, they were all lame messages; "Just came back from my trip." "Would you like to see my holiday photos?" And others, were, "Love to see them. How about Tuesday night?" or "How about next week?" Scanning down she found twenty-seven such exchanges over the past six weeks. A fast cross-reference with the Sent Items folder; the same thing.

She chuckled as she soon recognized this as security 101. The dates to "look at pictures" were probably when they'd get together to exchange information or discuss their work. Nice low tech way to avoid any sniffer programs searching cyber space for key words.

Unfortunately the Address Book contained information only for these three people. Two of them had full details including home address and both land-lines and cell numbers. One was Alice Vanderlund, probably the friend from work who was supposed to help Valerie out of her condo. She tried that number first. No answer. Not sure how to word a message, she hung up.

She started to call the next person using her house phone, then gave it a second thought. She retrieved her cell phone from her backpack. Her cell had caller ID block. A little anonymity wouldn't hurt.

Bill Chang was quite friendly and open, though not at all helpful. He and Valerie had worked together but he didn't really know much about her. They'd spoken a couple of times by phone. He thought that Valerie was nice. That was it.

The third person, Howard Dixon, only had a single phone number listed.

Dixon answered after five rings. There was the sound of cars and blaring horns in the background.

She cleared her throat and spoke quickly.

"Hi, my name is Naya. I'm a friend of Valerie Peters. I've been trying to get in touch with her and I was wondering if you've heard from her?"

"No," he answered, hesitating briefly. Something in that single word suggested that she'd caught him off guard. And something else in his tone told her that he wouldn't be honest with her. Then he demanded, "How'd you get this number?"

Usually people say "my number." She opted not to mention the computer.

"From Valerie's address book," she said innocently. Technically it wasn't a lie. She continued, "Do you have any idea where she might have gone?"

"Sorry, but I hardly know her," he said smoothly. "We just exchange the occasional cards at holidays, you know. But if I hear from her, I'll call you." Click. He hung up before she had the chance to give him her number. Rude and suspicious.

Naya obviously wasn't a professional interrogator. It was time to let the police take over, now that she had contacts from Valerie's life to give them. She called the police and this time asked for Missing Persons. She spoke to Sergeant Philadelphia Ashantre.

She summed up quickly, ending with the fact that she hadn't been able to get in touch with her since yesterday. Naya started to list the three names in Valerie's address book when the detective cut her off.

"Ms. Assad, I see here you that you called 911 on Monday at 6:16 pm."

"Yes, that's right. She was supposed to come over yesterday afternoon. I went over to her apartment last night to check on her and while I was there..."

"Did you go inside?" the sergeant asked.

"Yes, I found the door unlocked. She'd never leave without locking her apartment. And while I was there, someone broke in..."

"Did they attack you?" Ashantre interrupted, sounding concerned.

"No, I pretended to be asleep on the sofa and I suppose he thought I was Valerie. But now I know she really is missing."

"Ms. Assad, all you know is that she wasn't home. As an on-line friend, it's hard to know about her real-world life."

Damn! She had hoped that the 911 operator hadn't put that in the report. "Look, I have some names..."

"Random names that you found at your friend's apartment."

"One is the person that was supposed to help her come to my home. Alice Vanderlund..."

"Do you know any of them personally?"

"Well, no, but what about the burglar?"

"Any evidence the lock was broken? No? Then how do you know it wasn't her boyfriend?"

"Using a flashlight?"

"Perhaps he didn't want to wake her." The forced patience in her voice vanished. "Look, Ms. Assad, I understand you used to be close friends. But that was a long time ago. You don't really know much about her life now. Or," she paused for a beat, "that she's actually agoraphobic. I'm sure she'll contact you when she's ready."

"Thanks for your time," Naya shoved the words out through her teeth and hung up. She didn't care what some judgemental stranger thought. She knew Valerie better than anyone — and it didn't matter how long they'd been apart — they were still friends.

She wondered if the first 911 call would have gone differently had she known Alice's last name then. Somehow, she doubted it. Since her phone interrogation skills obviously weren't the best, she opted for an unannounced visit to Alice Vanderlund's home. It would be harder to be evasive in person.

Mid-morning Alice was probably at work but Naya planned to wait, all day if necessary. She packed a snack, a metal water bottle and a thermos of coffee into her backpack. Then called a cab.

She'd taken Valerie's computer without permission. It obviously held sensitive data making it Naya's responsibility to keep it safe. Perhaps she was being paranoid, but she knew she'd feel better if it was out of sight. Looking around the kitchen she opted to hide it on the top shelf of the pantry behind the cereal boxes.

Thirty-five minutes later the cab pulled into the driveway of Alice's bungalow. She asked the driver to wait for her then slipped the backpack on. Gripping the cane, she negotiated her way across the cobblestone driveway all the while muttering that she shouldn't have left her walker in the trunk. With a sigh of relief she made it to the front door with only a couple of near falls. She rang the doorbell. Immediately she heard heavy footsteps rush to the door.

The door sprang open to reveal a vaguely familiar young man. He was thin, with fuzzy, short blond hair and a goatee. As he stepped closer, she got a lung-full of a musky, burnt wood aftershave.

It was the burglar from Valerie's apartment.

CHAPTER FOUR

Naya debated running, screaming, or smacking him with her cane. He stared back, eyes wide, slowly blinking as though struggling to process information overflow. Finally she swallowed hard, licked her lips and forced her voice to be calm.

"Hi, I'm a friend of Valerie Peters and I'm..."

"Do you know where my sister is?" He lunged forward, grabbed her arm before she even had time to gasp. Naya's stronger right foot caught on the door step so suddenly she didn't have time to move the weaker leg to steady herself. In stomach churning slow motion she fell forward and crashed against his chest. The momentary relief ended when he lost his own footing. Both fell, a lot faster this time. He hit the floor first. She landed on top.

The sharp angles of his ribs and shoulder dug into her. His elbow smacked her in the head making sparks flick before her eyes.

"Oh my god!" He cried out. In a panic he rolled her off of him, got to his knees and said, "I'm really sorry. Are you okay? Can you hear me?"

She started to answer until a lacy darkness in front of her eyes distracted her.

He helped her to sit then handed her the cane. Coming around behind her, he slipped his hands under her arms and lifted her easily to her feet. Guess those skinny bones had some muscle connected to them after all.

"I'm really sorry. You better sit down." He guided her into the family room to sit in the armchair. "Can I get you something? An icepack? A drink? A Tylenol?"

She rubbed her temples, blinking hard. Finally the cobwebs cleared from her vision and thoughts. This was the burglar from Valerie's apartment. She had to stand. To get back to the taxi. First — she needed to get rid of this guy. "Maybe a glass of water, please?"

"Sure," he said and ran out of the room.

For a terrifying instant she understood how a turtle felt when it was trapped on its back. Unlike the poor animal she had one advantage. She shrugged off her backpack. Abandoned it. Stood up. Now to escape in the waiting cab.

The stranger returned with a dripping glass of water.

She sat with thud and took the glass. She cupped her hand underneath it to catch the drops and sipped as she eyed her cane on the floor at her feet. One good hit. That's all she needed. She handed back the glass. Reached for her weapon.

"I saw the cab in the driveway," he paused then added, "I paid him then sent him off."

"What?" Eyes round with panic she struggled in vain to get back to her feet. The extra surge of fear stole her strength.

"It's okay. I'll drive you home." He sat in the armchair next to her. "I wanted to talk to you about my sister."

"Your sister?"

"Alice," he said. He leaned forward, staring unblinking into her eyes. "She's been missing since yesterday."

She concentrated on his words trying to force her brain to understand through her fear. His sister? Missing the same day as Valerie? That meant that whatever happened, it was after she'd gone to help her leave the condo. Discovering that he was Alice's brother helped her fear inspired urge to escape, vanish.

"That's why I came," she said. "My friend's also been missing since Monday. I was hoping that Alice could help me find Valerie..."

"Valerie Peters?" he interrupted, his voice harsh. "When Alice — uh — didn't meet me for dinner on — on Sunday and — and didn't call — I — I came here looking for her — uh yesterday. I checked her computer and found a bunch of emails from this Valerie person asking her to go with her to meet some friend. Probably some online predator."

"Uh, no, that friend was me. The thing is," she broke off. She almost blurted out her friend's secret to a stranger again. Instead of mentioning the agoraphobia, she said instead, "Valerie doesn't drive so Alice was supposed to pick her up. But now they're both missing."

"She's *not* missing. When that woman ignored all my calls, I — I took Alice's spare key and went to her apartment and — and I — I found Valerie asleep on the sofa. I should have woken her and demanded answers. But I panicked and left. "

She sighed. "That was *me* on the sofa." She felt sorry for him as his shoulders gradually slumped forward, like air leaking out of a balloon. "Why didn't you call the police?"

"Uh, I tried, but — but they told me she's an adult and — and to — uh, check with her friends." He paused, taking a big breath. "Did you go to the police?"

"Yes, but ... They just told me to wait a few days and see if she comes back." She was too embarrassed to tell him the full conversation. Brightening, she began, "You know, if we go to the police together..."

"Oh, uh, they — they'll probably insist they took off together. Like, like I first thought."

"I guess we'll just have to get proof that they're actually missing. Then the police will listen," she said.

"How?"

"We start with Alice's computer," she said.

"Beyond getting into her email, I couldn't figure out how to look at any files."

"They're probably encrypted." She gave him a small, tentative smile, saying, "I don't even know your name."

"It's — it's Kevin. And you're?"

"Naya."

"If you know anything about computers maybe you could figure it out. I'll show you to Alice's office," Kevin said. He stood and extended a helping hand.

She hesitated. What the hell was she doing? She was alone with a complete stranger and, judging from his reaction at the door, he also had a temper. Before the MS it wouldn't have been an issue. She could have defended herself then. But now...

The wisest thing was to leave. She edged forward, preparing to stand and make some excuse.

The doorbell rang.

"Excuse me," he said and rushed to answer.

Re-energized, she got to her feet easily using her cane. She put on her backpack and followed Kevin, intending to hitch a ride with whomever was at the door.

It was her taxi driver standing next to her walker.

"Ma'am, you left this in my cab. Thought you might need it."

She should leave with the driver. She should come back with a friend and then go through the computer. But did Valerie have the time to wait? She studied Kevin. He looked like he needed an ally. She knew that she definitely did.

"Thank you, so much," she said to the cabbie and pulled the walker inside. She watched the driver pocket a hefty tip from Kevin. As he drove away she hoped this wasn't a mistake.

"So, let's go check out Alice's computer," she said.

It didn't take long to access most of the files which were simply vague progress reports for past projects. However, the larger recent files were highly encrypted. Given enough time, she knew she could open them. Unfortunately all her hacking tools were at home.

Naya checked the emails. Unlike Valerie, Alice seemed to use this computer for both business and social contacts. The Inbox was jammed full of messages dating back several months. The Deleted and Sent Folders contained hundreds of old messages. It would be a tedious job to go through everything now. Naya snuck a glance at Kevin. He was pacing near the window, oblivious to what she was doing. She compressed all the message folders and emailed them to herself.

Scattered among this week's messages of spam and social messages were a few from Howard Dixon; the same man that had denied having recent contact with Valerie. These messages also suggested getting together to look at vacation pictures. Alice had sent messages to the names Naya had, as well as two other contacts. From this series of messages it became clear who was co-ordinating everything.

"Do you know a Howard Dixon?" She asked.

"Uh," he stopped pacing and turned away from the window. "Is — is he Alice's uh, new boyfriend?"

"No..." she said.

"I — I was hoping that — that if he was her boyfriend, maybe she was with him."

She gave him a consoling nod noting that his stutter became worse when he was nervous. She continued. "It looks like he worked with both Alice and Valerie. From what I can tell, each worked independently on a different part. Then they would send these coded messages." He peered over her shoulder as she showed him a couple of examples. "I tried talking to Dixon before but he denied even knowing Valerie. Maybe you'd have better luck, do you want to try?"

"Uh, oh, okay. Do — do you have his number?" Kevin said. She opened up the Address Book on the computer. This one listed a second cell number. She prudently chose that one to give to Kevin. He called using the house phone.

He spoke with a much deeper tone, as though trying to sound business-like though the stutter was more pronounced. "Hi, this is — is Kevin, a — a relative of Alice Vanderlund. I understand that you've worked together." Short pause. "I haven't seen her for a couple of days and was hoping you might know where she's gone." Much longer pause. "Are you sure?" He looked at Naya, lips drawn tight as he shook his head. "I see. Thanks."

He hung up and said, "He claims that he hasn't talked to her for a long time. I should have mentioned the recent emails he sent." Kevin picked up the phone again. "I'll — try again."

"Wait." She put her hand on the phone to stop him. "I've got some friends that can check him out. In the meantime let's call the other two."

"Okay," he checked the screen to get the number.

She held out her hand for the phone and said, "Sometimes people are more receptive to a woman asking questions."

She called Kirk Stroud who was very helpful. He'd finished his portion of the project and was waiting to pass it on to Alice when she was ready. The fact this guy admitted it quickly meant the portion he was working on probably wasn't secret. She tried the next number.

"Hi, could I speak to Rose Nellis, please?" Naya asked.

"Who's this?"

"My name's Naya Assad. I've been trying to get in touch with Alice Vanderlund for a couple of days. I was wondering if you've heard from her."

"Alice? She's missing?"

"Yes, even her brother hasn't heard from her."

"Her brother?"

"Yes," Naya was getting really annoyed that every answer ended with a question mark. "Do you know where she might have gone?"

"My goodness," Rose said. "I haven't seen her since we had lunch last week."

"How about Valerie Peters? Do you also see her?"

"Do you know her?" Rose asked.

"Yes, she's my friend."

"Oh course, Naya. Valerie frequently talks about you."

"She's missing too."

"*Both* of them?" Rose said, her voice an odd mixture of concern, surprise and something that might be described as anger.

Naya hesitated for a moment then asked cautiously, "Do you think we could get together over coffee? Maybe together we could figure out where they are."

"All right." No hesitation.

They arranged to meet at the Tim Horton's on Bank at Cooper at two o'clock. She hung up and said, "She seems willing to talk. I'll call a cab..."

"I'm coming too."

"She'll probably open up more if it's just the two of us," she said, fighting not to be dissuaded by his hurt look.

"Let me drive you. I'll wait in the car."

Her instinct told her to say no. To go on her own. She saw the candid desperation in his face. The way he clenched his hands together pleadingly. The expression in his puppy brown eyes. She debated saying no but he did have a stake in this too.

"Sure," she said finally.

❖ ❖ ❖

Exhausted from lack of sleep and the stress of the last couple of days, Naya wanted more than anything to close her eyes for a few minutes. A few minutes was all she got when Kevin dropped her off in front of Tim's. She negotiated around the coffee shop, grimacing each time her walker banged into the display near the door, the chairs and even the stupid counter. She could feel her cheeks burn hotter with each hit and apology. She should have left it in Kevin's car. Then she cringed at the thought of tripping and landing in someone's latte. Guess the walker was less embarrassing. At least no one was staring.

Breathless and sweating she reached the cash and had to sit on her walker to muster up the strength to order a large Cappuccino. She scanned the café for a woman dressed in a blue windbreaker, in her early forties, with burgundy hair in a page-boy hairstyle. There was a woman matching that description at a window table. She held a white porcelain cup in her hand looking as if she was about to take a sip. A croissant sat delicately poised in the other hand, ready to be eaten. But neither hand moved as she read a magazine on the table.

Naya placed her cup on the walker seat and rolled towards the woman, apologizing repeatedly for all the chairs she smacked.

"Excuse me, are you Rose Nellis?"

The woman looked up from the magazine filled with pictures of puppies in adorable poses.

"You must be Naya Assad," she said, with a bright smile. She put her snack down then stood to take Naya's cup off the walker and place it on the table. Rose pulled out a chair, saying, "Please."

"Thank you." Naya felt very uncomfortable with all the attention. She parked the walker close to the table. "It's nice to meet you."

"Always nice to meet a friend of Valerie's," she said.

As she sat down, Naya indicated the magazine saying, "Are you planning on getting a puppy?"

"It's always been a dream of mine," Rose said. Sighing, she added, "But my husband's allergic. So I'm quite content to admire them in pictures."

On closer look she realized Rose was a lot older than the admitted early forties. Though she did have playful blue eyes and a youthful smile.

"Have you known Valerie and Alice long?" Naya asked.

"We met last year on a project. After it ended we stayed friends. Since Valerie couldn't go out we always went to her place."

Rose paused to take a sip from her cup then continued to hold it up near her mouth as she added, "The last time all three of us got together was last month. Valerie mentioned she'd reconnected with you and was very excited about it. She'd been talking about trying to venture out to go visit you because you were a little immobile. Last I heard from Alice, she was going over to help Valerie get to your place."

Naya cringed at the reminder that she was responsible for the disappearance of not just Valerie but Alice as well.

"Valerie told me you used to be a marathon runner. But not what stopped you. If I'm prying tell me to buzz off."

"I have MS," Naya answered without thinking. Saying it out loud hadn't been as difficult or embarrassing as she'd thought. She was surprised to feel relief at sharing the secret.

"My cousin has MS," Rose said. "But he's given up. Won't even leave his house. It's good to see you're still going on with your life."

"Uh," Naya couldn't think of anything to say. She *had* given up. She *had* locked herself away from the world. Another reminder that this was all her fault. "I couldn't just sit still without trying to help Valerie."

"That's very brave."

"Not really," Naya said, uncomfortable with the undeserved praise. Changing the topic quickly, she asked, "You sounded surprised that Alice has a brother."

"She never talks about her family. I had the impression that she's estranged from them."

Moving back to the real reason she was here, Naya asked, "I have no idea of where to start looking. If I knew what they were working on it might give me some clue where to start."

"They wouldn't say much. We first met while working on a project to develop statistical models for human behaviour recognition. Basically it was to track a company's employees as they went around town then predict where they might go. The boss wanted to make sure they weren't going somewhere, well, inappropriate or meeting someone even less appropriate."

"Are you serious?"

"That boss has some serious trust issues. A little therapy would do wonders for his personality." Rose humpfed, then added pleasantly, "We may not officially work together but we still get together for wine and wonderful conversation which always drifts to shop talk." She took a long, slow sip from her cup watching her over its rim. Putting the cup down, she played with it for a moment as though making a decision. Finally she made unwavering eye contact with Naya and continued. "Valerie and Alice frequently asked about advancements in 2D/3D pervasive surveillance that I might have heard about. That could suggest that their current project is related to the previous work we did together."

Although Naya hadn't missed the phrase 'we may not officially work together' she knew better than to push.

"That's just a guess of course," Rose added in a tone that suggested it wasn't.

"I ran across a few other names of people they worked with — there was one common person. Do you know Howard Dixon?"

Rose brought the cup close to her mouth and said, "Can't say that I do."

Again she chose not to push and risk alienating Rose by pressing the point. She asked instead, "How well do you know Alice?"

"She's a happy, bubbly young girl. But I always thought there was a little sadness behind her eyes. She's always ready to help. If I hadn't been busy I would have gone to get Valerie to your place." Rose took a sip of her cup as her eyes darted to the window.

"It wasn't your fault," Naya said, gently. She was surprised to see determination in the other woman's eyes not tears.

"You keep in touch." Rose put a hand on Naya's. "And if you have any questions or need me to do something, you call."

Naya realized that she'd been dismissed. Rose had such a diplomatic way about her that she didn't mind. "Thank you. If you remember anything that might help..."

"Naturally, I'll call you," Rose said, giving her a smile that suggested Naya would be hearing from her again. Probably quite soon.

Standing near the curb Naya scanned the parked cars for Kevin's, trying to remember what it looked like. Then she spotted it around the corner. Of course, how could she have forgotten the ugly brown Dodge sedan? The old rust bucket had bits of peeling paint that revealed it might have been red in another life. The roof-rack, broken on the driver's side, was even more rusted than the car. Kevin had spent the first part of the trip apologizing for its condition. He then lamented on how he'd had to sell his brand new Lexus due to some unexpected expenses. After a while she'd stopped listening out of sheer self-preservation. What is it with guys and their cars? Once Travis got going, he'd recount each and every detail of how he'd rebuilt his Mustang — bolt by excruciating bolt. Of course she didn't mind listening to Travis, but drew the line at strangers.

When Kevin saw her, he waved and within seconds pulled up in front of her, stopping in a no parking zone. With his flashers on, he jumped out, helped her into the front seat, stowed her walker in the trunk and jumped back into the car. He certainly was attentive.

"Did you find out anything?" he asked as he pulled away from the curb.

"She doesn't know where they might have gone." She sat slumped in the seat, feeling the exhaustion grow inside her like a spreading wave.

"Does she have any ideas?" he asked. "Like you said, if we can figure out what they were working on it might help us find them."

Naya tried to replay the conversation in her mind. Rose had only given hints of possible secret work that Naya didn't want to divulge at this time. She took a deep breath, fighting to push the words out past the fatigue. "They met about a year ago through work and stayed friends. But they never told her what they're working on now."

"She wasn't too helpful."

Naya tried to answer and muttered something that even she found unintelligible.

"Are you okay?"

Too tired to answer she began to nod, only to end up leaning back on the head rest. She felt too heavy to move. Inhaling, she tried to speak but the rhythmic sway of the car made her words drift away from her. Strands of exhaustion invaded her brain. She barely had the strength to think. All she could do was sit there and let the sounds of the car and Kevin's concerned voice in the distance, drift through.

It felt like mere seconds later that the car stopped moving. She dragged her legs out of the car and stood. Without idle conversation to fill the embarrassing silence, Kevin helped her into Alice's house. She should have asked him to take her straight home from the coffee shop. She walked on increasingly leaden legs into the house and by the time she made it to the living room sofa, all her energy was spent. As much as she craved rest, she knew she couldn't. The soft, plush sofa beckoned to her and she couldn't help but allow herself to sink into it. She blinked slowly, enjoying the brief rest. She blinked again, lingering a few extra seconds in the comforting darkness.

Naya became aware of a blanket on her. Her shoes were off, her legs were up on the sofa.

"Hi."

Startled, she jerked up into a sitting position. The curtains were drawn to darken the room. Kevin sat in the armchair reading, a corner lamp making a tight circle of light around him.

He closed his book and said, "I tried to wake you but you just kept mumbling 'five more minutes.' So I let you sleep."

She checked her watch. 6:45!

"Oh, my God! I'm so sorry." She swung her legs down, slipped on her runners and fumbled with the laces while speaking quickly. "I really didn't mean to fall asleep. It's the MS — I have MS. On top of difficulty walking, the fatigue really gets to me. Sometimes I'll be going along just fine, then it seems like all of a sudden, without any warning, I just have to close my eyes, though now I know how narcoleptics feel and I'll just get my stuff and get going and ..." She found her cane on the floor. "Thank you very much for everything..."

"I guess it must be difficult."

Embarrassed, she gave him a flicker of a smile. She was also mad at herself for wasting time napping. *Again.* "I really should get going." She started to stand up but Kevin's sombre tone interrupted her.

"You know, ev — everyone's had a tough life, one way or another." He glanced away for a second, then back again. "Look, I wasn't completely honest with you. When I called the police, they took a report but I kinda doubt they're going to do much. You see, she — she has a history of running away when — from when we were kids. She'd disappear for weeks at a time, especially when — when our dad was, uh, really drunk and... But this time, it — it feels different. I know you're tired, but maybe you could go through Alice's computer again. You might find something helpful. We could order in?"

His stutter was much worse when he talked about his difficult childhood making her imagine that he'd left out many painful details. She should leave. It was the smart thing to do.

She studied the floor trying to think. Alice's computer could hold the clue to finding Valerie. And Kevin wasn't really a complete stranger. This was personal for him too. There was only one decision.

She asked, "How about Pizza?"

❖ ❖ ❖

Naya yawned widely, stretching her back muscles. Kevin had fallen asleep long ago in the corner armchair in Alice's office. It was already after eleven o'clock. She was always amazed at the black hole that seemed to swallow up time whenever she worked on the computer. Unfortunately tonight her work hadn't made much progress. She planned to be sure to carry her decryption files with her from now on.

She searched through the desk drawers hoping Alice wouldn't mind the intrusion and found a new memory stick still in its package.

She checked to see that Kevin was still asleep in the armchair not wanting to explain why she was taking the files without permission. She plugged in the stick. Copied all the files. Time to go home.

The question of whether or not to wake him depended on if she needed a key to lock the front door. She checked it on the way to the kitchen. Good. A basic push button. In the kitchen she used her cell to phone for a cab. She returned to the office to leave Kevin a note thanking him and promising to call tomorrow afternoon.

She shrugged into her back pack, folded up the cane, put everything onto the walker and left to wait for the cab outside.

❖ ❖ ❖

She arrived at home, thanking the driver with a big tip for helping her get inside in the dark. Had she known that she'd be out this late she'd have left some lights on. She pushed her walker to the staircase and sat on the bottom step to take off her shoes. She tossed her windbreaker on the railing. Brushing her teeth could wait till the morning. Yawning widely, she even considered sleeping on top of the blankets fully clothed.

Eyelids half closed, her legs were getting heavier as she shuffled behind the walker to the family room. She dropped her bag on the floor near the room's entrance. Flicked on the lights.

And gasped.

CHAPTER FIVE

Mouth open in a silent cry, Naya gaped at the mess in her family room. She blinked rapidly trying to make the hallucination go away. The image was real. The mattress, flipped on the floor. Clothes, strewn everywhere. Empty suitcase, tossed in the corner. The DVD and stereo system, had toppled off the TV stand, still tethered by their cables. The bookcase, swept clear. Every book, CD and DVD huddled in piles on the floor.

She had to escape. Get outside. The burglar could still be here. She grabbed her cell from her backpack and retreated slowly, pulling the walker with her. She listened for footsteps upstairs. Eyes darted back and forth. Any movement in the dark? At the front door, she dialled 911 then made a quick exit.

She stumbled down the steps, dragging the walker behind her. Then she rushed to stand against the garage door, glad she'd forgotten to turn on the outside lights.

Now she felt safe enough to whisper into the phone, "I'm alone at home and I've had a break-in."

The operator answered, "I've dispatched the police. Can you get to safety?"

"I'm outside. On the driveway," she continued to whisper.

"Do you have a neighbour you can go to?"

"I can't wake them at this hour."

"The police car will be there in one and a half minutes. Try to stay out of sight."

"Okay," she said and pressed herself closer against the garage door praying she was invisible in the dark.

True to the operator's word, a minute and a half later flashing lights silently pulled into her driveway. She waved at the officer needlessly. There was no missing her in the headlights. He got out and approached.

He whispered, "Wait in the cruiser till I check the house." She nodded, left the walker behind, and took his arm. She got in the front passenger seat.

She recoiled instinctively when he drew his weapon before entering the house. Barely remembering to breathe, she waited. She listened to the crackle of voices on the radio, studying the computer console resisting the urge to check out its programs. The computer kept her distracted from worrying about what might be going on inside the house.

She sighed loudly when the policeman come out of the house with his gun holstered three minutes and thirty-two seconds later. Not that she was keeping track of the time or anything.

He opened the door and extended a helping hand. "It's safe to go in."

"Thank you." Despite his assurance she gripped his hand tightly and glanced around with saucer eyes as she stepped into the foyer.

"You did the right thing getting out," he said after he brought in her walker and locked the door. "You never know if the burglars are still in the house."

She sat at the base of the stairs. All the inside lights were on now. Only then did she realize that she'd gone out in her white socks which were now damp and brown on the bottom. She took them off and put them on her runners.

"Do you need some water?" he asked. "You look a bit pale."

"Yes, please," she answered. The adrenaline rush had worn off and shock was setting in. She could hear him open a couple of cupboards then heard the tap go on for a few seconds.

He knelt before her to hand her the glass and said, "I've called for the detectives and they should be here within an hour." She clutched his wrist and he added quickly, "Don't worry, I'll stay with you until they get here. On this floor, only the TV room's been trashed. The basement looks okay. Your bedroom and office are messed up. Did you have a computer in the office?"

"No, I had it brought down to the kitchen after I got sick."

"I didn't see one there."

"What?" She shoved the glass back into his hands as she used his shoulder to leverage herself to her feet. She steadied herself with the railing and walls to rush to the kitchen.

She held onto the counter and stared at the empty table. She refused to believe that it wasn't sitting exactly where she'd left it. She stared for a moment longer just in case it might magically return. But it *was* gone. So were her notepads, her printer and even the packages of printer paper. The rest of the kitchen was untouched. Maybe that's why most of the house wasn't ransacked. They'd left as soon as they found her computer.

Startled by the officer's hand on her arm, she realized that she was swaying. Her legs felt weak. She leaned heavily on his arm as he helped to the table.

"My name's Charles Forgham," he said as he sat in the chair across from her.

"Hi. Naya Assad," she introduced herself and was glad that he didn't feel the need to fill the silence with pointless chatter. Charles? He looked more like a Todd or even a Fabio, especially with his broad shoulders, light brown wavy hair and sensitive brown eyes, which offset his strong jaw. Exactly the kind of knight every damsel in distress wanted to have racing to her rescue. Too bad she didn't care about romance at this very moment. And she had to be in shock to even be thinking this way.

She pressed her hands flat on the table top. She felt numb inside. No. She felt nothing but a blank sensation that matched the empty table.

"Ms. Assad, are you all right?" The officer asked.

"What?" She recovered quickly. "Yes. I was just thinking about my computer."

"Did you have a lot of important information on it?"

"No, luckily all my files are on the network drive," she said. She shook her head trying to put into words what she was feeling. Yes, now she did have emotion. She felt queasy, frightened and angry. Queasy to know that strangers had touched her personal possessions. Frightened because she no longer felt safe in her own home. And angry because her sanctuary had been violated and she couldn't do anything about it.

"It's okay," Charles said. "It's difficult to process your emotions when you're the victim of a crime. If you need to talk, or have any questions, you can phone me." He pulled out a business card from his breast pocket and scribbled a number on the back. "I've also included the number for the Victim Crisis Unit if you feel you need more than just talking."

"Thanks." She took the card, tracing her finger over the raised logo of the Ottawa Police.

"Usually the detectives would contact you later. But there've been a rash of break and enters about a kilometre away, so someone will be coming to check if this might be related."

"Okay, thanks," she said, wondering if she should feel honoured about the special treatment. Or should she be insulted that her home had just become part of a trend.

"Is there someone you can call now?"

"Not at this time of night." She paused before quietly adding, "If you need to go..."

"No, it's part of the job to stay. I was just wondering if you have someone to help you clean up."

"Yes, I do." She'd phone Travis in the morning and tell him about the burglary. She knew he'd be over to help before she even asked.

They chatted about many things including movies and best vacation spots. She relaxed enough to almost forget why he was here. It made the hour and half wait for the detectives pass quickly.

Detective Sully proved to be a shorter, rounder version of Columbo, but with a lot less hair. And a pencil, instead of a cigar, hung out of his mouth. He wore a dark grey, loose-fitting suit, as though he'd recently lost weight. He looked exhausted, overworked and bored as he took his notebook out of his jacket outside pocket. He sat at the kitchen table and scribbled her answers to his quick, curt questions.

When did you go out? When did you come home? Who did you tell that you were leaving? What's missing?

She answered just as succinctly that she'd left yesterday in the morning. Was out all day and came home just past midnight. And no, she hadn't told anyone she was going out.

"My computer and all my notes and even the printer are gone. I haven't had a chance to check what else is missing."

"When you do know make a list. Especially cash and jewellery."

"Do you think you'll find the people?"

"There've been several burglaries in the area. A few witnesses have spotted kids making a run for it. They probably branched out because the neighbours were getting more vigilant."

Naya nodded even though she doubted that. She'd read about the places the kids had hit. Those kids would have taken her DVD player, PVR, even the 52 inch flat screen TV which was light enough for two to carry. A quick estimation of the mass of scattered music and movie disks she assumed that few, if any, had been taken. Also, the kitchen would have been a favourite trashing spot with food thrown everywhere. And they definitely wouldn't have left beer in the fridge or wine bottles on the wine rack.

"The computer!" she exclaimed suddenly. Standing up, she manoeuvred her way to the pantry. She dragged out Cheerios, Corn Flakes and Orville's extra butter popcorn, ignoring them as they bounced on the floor. She stretched and reached into the cupboard, giggling as her fingertips made contact with Valerie's laptop. It was still here. She pulled it out, hugging it like a delicate baby.

Sully was peering over his reading glasses at her, his mouth open like he wanted to say something. Officer Charles also watched her silently, though he fought to hold back a half smile.

"This isn't my computer," she explained, smiling brightly. "I thought I was being paranoid when I hid it before I left. Guess I wasn't."

"Okay, right," Sully said, closing his notebook and standing up as he headed towards the foyer. Naya hid the computer in the cupboard again and followed, Officer Forgham behind her. The detective called out, "Kate, you finished?"

The policewoman leaned out over the railing from the second floor and called down, "I've just got a few more photos to take and I'll be down."

"She's still training," Sully told Naya. "She takes a little longer to process a scene. We'll be out of your hair soon."

Naya got her walker and sat on it to wait, giving him a tiny, closed mouth grin.

Within moments Kate cheerfully bounded down the stairs, her dancing, short blond hair worthy of a shampoo commercial. Naya tried not to feel jealous of the girl's agility.

"All done," she told Sully.

"All right, Ms. Assad." He handed her his business card. "Email me the list of everything that's missing as soon as you know."

She examined the plain, nondescript card. It only had his name, phone number, fax and email printed in small unassuming font. Nowhere did it mention that he was a cop. She walked with them to the door with a quick glance at her watch: 2:42 am. They'd been here less than an hour. "Is there any chance of finding my computer?"

"Sorry, not really," Sully said. "Have a good night, Ms. Assad."

She nodded and locked the door after everyone had left. Resting heavily against it, she listened to the quiet in the house. Turning on the stereo full blast would help cure the silence. She pushed the walker back to the family room. To listen to music meant putting the system back together. And she didn't even know if it was broken. This wasn't the time to find out.

She surveyed the damage. No way could she sleep here even if she could wrestle the mattress up off the floor. She yanked the blanket out from under the mattress and considered curling up in a corner somewhere to sleep. She held the blanket at arm's length, wrinkling her nose as though it stank. No way. She'd need to wash this before using it again.

She managed to pull the sheets off the mattress then pile them, the blanket and pillow cases onto her walker and take everything to the laundry room. She set the washer to hot and watched the machine start to fill. There wasn't a setting hot enough to decontaminate the bedclothes. She shut off the machine. Got a large black garbage bag from the cupboard above the washer and shoved the sheets, pillow cases and blankets into it. Making a tight knot, she dragged the bag to the garage and tossed it out with a grunt of approval.

Naya double checked the locks on the windows and doors on the main floor. Then, leaving all the lights on, she paused at the bottom of the staircase. What originally was a major appeal to buying the house had now become a daunting mountain to climb. No, she reminded herself, she'd climbed up four stories just yesterday. This was a piece of cake.

Breathless and ribs aching by the time she got to the top, she was clutching the banister with a white knuckle grip, terrified she'd topple down the stairs. That would be horrible because if she didn't break something she'd have to climb back up. She doubted that she had any strength left for that.

She limped to the linen cupboard to get a blanket. As she passed the guest bedroom she noticed that it was untouched. Of course, Officer Charles had said only the master bedroom and office had been wrecked.

Leaving all the upstairs lights on as well, she slipped under the covers fully clothed.

She lay on her side facing the door. She gripped her cane with both hands. Eyes wide, she watched for anything that moved in the hall. Her ears were on high alert. She tried to block out the magnified sound of her heart pounding in her chest and listened for any noise that didn't belong.

She was ready to make a quick escape.

❖ ❖ ❖

51

Naya woke with a start. Her heart thumped sharply against her chest. Her headache approached migraine level as her eyes flicked back and forth trying to transfer information to her brain so that it could tell her where she was. It couldn't be the hospital because she'd moved to the rehab centre. Eventually she was awake enough to see that she was in her spare bedroom. A few heartbeats later, she remembered the burglary.

She checked her watch. 7:16 am. She'd managed a few hours of sleep. She threw off the covers and carefully swung her legs over the edge of the bed.

She found her cane on the floor and pulled herself to her feet, waiting the obligatory few seconds to find her balance. Relieved to find the bathroom also untouched, she examined her image in the mirror. Her extreme pallor shocked her. She needed food. But first she needed to wash off the sensation of grime from last night's ordeal.

After several failed attempts to lift her weaker left leg into the tub, she stepped in with her right leg first. Unable to lift her other leg and afraid to lose her balance if she removed her hands from the wall, she surrendered to her physical limits. Sat on the edge of the tub and used both hands to lift her leg in. After only a half-hearted attempt to stand she wisely chose not to become part of the home accident statistics that occurred in the bathroom.

She imagined herself under a refreshing waterfall after a long jungle hike. The pounding water massaged away muscle knots and soothed her aching head. The real water pressure up here, as compared to the drizzle of the portable shower downstairs, made it much easier to rinse out the shampoo.

Like many people, she used to take doing the basic tasks for granted. Such as walking down the hall. Climbing a set of stairs. Getting into a bathtub.

Along with the dirt, the last of her misguided pride was washed down the drain. Before she'd been discharged from the rehab centre she'd accompanied an occupational therapist to ensure that her home was accessible to someone with limited mobility. At the time Naya had silently rejected each modification and adaptation the therapist proposed, deciding to make her home accessible in her own way.

Now, as she literally crawled out of the tub, she reconsidered some of the suggestions. Grab bars in the tub for sure.

Her energy levels drained to an all-time low after the warm shower; she was surprised at the effort needed to wrap a towel around herself.

The wall provided the extra support she needed to make it to her bedroom. Panting and light-headed, she collapsed into the corner armchair near the door. Taking long deep breaths, she gradually felt better.

She surveyed the typhoon-inspired decor of her bedroom. All the dresser drawers were open and much of their contents were scattered on the floor. The wall-to-wall closet was open with most of the clothes still hanging, though slid aside as though searching to see if anything was behind them. Strangely enough her jewellery box was untouched.

Were they looking for something in particular and stopped searching when they found it? Or were they after the computer and made a mess just to make it look like burglary?

After a few minutes she felt ready to get dressed. Acutely aware of her tentative balance, she felt like a tight rope walker as she made it around the piles of clothes to her dresser where she was relieved to find some untainted clothes. She dressed in black slacks and a beige t-shirt. Righting the chair in front of her dresser, she sat down. A wave of warmth filled her as she untangled her hair. She hadn't realized how much she'd missed her room. Or being able to do the simple things like shower and comb her hair upstairs.

She felt human again. She felt whole.

Naya went downstairs, a much easier journey than going up, in search of breakfast. While waiting for the toast to pop, she phoned Travis to tell him about the break-in. Predictable as ever, she barely got the words out before he snapped, "I'll be right there." And hung up.

Sitting down to eat the toasted cream cheese sandwich, an irrational feeling of claustrophobia hit. Only a few hours ago strangers had been in her kitchen. In her house. Breathing this air. Touching her things.

With toast in one hand, cane in the other, she slid the patio door open. The scents of flowers and fresh cut grass called to her. Cautiously, she stepped out onto her patio stones. There were so many different birds chirping and singing. As a child she'd thought that the birds woke the sun each day, and if they didn't sing it might sleep in. She used to wonder if they'd cancel school if that ever happened. Even now, early morning nudged those warm feelings to the surface. She'd been a fool to avoid coming out to her own backyard to enjoy breakfast the way she used to.

She took in her backyard, enjoying the familiar feel of home. Travis had been cutting the grass every two weeks and it was about due. Her usually flourishing vegetable garden accused her of abandonment and allowing thriving weeds to enjoy the full sun. The cedar fence that bordered her property was accompanied by more weeds with the occasional splash of colour from growing perennials. There was a patch of golden yellow lilies and another of dark orange ones, plus a healthy red rose bush, thriving only because it had been trimmed last fall.

In the far corner the apple tree was full of tiny green spheres, as was the ground below it. She should have thought to hire someone to prune and feed it.

"Hello there."

Mid-spin she recognized the voice of her elderly neighbour. She expected to catch the usual glimpse of his eye through the wooden fence slats and was surprised to see his head and shoulders above the fence.

"Hi Ray," she waved awkwardly with the sandwich. She really hadn't wanted to talk to any of her neighbours. She hobbled back towards the door to escape any prying questions.

"Your apple tree is doing quite well," he said.

"Umm, yes, it definitely looks healthier than last year." She reached the door and was ready to bid a quick good-bye.

"I remember how upset you were last fall when you thought it was going to die. I hope you don't mind that I came into your backyard without permission to fertilize and prune it. And I sprayed it with captan. It looks like you won't be having fungus trouble again this year."

"No, of course I don't mind. Thank you very much." she said. Changing her mind about fleeing, she moved closer to the fence. Early spring last year she'd been devastated when she found lesions on the leaves. By September the apple tree had dropped all its leaves before any of the other trees had started to even change. Ray, a retired pilot, reminded her of Jimmy Stewart but without the relaxed stuttering speech. Always ready to help with any gardening question, he'd come to the rescue immediately recognizing the fungus infection. He helped her keep the ground clear of infected leaves and sprayed the tree.

"Naya, I hope you don't think I'm prying," he started.

Oh great, here come questions. Where had she been for three months? Why the cane? She prepared to deliver the usual story: back injured in fall during race.

"Last night I noticed a police car in your driveway," he said. "Is everything all right?"

"Oh." Why was she being such a jerk? Why hadn't she remembered that he was never nosey? The rest of her neighbours were a different matter. She suspected that they had a 'Naya watch committee' ensuring someone was always outside waiting to ask her questions, no matter the time of day or night. Back then she didn't mind stopping to chat. Now, the last thing she wanted was to be spotted going for a walk with her cane. Or worse with her walker.

"I had a break-in last night," she said.

"Oh, my goodness! Are you all right?"

"Luckily I was out at the time," Naya said. "They only took my computer. But they made a big mess. The police think it's kids."

"My, my," Ray shook his head. "I really don't know what has become of children these days. When I was young the biggest crime was climbing the neighbour's fence to get to the orchard." He tsked and added, "Such a shame. Kids just don't steal apples anymore."

"No, guess things have changed."

"Do you need help cleaning up?"

"Thank you, no," Naya said. "A friend's coming over. Actually, I should get going..."

"Just keep in mind if you need anything you have my number. Or feel free to pound on my door, even if it's the middle of the night. At my age I don't need much sleep." Then his head dropped below the fence. She could see him moving around in his backyard.

She was relieved that he hadn't questioned her cane. She really didn't want to lie to him. There was only one other time where her cover story had made her feel guilty.

It had been a few days before she'd been transferred to the rehabilitation centre when Taylor and Mackay had visited. She'd sat up in the hospital bed struggling to look interested when all she wanted to do was sleep after an especially difficult day. Taylor wore jean shorts and a tank top, and sandals, all in her usual choice of colour — black.

Mackay dressed more mundanely in jeans and white dress shirt with rolled up sleeves. He wore a thin red tie, which she guessed was his way of dressing up for her. From the moment he'd first come into the room he'd found it necessary to fill every silence with various topics that she'd lost track of ten minutes ago. If he'd only take a breath between sentences then someone else could jump in.

She glanced hopefully at Taylor. She sat slumped forward in her chair, legs crossed, top one pumping up and down, head titled to one side, twirling a strand of smooth black hair as she vacantly stared out the window.

Mackay's constant chatter had always provided a sort of white noise at work. Today it took on a hypnotic quality able to lull the most avid insomniac to sleep. So what chance did she have?

Naya heard a new voice speaking. Relieved about the change in topic she tuned in to the conversation. It was Taylor. Mackay must have paused to breathe.

"So, what did they say?" Taylor asked.

Naya stared at her blankly.

"The doctors. What did the doctors say?" Taylor said.

"They said it's severe exhaustion," Naya started, trying to make sure the words didn't sound rehearsed. "Trained too hard after the marathon last fall. I need to take a few months off." She smiled and added on a whim, "Maybe I'll find a nice beach to spend the summer."

Taylor stared at her in silence, her pale face expressionless. Finally, she blinked a few times and said, "Do you really think we're that stupid?"

Naya was silenced by what was essentially for Taylor an emotional outburst. Mackay stared at the floor, his face crimson.

"Well," Taylor said, slapping her thighs in what was meant to be a nonchalant gesture, though successfully broadcast her anger through the room. "We should get back to work. See you in two days." Mackay gave Naya an awkward nod and hurried out the door after Taylor.

Naya rested her head back on the pillow feeling chastised. No, she didn't think they were stupid. She hadn't told anyone about her true condition — except for Travis. The entire time she'd been in the hospital, Taylor and Mackay had visited every other day. Whether they were coming out of loyalty or because Travis had asked them to, didn't matter. She should have offered them the courtesy of the truth.

Two days later she came clean with them. The slight relaxation of Taylor's frown had told her that she'd been forgiven for the lie.

About to call Ray back, she peered through the fence slats and saw him go into his house. He also deserved honesty and she planned to give him that respect the next time they spoke.

For now, there was no point in putting off the inevitable. Time to clean up the family room. She finished her toast in a couple of large bites and went in.

She barely managed to sort out the mess of wires under the TV and replace the PVR and DVD player before she became exhausted. Crawling around on the floor and moving fairly light equipment shouldn't have been such an arduous task. But it was. She leaned against the wall. Wiping the sweat from her forehead, she wished that she'd remembered to bring some water. In the middle of debating whether she should get a drink or have a brief nap she heard the front door open.

She checked her watch. It had been barely twenty minutes since she'd phoned Travis. He lived forty-five minutes away. She reached for her cane as she strained to listen.

Naya tightened the grip on her weapon.

CHAPTER SIX

Within seconds Travis appeared at the door to the family room, dishevelled and breathing in panic mode.

"Travis!" Naya exclaimed. She loosened the grip on her cane and sighed loudly. "Did you get a speeding ticket?"

"Are you okay? Did they hurt you?"

"Travis, I told you I was fine. Seriously, you could have had an accident."

He sat on the floor beside her. "They made a hell of a mess."

"You should see upstairs."

"The police have any leads?"

"No," Naya said. "There've been several burglaries in the area. They think it's kids.""Kids would have taken your expensive sound system. What's missing?"

"My computer, all my handwritten notes. They even took all the supplies you'd brought down and the printer. They're gonna go blind trying to read my chicken scratch handwriting. At least all my files are on the network drive."

"Good. But don't worry, all the equipment can be replaced. What else did they take?"

"I haven't had a chance to check yet."

"You'll be able to tell after we clean up." Travis stood, offering her a hand.

In seconds Travis closed up the sofa bed which immediately gave them more floor space. With his help the entire room was returned to its normal look in less than thirty minutes. She was relieved to find that there weren't any gaps on the shelves which meant that her entertainment was all present and accounted for.

"That didn't take as long as I thought it would," she said, breathless but invigorated. She relaxed on the closed sofa bed glad to have her second couch back. Travis brought them each a mug of coffee and sat on the other sofa.

"Thanks," Naya said.

"What're friends for? So, we'll take a short break and get started upstairs." The words were barely out when his cell phone rang. He checked the call display before answering. "Hi, Taylor."

He listened for a long time and then said, "Okay, yes, I did forget. I'm at Naya's place now. She had a break-in last night — No she hadn't been home — Just her computer. But they made a hell of a mess." He glanced at Naya, then added, "That's a great idea." He hung up.

"That was Taylor. I forgot about a meeting with a perspective client."

"I'm sorry. I didn't mean to make you late."

"Don't worry. The meeting's not for another couple of hours. But I need to get into the office and finalize our proposal."

She walked with him to the door. "Thanks for your help here. I'll just take my time cleaning upstairs. Don't worry."

"Oh, I won't. Taylor's coming right over to help you." He gave her a smile and quickly shut the door before she could utter a word of protest.

Naya stared at the closed door. After a moment she locked it. Took a step back and continued to stare at it. Cleaning would be stressful enough. But now she'd have to come up with conversation to help fill all those awkward silences Taylor was famous for.

As the saying goes, she shouldn't look a gift horse in the mouth. Checking the lock again, she went upstairs to get a head start on cleaning the bedroom.

They'd hired Taylor two years ago once their fledgling company had become successful. So successful in fact that they couldn't keep up with the work on their own and decided to hire two people. Three weeks and forty-one applicants later, they were still holding interviews. Had Naya realized it would be this hard she would have cancelled the rest of the interviews and given up sleep to meet their deadlines. Far less painful than enduring the endless parade of characters.

"We're a tiny company," Travis had said in answer to her constant question of why couldn't they find one normal applicant? "We can't afford to offer a big salary. You didn't really expect to see people at the top of their game apply."

"Look, I know that. But in *one* day we've interviewed four goofy guys and one weird girl that all snort instead of laugh — I'm going to be having nightmares for a long time. And I refuse to believe that none of them has ever heard of shampoo or seen a commercial for soap. Aargh!" Naya covered her face with her hands, shaking her head.

"Okay, who's next?"

Naya opened the schedule on the computer. "Taylor Mannion." A few mouse clicks later, she said, "Seems like she forgot to attach her resume. Hope she brings a copy with her."

As though on cue there was a knock on the door. Travis whispered, "Here we go. Good luck to us."

"Come in," he called. The door opened to reveal a young woman in her early twenties. She was dressed in a t-shirt, vest, knee-high boots, jeans, all in black. Even the backpack, slung over one shoulder was black. Her waist-length jet black hair was worn in a single braid which hung over the other shoulder. She took in the room with a slow sweep of her eyes. Then her aqua green eyes snapped back to focus on Travis and Naya.

"Taylor," Travis said, indicating the chair on the other side of his desk. "I'm Travis Bloom, this is Naya Assad."

"Yeah," Taylor said. She dropped her bag on the floor beside her and sat down.

"We don't seem to have your resume," Naya said. "You didn't happen to bring a copy with you? Or you can just fill us in on the highlights now and email it later."

Silently, Taylor reached into her backpack, pulled out a notepad, wrote a few words, then tore the sheet out and handed it to Naya.

Naya read it, eyebrows raised. Passed it to Travis, who read it with a chuckle.

Naya said. "Usually we ask a few questions first. But how about we get right to the point?" Gesturing to the computer in the corner, she added, "I'd like you to debug that program for us."

"Yeah," Taylor said. She got up slowly, picked up her backpack, sat down at the computer station dropping the bag on the floor beside her.

"Would you like some coffee?" Travis asked her.

"Yeah," Taylor said as she slid her chair closer to the desk.

Travis held the note she'd written and whispered to Naya, "This is either the best resume I've seen, or the dumbest."

"We'll just see how well she does with your program," Naya said. "I figure it'll take her twenty minutes if she's good. Half an hour if she's average." They both walked over to the low bookshelf where the coffee maker sat. She poured three cups.

"You know if she works out then we'll get to live out all our fantasies," Travis whispered. Then he lowered his voice further. "Never met a dominatrix princess before."

"She's a goth. And that's *your* fantasy," Naya whispered back, elbowing him in the ribs. "You idiot."

"Oooh, a goth princess." Travis picked up two cups to take one to Taylor. Naya carried her own as they turned. They stopped short and glanced at each other with disappointment. Taylor was leaning back in the chair playing with the end of her braid.

Naya sighed as she said, "Guess we gave you a pretty hard task."

"I fixed it," Taylor said, looking up at her.

"What?" Travis said. He put both cups down and practically pushed her out of the chair to check the screen. "There's no way..." He looked at Naya. "She did it."

"Move," Naya shoved him out of the way. She checked the program herself. He was right. It compiled correctly. Naya gave Travis a questioning look. He nodded. All the while Taylor leaned against the wall, absent-mindedly played with her hair and staring at her boots.

"A few questions," Travis began. "Do you listen to rap music?"

Taylor gave him an expressionless look. "No."

"Good. I hate rap."

"You don't snort when you laugh, do you?" Naya added.

"I don't laugh," Taylor answered, looking at Naya.

"Works for me," Naya said looking at Travis.

"Me too." Travis nodded. To Taylor he said, "Can you start Monday?"

She remembered Taylor's resume. It had read simply, "I can do the job."

And she had. Back then they couldn't afford a larger office space, but it had been easy working in close quarters with her. Taylor was quiet. Too quiet. She never laughed. Rarely talked.

Worried that she was either very shy or didn't know how to socialize, Naya had spent months trying to get through to her. Trying to bond with her on some level. She'd tried talking about music, books, movies, only to be met with, "I'm not really into that." Naya had tried talking about every sport she could think of. Nothing could stimulate conversation.

They'd been to her house a handful of times. They knew she was estranged from her entire family with the exception of her maternal grandmother. Other than that, they didn't know anything about her life.

With time, they got used to her silence. At work, it was comfortable. But here...

The doorbell brought her back to the present. It had to be Taylor. Naya surveyed her progress cleaning up her bedroom. Who was she kidding? On her own she'd be lucky to finish by next month.

Naya stood at the railing to wait for Taylor to let herself in.

"Hello?" Taylor called appearing in the entrance.

"I'm up here," Naya said with a wave.

Taylor slipped off her shoes, "Do you need anything from down here? Some ice water, maybe?"

"That would be great, thank you," Naya said. Only now did she realize how thirsty she was.

They sat on the floor in the hallway as Taylor handed her the glass.

"Thanks," Naya said, as she leaned against the railing. She admired the foresight of bringing a tray to catch any water drips from the frosty glass.

"I see you've started cleaning up," Taylor said, as she looked into the bedroom.

"How can you tell? It's still a disaster."

"I can see the carpet in that corner. Over there."

There were piles of clothes on the floor. The sheets and blankets in separate piles. Except for a narrow path to let her through, the carpet was still invisible. Taylor making a joke? That was unprecedented. And that thought made Naya start to laugh uncontrollably.

After a several seconds, Naya wiped the tears from her eyes. "Guess I needed that."

"Yeah, good to see that frown disappear," Taylor said, her lips relaxed not exactly into a smile, but not in their usual thin line. A small pause and she asked, "Have the police found your friend?"

"They don't believe she's missing, so I'm looking. No luck so far. Okay, I know it sounds crazy, but I think that all of this," she pointed at the mess in her bedroom and office, "is connected."

"Yeah?"

"I don't want to sound like one of those conspiracy types but the coincidences are a bit much. First Valerie and another girl who worked on the same top secret project disappear. The same day Valerie's desktop is gone. Then my place is robbed and the only thing I can see that's missing is my computer. It has to be connected. I just wish I knew how I got tangled up in this mystery."

"You were at your friend's house?"

"Yes and the other woman's, Alice," Naya could see where she was going with this. "Someone must have been watching their places and seen me."

"Yeah."

Naya took another sip of water. She felt obligated to safeguard Valerie's work. Only up to a point. No intellectual property was worth more than her friend. And that project was the only clue she had to find her friend. She knew she could trust Taylor completely. And not just because he passed intensive security checks necessary for their sensitive work, but on a personal level as well.

"I met with someone who worked with Valerie a year ago and then they stayed friends. Rose told me it was to write a pervasive surveillance program that used various video cameras around town to spy on this company's employees. She isn't working on this new project, but she suspects that it might be related to the old one." Naya paused for moment thinking. "They'd need to get all the access codes to all the different cameras."

"Or maybe the company just put up their own cameras in strategic locations around town."

"You'd definitely need a computer to sift through all the video," Naya said.

"Facial recognition programs are improving every day," Taylor said. "Yeah and you could also tag your targets. You know, embed something in their company ID card."

"Can you imagine how much a program like that could be worth? Not to mention the person who designed it." She shuddered at the thought. The theory made sense. All the pieces fit together. Naya sipped at the water as she considered everything, trying to figure out what to do next.

She shifted uncomfortably as the floor felt suddenly very hard.

"Yeah, maybe we had enough of a break. Can't keep putting off work."

"You're right," Naya said. She used to always prefer sitting on the floor to furniture. Not anymore. Her muscles had stiffened up enough to make her worry about how she was going to get up without embarrassing herself.

Without a word, Taylor came around behind Naya. With a lot of effort between the two of them, accompanied by protesting muscles, Naya stood.

"Yeah, you looked like you were going to need help."

"Thanks," Naya said. She held onto the railing stretching to get the circulation back in her legs.

In the bedroom Naya wanted to wash every piece of clothing, but Taylor, ever the environmentalist, had another suggestion.

"Yeah, I know you feel all icked out about the burglars touching your clothes. You should wash the clothes on the floor, especially your underwear. But anything left in the drawers is still clean. Things that fell off the hangars should be okay too. All that extra waste of water isn't necessary."

"Okay, in the interest of the environment," Naya agreed reluctantly. Looking at the mattress tossed on the floor she added, "But I don't think there's water hot enough to clean these sheets or the comforter."

"Yeah, how 'bout I take them to the Salvation Army?" When Naya nodded, Taylor tossed the bedclothes over the railing.

"There's also a garbage bag in the garage with sheets and stuff from the sofa bed," Naya said, "May as well take them too."

Taylor continued to help sort through things on the floor as she said, "You've never talked about your time at the rehab centre. Was it bad?"

"No," Naya paused. "Well, accepting things was really tough. I thought my life was over. I mean, how was I going to live in a wheelchair relying on people for little things? But Mike, my physical therapist, really challenged me to push beyond my limits."

"And he got you through the rest of your rehab?"

"Sure he helped me physically. But only one person kept me going mentally. Kept me from giving up. Valerie." Naya fell silent.

"You're a good friend to have," Taylor said quietly.

Naya wanted to say that she obviously wasn't. It was her fault that Valerie was missing.

"Yeah," Taylor added, "I'm sure she knows that you won't give up until you find her."

This time Naya gave her a smile because that much was true. She'd never abandon her friend.

They continued chatting on everything from their polar opposite tastes in fashion to advances in technology. In between, Taylor took down piles of clothes, put them in the laundry then came back upstairs to help fold and put away the clean ones. After a few hours, the bedroom was neat and tidy with the blanket from the spare bedroom covering the bed.

"I'll pick up a new comforter for you," Taylor said.

"Oh, you don't have to do that," Naya said, struggling to keep the feeling of dread out of her voice.

"Yeah, don't worry. It won't be black." Taylor gave her a hint of a smile.

Naya laughed. The thought must have been very obvious on her face. "Thanks. Just use my ATM card to pay for it." Sitting in the armchair, she said, "I just realized we missed lunch?"

"Do you like Chinese?" Taylor asked.

"Sure, love it. Order whatever you like, I'll eat anything," Naya said, moving out into the hall towards the office. "I'll get started in here now."

In the office Naya stood in the doorway, not sure where to begin.

This mess seemed exponentially worse than either the family room or the bedroom. She guessed that when they couldn't find what they were looking for, they'd changed from methodical searching to plain old fashioned destruction.

The bookcases sat empty and peered longingly at their belongings scattered across the floor. The desk drawers had been pulled out and their contents dumped on top of the books. Fortunately, most of the file folders remained in file cabinet, though they sat at haphazard angles in the open drawer. She didn't even want to imagine the nightmare that would have been if they'd been scattered.

She took a step into the room, bending to close a few books and place them in safe stacks. And that's when she saw him. Peeking out from beneath a stack of papers and books.

The pink nose attached to blue fur.

She dropped to her knees and dug out the Muppet.

"Grover!" She hugged him tight as tears flowed freely. She hadn't cried in years. Not even when they'd given her the diagnosis. Now, the frustration of the last few months came rushing back as she desperately hugged a symbol from her childhood that had been closed off to her by time. An athletic life that had been snatched away by her own body. And this little blue Muppet also symbolized her lost friend.

She sniffed and wiped her tears with the back of her hand and checked behind her. At least Taylor wasn't around.

Just as Naya gathered her composure, Taylor joined her in the office.

"Okay to start work?" Taylor asked, not looking in her direction.

Damn. She'd seen the breakdown. Forcing a nonchalant shrug, Naya held up Grover and said, "When Valerie and I were kids we loved Sesame Street. Grover was my favourite. She gave him to me on my eleventh birthday. I guess seeing him brought back a lot of memories and unburied a lot of — a lot of emotion."

"Yeah," was all Taylor said.

They worked with an awkward silence for a few minutes. Until Taylor spoke.

"Do you mind if I ask you a personal question?" When Naya nodded, Taylor continued, "Why don't you tell people you have MS? Why the big secret?"

Naya hesitated. How do you explain what it was like to go from running marathons to barely being able to walk? She glanced away for a moment, then back again.

"I won't deny that it's been hard accepting my new limits. You know, it's sort of ironic. I didn't tell people who didn't run about my competing in marathons because I hated getting lectured on the dangers of running on asphalt, shin splits, vitamin depletion and over-exercising. It was easier to just not tell people. Now, I guess I thought it would just leave me open to more criticism and well, pity. Being seen as something I'm not. Or less than I used to be."

Naya paused then added, "Yesterday I actually told a couple of people. Maybe because they were strangers I found it easier to get the words out."

"Yeah? How did you feel after?"

Naya thought about it for the first time and realized that she'd felt relief. "Like I could finally breathe easier."

"Maybe eventually you'll be able to tell people that you know."

"Eventually," Naya said. She thought about her parents that had moved overseas when they'd retired. They'd never been a close-knit family. They'd never approved of any of her choices — career, boyfriends and definitely not running. But they were still her parents. On some level she hoped that this might bring them closer together.

She also worried that this could drive them further apart. They'd have new things to criticize. They'd probably insist that all her training and running had caused this, or even blame working in front of a computer screen for too many hours.

Taylor continued placing books on the shelves after Naya sorted them. She was glad to see Taylor participate in an actual two-way conversation. Imagine that. It had only taken her two years.

Looking closely, Naya noticed a different tightness around Taylor's eyes. A serious expression was normal for her but this one echoed with sadness. She couldn't think of why, until...

"Taylor," Naya began, feeling a touch of foreboding. "How's your grandmother?"

She remained silent for a time, aimlessly moving papers around on the floor. Finally, without looking up she said, "She had a stroke last night. She's in a coma."

"Oh, my God. You shouldn't be here."

"Where else should I be?" She looked up, her eyes red.

"With her," Naya said.

"I can't do anything to help there. But I can help here."

"Taylor," she began. What was she going to do? Insist that Taylor go to her grandmother's side and sit helplessly by? She was right, it was better for her to keep busy. "Thank you for being here."

She nodded. Both continued picking up, organizing and putting away. By the time lunch arrived, the office was mostly back in order. Taylor went down to answer the door and by the time Naya reached the kitchen, the table was set and the kettle plugged in to make tea.

"It smells delicious," Naya said as she retrieved chopsticks from the drawer. "Remind me to pay you for the food.

"My treat. Besides, I ordered my favourites. Hope you don't mind." Taylor scooped the food out of the containers and into serving dishes.

"*These* are your favourites?" Naya said as she placed napkins on the table. There was BBQ Duck, beef in black bean sauce and Chinese greens. "I thought you were a vegetarian."

"Really? Yeah, guess at work I always eat light. You know, salads and stuff. If I eat more during the day I can't concentrate."

They ate in relaxed silence. After lunch, the last of the laundry was dry. Conserving her waning energy, Naya waited downstairs as Taylor put the clothes away.

By three o'clock the entire house felt like home once again.

"I really appreciate all your help," Naya said walking Taylor to the front door. "And I was really glad to have the company."

"Yeah. I liked helping," Taylor said, slipping into her runners.

"I hope your grandmother will be all right,"

"Yeah, me too." Turning from the open door, she added, "You know you don't have to face things alone." Then she was gone.

Naya locked the door, leaned against it with a small smile. She might feel alone, but she knew she wasn't. Even strangers were willing to be there for her. Like Kevin.

She hadn't given him a second thought all day. The poor guy had probably thought that she'd abandoned him. In the family room, she rummaged through her backpack for his number and phoned using her cell.

"Hi Kevin, it's Naya. Sorry I didn't call you back sooner."

"I figured you were so exhausted you just slept the day away. You should've woken me to drive you home."

"It was late and I didn't want to disturb you." Naya paused for a moment, then said, "I was a bit distracted today. I came home last night to discover my house was broken into and ransacked."

"Oh my God! Are you all right? I can come over to help you clean up?"

"I'm fine. A couple of friends already helped out. Thanks for asking, though.

"I was visiting a friend of — of Alice's. I could come over and we can talk about looking for Alice and Valerie. If you're up to it."

"Sure. Do you have a pen?" She gave him her address.

"I'm not far. Be there in ten minutes," he said and hung up. And sure enough, ten minutes later the doorbell rang.

"Have you got any news?" Kevin asked as they sat in the family room.

"I'm sorry, no. They can't have vanished without leaving some trace. We just have to keep looking."

"You're right but where do we look?"

"I'm not sure," Naya began. Yesterday, before going out, she'd phoned all the hospitals. One of her theories had been that Valerie might have panicked and caused an accident. She found no record of Valerie having been admitted and no unidentified patients. She had another thought. "You don't happen to know the licence plate of Alice's car, do you?

"Uh, well, uh, yes," he said. "The police won't look for the car. Unless, we — can report it stolen."

"I don't think filing a false report will endear us to them."

"Oh, wait, do you think the car got towed from someplace?" Kevin suggested.

"That's what I was thinking." She pulled out her cell to search for impound sites. "We can call around and see if anyone has Alice's car. As her brother, you should be able to get it out."

"Why?"

"Search it for any clues that might tell us what happened." She broke off at his expression. He must think that she sounded like a child playing cops and robbers. "Sorry, I'm just trying to help."

"No, it's — I should have thought about that myself." He got his cell phone. They split the long list of towing companies in the city. She never thought there'd be so many. Halfway through the list Kevin found it.

Alice's car had been towed from Valerie's street where it had been parked overnight.

Shaking his head with a frustrated sigh, he said, "They'll only release the car to the registered owner. What a waste of time."

"Maybe not. Feel like a little road trip?"

❖ ❖ ❖

Kevin parked on the far side of the impound office building, which was simply a small trailer, allowing Naya to get out of the car unseen. She headed into the lot to search for Alice's light green Saturn as Kevin went into the office to keep the attendant distracted. Armed with a licence number and a spare set of keys, she hunted through the rows of vehicles.

All she could think of was what a horrible place for a nice, law abiding car to wind up. Amidst the rows of vehicles were a select few that looked like they'd endured rough times. Next to an expensive Mercedes squatted a three door, one eyed, Hyundai whose original colour was unrecognizable beneath a thick layer of dust and debris. Further in, next to a sporty red Firebird, a Prius hunkered down for the long stay.

She negotiated the uneven gravel lot, constantly losing her footing. Why hadn't she brought her walker? She tripped and spiralled around her cane. Miraculously, she stayed upright. Could it be that her true calling in life was to become a pole dancer? She knew a few friends that would find that more than a little funny. She was never any good at dancing. It was that pesky thing called rhythm that she had issues with.

Almost five o'clock and it still felt as though an ocean of humidity was bearing down on her. She occasionally had to lean on various cars to rest, burning her hand on the metal.

Between tripping and burning, she wasn't surprised that she was running out of energy after a few minutes. Her backpack grew heavier and sweatier by the second. She should have taken Kevin's suggestion that she be the distraction, while he searched for the car.

The vehicles weren't organized in any obvious sense of order. New arrivals were dropped wherever there was an available space, randomly interspersed among long-time residents that were slowly decaying where they sat. As her frustration grew and her strength withered she realized that if she didn't start back now, she might not make it out of the lot at all. She really hated to give up but she had no choice.

And that's when she spotted Alice's Saturn. Right behind a Winnebago which appeared to have barely survived an encounter with Mad Max.

Kevin was obviously doing his bit keeping the attendant busy. Now all she had to do was search the car. Grab whatever wasn't nailed down. Shove it into her bag. And get out.

She opened the driver side door and recoiled when a wave of furnace heat smacked her in the face. Waiting a few seconds, wishing she could risk more time, she got in the driver's seat and checked under the seat. Nothing hidden there. Glove compartment contained only the registration and owner's manual.

Moving into the back, she found a sweater and sneakers on the floor. That was it. She peeled herself off the leather seats and limped around to the trunk. Inside she found a computer bag. Energy levels recharged as she reached for it.

"Hello."

She spun around, almost losing her balance, to come face to face with a young man. Maybe in his late teens. He grinned at her.

"Picking up your car, miss?"

"Oh, uh," she considered saying this was her car. But without the right paperwork to prove it, she knew that wouldn't work. The last thing she needed was to be arrested for grand theft auto. Maybe stretching the truth was more prudent. "No, this is my friend's car. You see she lent it to me and well, I spent the night at a friend's house and the car got towed. I left her computer in the trunk and just wanted to get it back." She smiled, adding, "Of course I'll pay for the towing charges but if she finds out I left her computer here, well, that wouldn't be good for our friendship."

"Okay, do you have a note from her saying she lent you her car?"

Damn. She hadn't thought of that. She could get Kevin to vouch for her. But she had no idea what kind of story he was telling the lot manager. Finally, she gave a Cheshire cat grin and said, "No, she's always going out of town and leaves me her keys." She held up the set. "See?"

"Well," he began, looking at her cane leaning on the side of the car. He studied her. As though deciding she wasn't some mastermind criminal, he said, "Sure, take the computer. Just hope it didn't get wrecked with today's heat. But the car has to stay until she gets back. Sorry." Looking her up and down, he added, "Do you need help getting back?"

She hesitated. All she needed was to get caught in her lies if he was the chatty type. She was sweating and finding it harder to stay upright. Looking back toward the office she hadn't realized how far she'd walked. She nodded to him, then shoved the computer case into her backpack as the man slammed the trunk shut and locked up the car. He offered her his arm. Even if he'd asked her any questions on the way back, she wouldn't have found enough strength to answer.

Breathless, her from simply walking, him from struggling to keep her upright, they finally reached Kevin's car. She thanked him with a weak smile as he helped her in. She hoped her partner would get back before the attendants started comparing stories. As soon as the young man had gone back to the lot, Kevin rushed out of the office.

"We better get going," Naya said warding off any questions.

A few blocks away, with no sign of pursuit, not that she really expected there to be any, Naya pulled out the computer bag.

"I just hope it didn't get ruined after all this time in the trunk," she said as she unzipped the case. "Damn!"

"What's wrong?" Kevin asked, startled, making the car swerve slightly.

"The case is empty," Naya said, slapping the bag on her lap. "I should have realized that it felt light. But I was in such a hurry to get out of there... I'm sorry."

"Don't feel bad," Kevin said, patting her hand quickly before returning his attention to the steering wheel. "It was a good idea."

Back in her kitchen, Naya sat at the table while Kevin brought her a glass of ice water.

After draining half the water in a long drink, she felt revived.

"I guess now we know they didn't leave on their own. I doubt your sister would have left her car behind." Naya yawned widely. Feeling embarrassed, she apologized then added, "If we put our heads together, I know we can come up with some more ideas."

"You look exhausted," Kevin said, standing to leave. "Call me tomorrow, when you feel rested."

She walked him to the door, saying a quick good-night before she locked up. She was tired. She felt too hot and sticky to think clearly.

More than anything, she wanted to shower, but she doubted she'd have the energy to come back down. After the big lunch she wasn't hungry now but she knew she would be later. Why hadn't she left clothes downstairs? She could have used the portable shower on this floor. She made a mental note to do that in the future.

The next best thing: She made a ham sandwich and grabbed an apple for a light supper. Then she retrieved Valerie's computer from its hiding place and put it into her backpack. A tight fit next to Alice's case. After forcing the zipper closed she put the backpack on; a little heavy but she knew she could manage.

Showered and wearing fresh pyjamas, she got into bed revelling in the cool freshness of the sheets. Propped up with pillows, she especially enjoyed the firm mattress. Quite an improvement from feeling every spring of the sofa bed. For the first time since the morning that she'd left for the marathon, she actually felt like she'd come home.

Naya reached into her backpack to get Valerie's laptop out. She pulled out Alice's case first and before dropping it to the floor, she had a thought. Though there was no computer in it, something else could be. She searched through the various pockets and other than a wireless mouse, nothing was there. Checking the outside pocket her skin tingled with excitement when her fingers touched a memory stick.

Turning on Valerie's computer, she plugged the memory stick in. Just one file.

A decryption program.

Excited, she tried it on Valerie's files. No luck. Maybe she was tired or feeling optimistic because the failure didn't upset her. She put the stick into her own backpack, positive it would come in handy at some point.

With her attention on Valerie's computer, Naya felt like her old self — at least on the inside. Positive that she could do anything. She'd once been called the best hacker in her field. Companies from around the world had tried to woo her to their side to design better, stronger, impenetrable systems. They'd been right to offer her the big bucks.

Confidence, not arrogance, assured her that she could still demand the top salary.

She gave the locked files one more try. Luckily the burglars hadn't taken any of her back-up memory sticks or disks from the office. After trying several decryption programs, the file opened.

Unfortunately, after all that effort she discovered that it wasn't a full program. Just a few sample lines of code as part of the project proposal. It did, however, confirm Rose's theory that it was related to their last project building on the original concept.

It gave Pervasive Surveillance a new spin.

A target's every movement, phone call, email and keyboard stroke, even how many times they went to the bathroom, could be potentially monitored and recorded. Surveillance in high crime areas was one thing, but this really crossed the line. It made Big Brother and all his CCTV cameras look like some old gumshoe in a black and white film.

The contract was for a large security company. She laughed when she read the name of the company owner. The same man that claimed he didn't know Valerie. Or Alice.

Howard Dixon.

Unfortunately, when she went on-line to check his company out, there was little information other that the usual PR stuff. She checked the time. Just past ten. Never too late to phone Travis.

"Hi, it's me." Naya said. "Have you heard anything about the company, SecurITe. Owned by a Howard Dixon? There's very little on-line."

She could hear him typing. "Can't find anything either. But I do know someone who could help out. The Bloodhound of the Internet."

"You don't mean that guy we ran into last year at the movies. What's his name ... Elliot? The guy believed he was some kind of spy and was convinced that he was being watched by either the government, aliens, or maybe both."

"But he's the best. Anything you need he can sniff out. If it's okay with you, I'll give him a call and he'll call you. Your cell phone okay?"

"Better than my home number," Naya said. Not even two minutes went by before her cell beeped.

"Yes?"

"This is Elliot. Meet me by the fountain in the park just off of Elgin Street, downtown. Tomorrow. Seven-oh-six in the A.M., sharp. I'll be wearing a beige trench coat, black fedora and aviation style sunglasses."

He hung up before she could say a word.

No more entertaining herself on Valerie's computer. She couldn't risk staying up all night and sleeping through the alarm. She should probably make an attempt at a good night's sleep.

The good thing about the park was that it was only a few blocks from SecurITe.

Hardly a coincidence.

CHAPTER SEVEN

Despite her best intentions, Naya spent the night fighting to control all the mind traffic zipping through her brain. She barely had time to enjoy winning the battle before the alarm buzzed and she came fully awake with a grumble. Then the anticipation of meeting with super-sleuth Elliot and learning Dixon's secrets propelled her out of bed with only a slight moan of protest.

She arrived at the park twenty minutes early. She rolled her walker quickly towards the fountain and sat on its edge to wait. The park was deserted except for the occasional jogger in shorts or person in a business suit. No one matching Elliot's description entered the park.

She was grateful for the early morning meeting. She could already feel the impending humidity the weather channel had warned about. She used to love the sun back when heat and humidity were mere adjectives and not fear provoking words. At one time, not long ago, she'd considered running an ultramarathon. She'd checked out the Western States Endurance Run; a hundred mile course over rough, mountain terrain in California. She'd even considered entering the Four Deserts marathon. Most of her running friends had been impressed though some had questioned her sanity. Whatever their opinion, they all had to admit there was no better way to test her limits.

Now the challenge became staying awake and upright during a heat wave.

Humidity drained the life out of her. Although, she told herself with a tiny chuckle that the desert was a dry heat — so there was still hope.

After a total forty minutes, she became painfully aware of the fact that the fountain was made of concrete. She tried shifting her weight to lessen the pain but no position was comfortable. She tried sitting on her walker which also felt like a rock. She decided to stand for a while.

What happened to 'seven-oh-six in the A.M., sharp'? By 7:35 her last bit of patience vanished and she decided to leave. That's when she spotted a man hiding behind a tree. She sat down on the fountain edge to wait for him to approach.

She spent the next several seconds watching his fedora peek out, then duck back into hiding. Should she call to him? He'd never asked her what she looked like. If he wasn't sure it was her, she considered simply calling out her own name. She'd really feel stupid doing that. Honestly though, who else would be sitting on a fountain edge for forty-five minutes at this time of day?

Obviously this little game of hide-don't-seek was also part of the deal. Rather than risk spooking him, she stayed put. Remained silent. Pretended she didn't see him.

And waited.

She'd now spent a total hour waiting. She'd never realized how tired you could get just sitting. And she was stiff. Fed up with the charade, she decided to go directly to Dixon's company and wing it. She stood to leave.

At that point he stepped out from behind the tree. Without looking in her direction, he walked towards the fountain trying to be inconspicuous. A little hard with his pant legs tucked into bright orange high tops. She remained standing. Waiting and wondering.

He continued his slow, meandering approach and finally sat down on the fountain edge three feet away from her. He kept his back to her looking everywhere but at her.

"Had to make sure you weren't followed," he said.

"Elliot?" She prudently erased the smile from her lips as he tried to look like he wasn't talking to her.

"No names. Please." He glanced all around abruptly as though searching for eavesdroppers. Transforming to his nonchalant posture, he added. "I have some info about that company you were interested in." He moved to sit closer to her. Not until she sat down again did he continue. "I think I've been here long enough to strike up a casual conversation — for the sake of anyone watching."

"Uh," was all she could think to say.

"Keep it light. Smile," he said grinning. He remained silent until she mirrored his look. "SecurITe is in the new glass office building one block away. It was completed before last Christmas. They take up the top floor. The two floors below are still unoccupied."

"That's a lot of expensive real estate going to waste," Naya said.

"Exactly!" He gave her a nod of pride. "You are smart, just like I was told. What do you know about the company?"

"They specialize in network security. Their clients include some of the world's largest corporations."

"Sounds like you read their web page. The truth about any company is never advertised. You gotta know where to look. And that's where I come in. I know where to look." He glanced around again then slid a little closer, lowering his voice. "They're also one of the best, if not *the* best, in designing surveillance systems. The latest thing is combing two dimensional still photos, video, IR, Lidar and GPS data to get fairly accurate 3-D representation in real time. Their work is more international than they advertise. Companies and," he broke off, spun suddenly to look behind as though he'd heard a noise. Naya wasn't sure if she should be concerned about his paranoia or try to ignore it. Eventually he appeared to be satisfied, sat down and returned his attention to her.

"Not just Canadian and US military, they also do work for — different — military."

"What do you mean 'different'?"

"Other countries. Let's just leave it at that. Rumour has it that they don't care who they work for as long as the cheque clears. And the company founder, Howard Dixon, used to be a Ranger. You can't trust anything he says. Lies are his religion." He studied his surroundings again, then leaned in close to add: "Something else you won't find on their website is they do personal protection for individuals. The rich, famous and those that don't want to advertise they have bodyguards. These days, thanks to excellent divorce lawyers, their clients include affluent women that have issues with their ex-whatevers." He stood abruptly, glanced all around in a panic.

Startled, Naya also checked the area trying to figure out what had spooked him this time.

"Good luck." Elliot's long strides took him to the edge of the park before Naya could say anything.

All this cloak and dagger stuff and she really hadn't learned much. Dixon may have some questionable foreign clients but in today's world economy, so did a lot of companies. Her best bet was still a personal visit to SecurITe. If she started walking now, she should get there shortly after eight. It could be too early for the boss but she intended to wait.

She reached for the water bottle in her walker's basket. It was gone. She shook her head at the eccentric young man. He'd probably taken it to do a DNA test to confirm she wasn't an alien.

❖ ❖ ❖

By eight-thirty she stood outside the glass door leading to SecurITe — Protection Consultants offices on the eleventh floor. The reception area was decorated like something straight out of a science fiction movie. There was a large shiny silver logo behind a shiny metal desk. The secretary was a slim blonde, her hair tied up in a messy bun. Her makeup of kohl rimmed eyes and pink lipstick was simple and not overdone.

She took a deep breath. Pushed the door open. When the secretary greeted her with a bright smile, butterflies suddenly flitted in her stomach. Naya considered saying, 'oops, wrong room,' turning tail and running. No, she'd come too far for that. Concentrating on each step she continued forward.

"Good morning, may I help you?" she asked in a heavy Texas accent, her voice deeper than expected.

"Good morning," Naya noticed the name plate reading Mussette Cooper. It had a nice sound to it. "I'm here to see Howard Dixon," Naya said, hoping her business-like tone camouflaged her terror.

"One moment, please."

The secretary placed her fingers on the black desk top. Immediately, a keyboard appeared on the polished surface. Naya envied the touch sensitive technology and was impressed to find the secretary wore short, practical nails, painted in a light pink sheer polish. She typed quickly, checking the thirty inch flat screen before smiling at Naya.

"He's free now until 11:15." She gestured to the left as the wall slid open to reveal a corridor. "Turn right. His office is at the end of the hall."

Naya's first thought. That was easy. Her second thought. Cool door. How many of the other walls were camouflaged entrances? "Thank you very much."

She was barely through when the wall whooshed shut. Turning right, she passed several normal-looking doors with handles and hinges. Silver name plates bore an eclectic list of boldly engraved names that ranged in ethnicity from Kapoor, to Leung, to Dutrisac, to plain old John Smith. She suppressed a laugh wondering if that last one might be an alias.

Within moments she stood in front of Howard Dixon's door. She knocked. Heard a muffled "come in" and entered.

She stopped short in the doorway of a dream corner office. No need for curtains with smart-windows making up the three outer walls.

The east facing windows had darkened to keep out the bright morning sun. There was a large, semicircular desk straight ahead in the centre of the room. To the left was a lounging area with plush armchairs. To the right, a rectangular table with ten plump leather chairs. Now this was the place to hold a staff meeting. Probably with the best coffee and danishes served on the best china as well. When she wanted to have a more comfy staff meeting they'd all trek down to the nearest Tim Horton's.

A man in his early fifties sat at the head of the conference table three file folders before him. His thick gray hair, a little longer than a brush cut, still had evidence of its original red. When he saw her he calmly closed each folder and approached her with a tentative smile. Under that off-the-rack dark suit, he still had the physique of a Ranger.

"Hello, may I help you?"

"Hi," Naya began. She pulled her attention away from the view. "Thank you for making time in your busy schedule to see me, Mr. Dixon." She could see the slight confusion in his eyes. Probably wondering if he'd forgotten an appointment. Keeping her own expression relaxed and pleasant she shook his offered hand. She pressed on not giving him the chance to deny anything. "I'm Naya Assad, a friend of one of your employees, Valerie Peters. I've been trying to get in touch with her for some time and I was wondering if you know where she is."

His hesitation faded as he eyed her walker. She'd seen this type of expression time and again with visitors at the rehab centre when they came to see other patients. Some rushed to move out of her way or open doors or constantly offered to help her. They viewed her as fragile. And theses were people used to dealing with the disabled. So what chance did the average guy have?

He ushered her to a chair by his desk and she walked slower than necessary leaning on the walker as though any minute she was going to topple over. She parked the walker behind the chair, then with exaggerated difficulty, sat with a heavy sigh of relief. He hovered near by ensuring that she was safely seated before returning to his own chair. From the way he watched her she could tell that he believed that she was frail, in need of constant help. Definitely not a threat. She counted on that false impression to make him let his guard down.

"Ms. Assad, I really don't know how I can help you," he said. "As I told you on the phone, I don't know your friend very well. I have over a hundred permanent employees and more than five hundred contract employees."

"I don't really expect you to personally remember Valerie," she said. Elliot was right. This man didn't know how to tell the truth. "And I'm sure she dealt with someone else. She probably wrote your name down because you're the boss. Would you mind checking your records to see who she worked with?" She gave him the sweetest, most innocent smile she could muster.

"I'll see what I can do," he said then typed, hunt-and-peck style, with one finger. After a few seconds he nodded at her and said, "Yes, she did have a contract with us. She finished it last month and we sent out her final cheque."

"Could I speak to the person she dealt with?"

"Sorry, no. Security, you understand." Now it was his turn to give her an innocent smile. She just hoped hers hadn't looked as wooden as his did.

"I understand," she said. She tried to think of something else to ask, knowing he'd be lying anyway but hoping he'd let something slip. Finally, "Could you check if her work involved travel?" She watched his reaction carefully and caught the slight tensing of his jaw.

He studied the screen briefly, but she knew he wasn't actually reading anything. After a few seconds he said, "No." Fake smile again.

"Why I'm asking is because she's agoraphobic and if she was forced to go outside she could have panicked and be hiding out somewhere." She saw his face relax, suggesting he was satisfied that she really was a friend. Only those close to Valerie knew about her problem.

"Now, if there's nothing else, I'm preparing for a meeting in a few minutes." He stood coming around the desk to offer a hand to help her up. Nice to see that he was a gentleman about throwing her out. She took her time getting to the door.

"But if you do hear from her..."

"Of course, I'll call you. Leave your number with my secretary."

"Thank you for your time." She shook his hand which now felt cold and clammy compared to when she'd first arrived. She felt a great satisfaction knowing that her questions had struck a nerve.

In the corridor she moved quickly back to the exit. She didn't see any control panel and was about to pound on the wall when it slid open. The secretary cheerily greeted her.

"I could see you looking concerned," Mussette said, her voice pleasant. "Everyone does the first time."

"Hidden cameras," Naya said, nodding. She pushed her walker towards the desk and came around to see the computer screen. Along the top were six camera views of identical looking corridors, with different number codes in the corner of the screen.

"Do you have to watch and open a door anytime someone comes by?"

"Are you kidding? How boring would that be? Employees use their biometric ID for access. If I'm not around and someone shows up without an appointment they wait."

Noting her friendly nature Naya felt comfortable talking to her. "Speaking of no appointment, I noticed that Mr. Dixon was surprised when I knocked on his door. Didn't you announce me?"

"Well," Mussette began, with a mischievous smile. "I guess it's my way of getting even with him. Yesterday he got mad with me for not reminding him about a meeting that he forgot to put in his scheduler. I'm great at remembering. Not so much with telepathy." She laughed.

"Judging from his expression I'd say you got even." Naya chuckled. Feeling a little headache and suddenly very thirsty she reached for the water bottle in the walker basket. Damn that Elliot and his paranoia. She asked, "Is there somewhere I can get a drink?"

"Yes, there's a cafeteria in the basement."

"Is it far from the elevator?" she asked, not relishing the thought of walking long meandering corridors.

"I'll take an early coffee break and join you," she said.

"It's pretty early, I don't want to get you in trouble."

"I've been here since 7:00," she said. "No one better complain." She got her wallet and cell phone from the bottom drawer then came around the desk. She wore black flats, navy pants and a short sleeved knit top with blue and white horizontal strips. Very summery, but still quite professional looking.

The spacious cafeteria contained a decadent selection of pastries, donuts and muffins, not something Naya normally ate. She decided to splurge on a piece of apple crumble and a large, black Columbian coffee while her companion ordered the same. Mussette thoughtfully carried the tray with both orders to a table close to the cash as she followed on wobbly legs. After a sip of coffee her strength began to seep back.

"Were you here to see Mr. Dixon about a job?" Mussette asked, taking a sip of coffee.

"No, I was hoping that he might know where a friend of mine has gone. Valerie seems to have vanished from the face of the earth."

"You mean Valerie Peters? Where could she go with agoraphobia?"

"You know her?"

"I usually arrange for courier deliveries from Mr. Dixon. But one time there was an emergency delivery so he asked me to go. We hit it off right away. She's such a character. What a great sense of humour."

So much for Dixon barely remembering her. Guess someone should have reminded him that if he really wanted to lie, he should have told his secretary.

"Did you phone her?" Mussette asks.

Naya sighed thinking, what am I, an idiot? Trying not to sound annoyed she said, "Of course, but she's not home."

"No, I meant on her cell. All employees have a company phone. It makes it easier to discuss their progress anywhere."

"Cell phones aren't secure."

"Maybe most aren't..." She took her cell out of her pocket and retrieved the number. Naya keyed it into her own cell phone's address book.

"Coffee break's over," Mussette said, as she picked up her untouched snack. "Hope you find Valerie safe."

Naya watched as Mussette left the cafeteria tossing in her full coffee cup and the apple crisp into the garbage. Eating the last bites of her own dessert, she tried the cell number. It went directly to voice mail. She hung up without leaving a message.

Next she phoned Rose. After studying Alice's files last night, she'd discovered that Rose had in fact been working with Valerie and Alice on a small part of the current project. Naya didn't plan to confront her about it — she was probably following security protocols, or perhaps didn't know exactly what she was working on — either way Naya wanted to talk to her again.

She muttered a curse as Rose's phone also went straight to voice mail. She left a brief message.

She warmed her hands on the coffee cup, wondering about her next step. The obvious would be to go home. Or maybe just go to Rose's place and take a chance that she was there. Before she could decide, her cell phone beeped. Checking the caller ID, she answered.

"Hi Travis, what's up?"

"What's up? I'm at your place. Where the hell are you? Are you okay?" His voice was a little higher than its normal alto timbre.

"Yes, *dad*. I'm fine." She paused, shaking her head. Then she realized that after the break-in, he would be concerned. "Sorry, guess I should have told you I was going out. I found a lead that I had to follow."

"You were supposed to talk to Elliot and get info. Not run around all over town following leads. Alone."

"Elliot did call last night telling me to meet him downtown. And it was close to..."

"Naya," Travis cut her off, "you're not a cop. And we don't really know what's going on. It isn't safe for you to be roaming around all alone. And I'm not saying anything about your physical ability. You *know* that."

"I appreciate your concern, but I'm fine. I thought I'd drop by SecurITe and check out the company."

She could hear him sigh, sounding like he'd lost the battle then asked, "Find out anything?"

"Not from the boss. He kept lying about knowing Valerie. But forgot to tell his secretary to back him up. She gave me Valerie's company cell number."

"I take it you called it."

"Yup, went straight to voice mail." She broke off, thinking for a moment. "Remember your buddy that loved to hack into GPS systems? Ben, Fred or something like that?"

"You mean Clive? Yeah, he's doing time for breaking into the military's email and well, let's just say sending messages that only he thought were funny. The guy you want is Raj. Remember him?" That last question had a teasing tone.

"How could I forget?" She laughed. "I still have his number."

"Are you coming home now?"

"I'm going to phone Raj now and then afterwards I'm going to go visit someone who worked with Valerie. Why, do you need me for something?"

"Oh, uh no." Travis hesitated. "Actually, give me the address where you're going." She gave him Rose's. Then he continued, cheerfully, "Okay, take your time. Don't go wandering around town without letting me know. And be careful."

After he hung up she thought about his concern. His overprotectiveness. It was something new that had developed after she'd got sick. First he was concerned that she wasn't going out. Now he was concerned because she was. This, in a nutshell, was why she didn't want to tell people about her MS and have them treat her differently. Come to think of it, even Taylor was different. The only one that hadn't changed was Mackay. She couldn't wait until everyone got back to acting normal. Hopefully they would.

No time to worry about that now. She called the number.

"Hi Raj, it's Naya."

"Naya, how you doing?" Raj said. "Haven't heard from you in months."

"I'm fine. Been keeping busy." It wasn't a lie. She *had* been busy recovering. "I was hoping you could do a favour for me."

"For you — after all your legal advice — anything."

She laughed. Her alleged 'legal advice' had been a passing comment that he should get his own lawyer in his divorce. That small suggestion had saved him from losing his house and half his salary to his wife whose hidden assets proved that she made three times as much as he did. In the end, she paid *him* alimony.

Naya quickly explained, "I have a friend who's missing. I have her cell phone number but I believe it's off. Could you keep an eye out if it gets turned on?"

"Hmm, it's been a while," he said.

"Come on Raj, if anyone can do it, you can."

"I said it's been a while, not I couldn't do it." She could hear him typing as she gave him the number. "Hmm. This phone has a high level encryption lock. It'll take me some time to break in. I'll get back to you."

Naya drained the last of her coffee and left to flag down a cab.

She asked the cab to wait for her in Rose's driveway. Feeling energetic again, she left the walker in the trunk and used the cane to go up to the front door. After a few moments the door opened to reveal an elderly man with red-rimmed eyes.

"Good morning. Is Rose home?"

The man suddenly burst into tears. Shocked, Naya stood there for a moment, afraid to talk, or even pat his shoulder. Eventually, he managed to choke out a few words.

"My wife's been kidnapped."

CHAPTER EIGHT

Naya waved the cab driver off. Good thing she'd paid him before getting out though that had been his idea. As he sped around the corner she remembered the walker. She really should consider getting several of them. That way she could leave them in cabs all over town.

She followed Barry Nellis into the kitchen. He looked to be in his seventies, with thick curly grey hair that she knew her chrome-dome father would envy. Barry walked with stooped shoulders and a pronounced limp. From his gait she wondered if maybe he'd hurt his hip or had hip replacement surgery. He gestured at a chair as he got the boiling kettle from the stove. Shutting off the stove with trembling hands, he poured the water into a china tea pot.

She sat at the small, round, glass table and studied the ultra-modern kitchen. A double oven, a ceramic top stove, a huge side-by-side refrigerator. Every appliance shone so much she believed that they had been polished to within an inch of their life. He started to open a cupboard but got distracted and scrubbed at an invisible spot on the light brown marble counter.

Selecting two china cups and saucers with delicate pink roses, he filled them with tea, then shuffled cautiously to the table, threatening to trip any second. Naya longed to help him, but the fear that she could lose her own balance and smash the delicate cups kept her still. He placed them on the table and rearranged the matching creamer and sugar bowl in the centre of the table, then closer to her, then back in the middle. He sat and reached to move them again. She rescued him by taking the creamer and pouring a drop into tea that she normally would have taken black.

"You said Rose was kidnapped?" Naya asked.

"My Rosie came home yesterday after meeting with a friend," he began. Naya realized it was her meeting with Rose that he was talking about. "As soon as she got home, her cell phone rang and she went out straight away, promising to be home for supper. She hasn't been back since. I left countless messages for her to call me. She would never go anywhere without telling me."

"Did you call the police?"

He nodded. "They were here all last night. They just left. Oh, my goodness what could have happened to her?" He covered his face with his hand. Though he wasn't making any sound, she knew that he was crying.

Naya patted him on the shoulder in an ineffectual attempt to console him as her mind reeled. Now three people that had worked for SecurITe had vanished. Eventually Barry calmed down and she asked, "You said you left her a message?"

"Why, yes," he said with a sniffle. Wiping his nose with a handkerchief from his pocket.

"Could I get her cell phone number, please?"

He stood slowly as though every joint needed to be engaged one at a time, then limped over to the counter. "I don't think it'll do you much good. She left her cell here."

"Oh. Uh, guess not." She took the offered phone. Great, the man was either senile or the stress was playing with his mind.

"Unless," he asked slowly, "did you want the number for her iPhone? That's where I left the messages."

"I thought you said..." Naya broke off. He didn't look like he was technologically minded. She added tenderly, "An iPhone is the same as a cell phone."

"Really? Technology changes fast. My Rosie is the only one who can keep up."

Such innocence made her heart ache for him as she accepted the number. She'd get Raj to track this number as well.

Barry began to aimlessly wander around the kitchen. He wiped a counter that was already clean, rearranged dishes in the cupboard. She took advantage of his distraction and checked the call history, jotting down all incoming and outgoing calls from this past week.

Finally he turned his attention back to her.

"Would you like a snack with your tea?" he said.

"Thank you, but I should get going."

"You need to eat. You're too skinny," he insisted. "I know you young people are always in a hurry." He sighed and added, "Even my Rosie forgets to eat. Do you know they gave her two large screens for her computer just to make her work even harder. And she's so dedicated that she tries her best."

She smiled at his innocent comment. Then she noticed his sallow complexion. "Mr. Nellis, when was the last time you ate?"

"I had lunch." He paused looking up at the ceiling with a thoughtful expression. "Yes, lunch yesterday. I waited for Rosie to get home for supper but..."

"I'll make a deal with you. Let me make you lunch, then I'll take a sandwich with me."

Naya stayed long enough to make him scrambled eggs and cut up a cantaloupe she found in the refrigerator. While she prepared his food, he packed a lunch in a paper bag for her. Then she called a cab.

When she opened the front door she almost whooped at the sight of her walker. Climbing into the new cab she hoped that she'd remember to take it out when she got home. Getting Rose's secure phone number was a good accomplishment. If only she could have managed a peek at her computer. Of course asking poor fragile Barry would have definitely crossed the line.

Naya phoned her GPS guru.

"Hi, Raj. Anything on the number I gave you?"

"The phone's still off," Raj said. "Don't worry, I'm keeping an eye out, twenty-four-seven. Got my computer set up to alert me even if I'm not home. Not that she wants me to ever leave her side."

"Raj, I hope you're not working too hard," she said. He always got a little weird when he had a tight deadline. He'd spend hours at the computer usually forgetting to eat or sleep.

"Just have to finish one more thing then I'll take a break. So, what can I do for you?"

"I have one more cell number for you, if you don't mind."

"Ah, she's a temperamental mistress, she is. But I'm sure I can persuade Emma to add the number."

Uh oh. He'd given the computer a name. "Thanks. And Raj?"

"Yes?"

"Get some sleep." She worried about the guy. He'd always been a bit of an obsessive compulsive personality. It's what made him an excellent programmer. She hoped he'd get some rest before he and Emma became engaged.

She watched the houses, with their perfectly manicured lawns, zip by. She admired a few of the late summer flowers and thought about doing a little garden work herself at home. The way she used to. As soon as Valerie was back home and safe that was exactly what she'd do.

Within five minutes, Raj called back.

"I got a signal on that second number," he said.

"You're kidding. I thought it was off."

"It was just turned on — oh, wait. I lost the signal."

"Did you get a position?"

"Of course. I told you Emma is good." He gave her the address of a motel just south of the city.

"Thanks, Raj. What number did she call?" Naya asked. When he gave her the number, she did a quick check. Rose had called home. Or someone did.

She considered phoning the police to let them know that now there were three connected disappearances. Hold on. Did she really want them to revise their opinion of her from simple annoyance to conspiracy nut? Forget it. Naya redirected the cab to the motel. If she found Rose there, then a nice anonymous call to 911 would be in order.

She got out of the cab a block from the Happy Slumber Motel, proud of herself for remembering her walker. At the opposite end of the motel parking lot she found a bench partially hidden by tall bushes. She settled in expecting a long wait. Opening the paper bag Barry Nellis had packed for her, she found a bottle of apple juice, a roast beef and cheese sandwich and a pear.

After an absent-minded bite, her hunger awakened. She ate, watching the comings and goings of the motel patrons for entertainment. Drug dealers in room three. Room six, well, the scantily clad woman greeting a different man every thirty minutes or so left little to the imagination. The August afternoon was nicely cooled by a breeze from the north. A definite shift from this morning's promise of humidity. After a few minutes the pleasant breeze had transformed into a cold wind. She pulled out her thermos of coffee from her backpack and felt a giddy sense of relief to discover it was still hot. It would both warm her and hold off the threatening nap that always lingered close by.

A few more sips of coffee made her realize that last night's lack of sleep had made her not only tired but naive. Did she actually expect to see Rose wandering around? What if she wasn't even here, just her stolen cell? There was only one way to know.

She stood, put the backpack on her walker. Time to knock on a few doors. Note to self: skip rooms three and six.

Barely a step away from the concealing hedge, a car screeched into the motel lot and parked in front of room twelve. Startled, Naya instinctively ducked back behind the bush. Spying through the branches she couldn't believe who got out of the car.

Howard Dixon.

He marched up to room twelve. He pounded on the door with his fist so hard Naya could practically feel it even from this distance. Immediately a man, built like a gorilla, opened the door. A second later, Rose appeared and shoved the large man aside. Though no words reached across the parking lot, there was no mistaking that Rose was furious. She stood with her fists on her hips and shouted at Dixon. In contrast, Dixon calmly made placating motions with his hands until both went into the room, shutting the door behind them.

She had to get closer to eavesdrop. With only three other cars in the parking lot and no chance of cover she couldn't figure out how, but she had to try. The temptation ended when Dixon came out of the room less than a minute later. Shaking his head, he drove away at a rational speed this time.

She had to save Rose. Her original plan was to call 911. That was the smart thing to do. That's what a sane person would do. Before she could complete her psychological analysis, the large ape man left the motel room carrying an ice bucket.

Sanity was definitely overrated.

Naya abandoned the walker — people with walkers were noticed. She unfolded her cane — people with canes blended in — and rushed as best she could across the parking lot. The second she passed Mr. Gorilla she released her held breath. A check over her shoulder confirmed that the guard was in no hurry as he sauntered along. He was still three rooms away from the office and ice machine when she reached room twelve.

The door opened and Naya came face to face with a very shocked Rose.

"Come with me," Naya whispered urgently. "I'll help you escape."

"I'm not a prisoner. I'm being kept here for safety." She stuck her head out the door looking for the guard. "And if that fool sees you, you'll get stuck here too."

"Why was Dixon here?"

"You went to see my husband and Dixon got worried." She glanced outside again. "Don't tell anyone I'm here. I'll phone you later and explain." She slammed the door shut.

Dumbfounded, Naya stood frozen. Trying to process the unexpected turn of events. Out of the corner of her eye she saw the guard returning, her brain came out of neutral. It instructed her legs to start moving. She hoped that he hadn't noticed that she'd been lingering in front of room twelve. She avoided any eye contact as they passed each other. His polite nod of hello startled her into returning the greeting. She held her breath as he continued walking.

She heard the motel room door open and close, a glance over her shoulder verified that he was gone. She stopped and leaned against the building hyperventilating. Indulging in a couple of seconds of rest, she then crossed the parking lot to seek shelter in her hideout.

Trembling, she collapsed onto the bench. Good thing she hadn't phoned the police. Whatever was going on, at least Rose hadn't been kidnapped.

Could that mean Dixon was also hiding Valerie and Alice?

❖ ❖ ❖

Naya got home to discover Travis's car as well as an INT Home Security truck in her driveway. So, he'd arranged to have a security system installed for her. That explained his mysterious tone when he'd called earlier.

Inside she called, "Travis?"

He appeared upstairs at the railing with a huge smile. "Surprise!" He bounced down the stairs. "Hope you're not mad but consider the security system an early Christmas gift. Or a late birthday present."

"Travis," she gave him a quick hug. "I'm not upset. I don't know why I never thought about getting one before the burglary. It's a great idea, but you shouldn't..."

"Hey, like I've said before, that's what friends do." Pointing upstairs, he added, "He's wiring up the windows, then it's done." The doorbell rang. "Talk about timing. I wasn't sure you'd be back before I had to leave so I called Mac to supervise the work." Travis opened the door.

"Hi," Mackay said. Today's t-shirt simply had a drawing of a telescope. "Where is he?"

"Upstairs," Travis said. As the younger man climbed the stairs two at a time, Travis called, "Mac, let him work. Don't tell him the right way to do things."

"I won't," Mackay called over his shoulder, "unless he really messes up."

"Mac!" Travis warned, but he'd already disappeared from view. To Naya he said, "I hope he doesn't cause too much trouble."

"I'll keep an ear out," Naya said, walking him to the door.

"Oh, I almost forgot, I brought you another laptop. It's on the kitchen table," Travis said.

"Great. I'll check it out. Thanks." She locked the door behind him and after parking her walker in the corner near the door, made her way to the family room to sit and rest. She checked her watch. Only 1:10? It felt so much later.

She slipped off her shoes and lay down on the sofa. She allowed herself to drift into that relaxing nether world between reality and dreams. Somewhere in the distance she heard Mackay's muffled voice talking non-stop. She felt sorry for the technician.

She'd always had a higher tolerance for his surplus energy and constant fidgeting. She remembered how much she'd had to fight to hire him.

"Of course he's annoying," Naya had whispered to Travis as they'd watched Mackay work on debugging the test program. Travis hadn't even wanted to test him. He answered every question quickly but with a tone that made it sound like it should be obvious and why couldn't you come up with a better question. She'd managed to cut the question portion short and suggested he move to the practical part of the interview a millisecond before Travis had a chance to thank him for coming in and dismiss him.

"Let's just see how well he does on the program," Travis said in a tone that he didn't expect much.

As though on cue Mackay had held up his hand, as though he was in a classroom and announced that he'd finished. He'd succeeded in four minutes. Second only to Taylor who'd completed it before they'd managed to pour her a cup of coffee.

Naya had spent the better part of the day defending Mackay's quirky nature. She liked to pretend that it had been her wonderful talent for persuasion that had won her case. However even she had to admit that it had been the next interview that had helped Travis come around. The twins had come into the office, sat in the same chair and insisted that they had to be hired together because they were Siamese twins; connected not physically, but mentally.

After they'd left, Travis had said. "No more interviews. Mackay's hired."

Smiling at the memory, Naya drifted into a light sleep.

Until loud voices startled her back to the present.

By the time she reached the bottom of the stairs the argument was at full boil. Mackay and the technician faced off at the top of the stairs, shouting insults and curses at each other.

"Hey!" she shouted and got immediate silence. Both men looked down at her. "Mac, what did you do?"

"Me? He started it!" Mackay yelled, his voice shrill. He raced down the steps.

"I started it?" The technician followed close behind to stand next to Naya and point accusingly at Mackay. "He said my brother's stupid."

"I never said anything about your brother. But *you* called *me* an idiot. Me. *Me.*"

"Stop it!" Naya snapped. Pausing for a moment to regain her own composure, she asked, "What happened? You first." She nodded at the technician, holding up a warning finger to silence Mackay's protests.

"Okay," the technician paused as though counting to ten. He continued, his voice slightly calmer. "I needed to check the I.D. of whoever signs off on the work. For our records and to make sure there's no problems later. When I handed his I.D. back all I said was, thanks Alfonso. And that's when he freaked out."

"I did *not* freak out. I calmly told him that I don't use that name, so he called me Al. When I explained why I don't use that name either– *he* freaked."

"Oh," Naya said. Covering her eyes with her hand realizing what was coming.

"Yeah, *Alfonso* here claims that he doesn't use Al because he didn't want people to think he was a plumber. I told him my brother's a plumber. And he said that it was good that he even had a job considering his limited intellect."

Naya glared at Mackay, then to the technician said, "I'm really sorry about this. Umm, maybe I should sign off on the work. After all, this is my house."

"He doesn't live here?" When she shook her head, he said, "Good. Because I was about to disconnect everything. Wait a minute. He's not your boyfriend, is he?"

"God, no!" Naya and Mackay chimed.

"Okay then," he said, handing her the electronic tablet to sign. He pulled out a basic instruction manual from his bag and handed it to her. "You can get more detailed instructions on-line. I'll just run through everything quickly now." He gave her a quick lesson on activating and deactivating the alarm. How to bypass the internal motion sensors when she activated the system while at home. "If you have any questions, *you* can call 24/7."

She thanked him, apologized again and locked the door after he'd left. She spun around to face Mackay. One hand on her hip, the other on the wall for balance. It took her a few seconds before she could speak, all the while Mackay was looking everywhere but in her direction. At least he knew he'd been an idiot. This time more than usual. She just wished she knew why he was always such a maniac when the subject of his name came up. Alfonso Mackay wasn't a common combination. And he never ever considered finding the humour in it.

Within minutes of meeting him, they'd learned to call him either Mackay or Mac. No Alfonso and never, ever, ever, Al. One day soon, she planned to get him full of enough beer and get some answers. For now, he appeared suitably chastised. Rather than pick him apart, she really wanted to pick his brain.

Removing her hand from her hip, she suggested, "Let's have a seat in the family room."

"Uh, sure, okay," Mackay studied the floor as he obediently followed her.

Each settled on a different sofa. Naya said, "I'm not planning to yell at you. Just promise not to go ballistic — the next time." When he nodded, she continued. "I have a technical question for you."

"Really?" he perked up.

"I wanted to know..."

"You have any idea what it was like growing up?" Mackay interrupted. "Kids were always joking about my name. Asking if my mom dated the mailman. And then that damn technician asked — asked if the mailman was Spanish."

"Mac..."

"What was your question?" His tone recovered its eagerness.

"Mac," Naya began. She gave him a tiny smile. "My question is about tracking cell phones."

"There are several commercially available programs out there. You know to track your teenagers, or keep track of cheating spouses."

"I know, but I was wondering if there was a way to track a phone when it's off."

"Not when it's off. The phone has to emit a roaming signal which is picked up by the closest antenna tower. It doesn't have to be making a call, just be on. Then using multilateration based on the signal strength to nearby antenna masts, you can pinpoint its location. The accuracy depends on the quality of the phone."

"Too bad," Naya said. Raj was keeping an eye out if Valerie's phone was turned on.

"If you don't have any more questions, I gotta get going." Mackay stood. "Travis said to remind you to activate the alarm."

"I will," she said walking him to the door. "Thanks for coming over."

"Thanks for not getting mad about, well, you know."

She gave him a 'you're welcome' nod, then locked the door behind him and turned on the alarm.

In the kitchen she checked out the new computer. It was a Notebook, only eleven inches in size. Much smaller than her previous seventeen inch laptop and a lot lighter. Now she could carry it around with her and not worry about waiting to get home to hack files. She loaded up a few programs. This would make her sleuthing efficient and much easier.

All the time she kept hoping Rose would phone soon. A long shot, but it would be nice if the woman could confirm that Dixon also had Valerie hidden for safe keeping. She could rest easy. And so could Alice's brother.

She should call Kevin and let him know what she'd found out. Of course she planned to leave out the part about finding Rose. She should probably leave out the part about going to see Dixon. Maybe she shouldn't mention her conversation with Mussette either. Come to think of it, there wasn't much she could tell him. Just the same she should phone him in case he had some news for her.

Startled when the house phone rang she grabbed it before the first ring had finished.

"Oh, hi, Travis," she tried not to sound disappointed that it wasn't Rose.

"Naya, it's good to see that with everything else that's going on, you have time to look for new clients."

"New...what?"

"I got a call from someone named Mussette. She wanted some info on our company."

"She didn't by any chance speak with a Texan accent?"

"Yes. So what kind of work is it?"

"Sorry, no job. She's Howard Dixon's secretary. What did you tell her?"

"To call back because I was heading into a meeting. Which was actually true, but I wouldn't have said anything without talking to you first anyway. Guess you struck a nerve if Dixon's checking us out."

She told him about Rose going missing, but decided against mentioning the motel over the phone. She'd wait to tell him in person.

"You think that all three missing women are connected?"

"First Valerie and Alice disappear, then Rose, two days later. They all worked on the same projects and all know Dixon. And he lied about knowing Valerie. I guess there's no point in listening to him lie about knowing the others."

"You can't blame him for that — not with corporate security and all that. But you're right, it's too much of a coincidence not to be connected." Travis continued, his voice taking on a lecturing tone, "This just goes to prove that you shouldn't be gallivanting around town on your own."

"You worry too much. Besides, I wasn't alone. Kevin was with me."

"Kevin?"

"Alice's brother. When I went to her house I found him there. He's looking for his sister so we teamed up to search together."

"What's his full name?"

"Uh," she paused. "I guess I never asked. I assumed that they had the same last name. It could be Vanderlund."

"I'll check into that."

"Why?" Even as she asked the question she realized that she should have checked more closely into the backgrounds of the players. Every bit of information would help. "Never mind."

"Not to change the topic, do you like the new computer? I know it's small, but it's still pretty powerful."

"It's great. Much easier to carry around."

"That's what I thought," Travis said. She could hear the relief in his voice. "Did the house alarm get installed okay? No fireworks?"

"Everything went smoothly. The tech gave me a crash course before he left." No point in mentioning the men's meltdown. "It's on now."

"Good. I think we can all sleep better now."

She hung up. Immediately, her cell phone beeped. She checked the call display.

"Rose! Are you all right?"

"Yes, I don't have much time. You need to know that I spoke with my husband and told him I'm on a business trip and there was a mix up getting a message to him. He told me you were nice to him today. Thank you for taking care of him. He's not well." She stifled a curse. "My babysitter's back."

"Wait..." The line went dead.

Good thing that she had the new computer to distract her. Travis wasn't kidding, it was much more powerful. She realized that she had to stop playing on it and go back to thinking about what was going on. She opened Word and typed in what she knew.

- *Valerie and Alice disappeared Monday*
- *met with Rose on Wednesday afternoon*
- *Rose disappears Wednesday evening*
- *find Rose at motel where Dixon has hidden her*
- *all 3 have worked on pervasive surveillance project*

Seeing everything written on the screen only brought home how little she actually knew. She had no idea where Valerie and Alice might be. Raj was keeping a watch for Valerie's cell phone. She also had no idea who took them. Just because Howard Dixon had Rose hidden at the motel it didn't necessarily mean that he'd taken the other two women.

The other project members hadn't been helpful when she'd first contacted them. Maybe now that she had a bit more information, such as it was, she might be able to get some new insight from them.

She called Bill Chang, the contact from Valerie's address book first. He'd readily admitted the first time she'd spoken to him that he'd worked with her. Obviously not a proprietary portion, but with a few carefully worded questions she might learn something new. After a brief conversation with his wife, she hung up with an unsettled discovery. He'd left for the airport yesterday while she'd been out grocery shopping. Apparently a last minute business trip to a location that he'd forgotten to include in his note. And no, he hadn't had a chance to phone her yet.

Next she phoned Kirk Stroud, the name she found in Alice's computer. The secretary told her that he'd left town last night on a business trip to a location that she wasn't at liberty to disclose.

Naya stared at the phone in her hand. Was it likely that both men had left on last minute business trips? Were they on the same "trip" as Rose? Was Dixon keeping everyone in protective custody? Or was Rose the only one truly safe?

She added to her list.

- *Stroud and Chang gone same day as Rose*
- *all disappearances definitely connected to project*
- *is Howard Dixon behind ALL the disappearances?*
- *WHY?*

She stared at the word WHY realizing how far out of her element she was. She wasn't a cop. She didn't have the resources to track down missing people. She wasn't even sure how to do it. She could try phoning the police again. Speak to the missing persons detective, Philadelphia Ashantre. But they didn't feel there was a problem and Ashantre had even doubted that the agoraphobia was real. They also didn't believe that her break-in could be related to her friend's disappearance. Naya could admit that she had Valerie's laptop. Unfortunately the only thing that would achieve was getting charged with theft.

The cell phone startled her out of her thoughts.

"Hi, it's Kevin. Just wanted to see how you are."

"Oh, hi. I'm a little frustrated."

"Sorry, didn't mean to bother you."

"No, I mean because I can't seem to put the puzzle pieces together. I can't figure out where to look for Valerie next. I've exhausted every clue. Some are just dead ends. Some just lead to more questions."

"Well, I don't want to impose, but could I come over? I may have some ideas."

"Of course."

"Be there in about an hour."

She hung up feeling more positive now. Despite generating questions not answers, the last time she'd worked with Kevin she'd found Rose.

She reread her notes. Deleted them. Why keep a record of how much she didn't know?

An hour later the doorbell rang. Talk about being punctual. She deactivated the alarm and opened the door with a smile.

"You're right on time..."

A shadow descended on her and knocked her to the floor. She heard a deafening crack as the back of her head hit the floor. She heard the door shut and felt someone step over her. She made a move as though to sit up, but fell back dizzy, her vision dimming at the edges.

She had the vague sensation of someone stepping back over her towards the door. Then she heard the front door open and slam against the wall.

Everything went dark.

CHAPTER NINE

Thick white fog surrounded Naya. Barely visible was the outline of someone leaning over her. The attacker was still here! She started to punch at them only to have large hands pin her wrists to her chest. She began to writhe in panic, fighting to get free. He was too strong. She hoped a neighbour could hear her cries for help.

A familiar voice broke through her screams. She blinked rapidly and her vision cleared. She calmed at the sight of Kevin's face over her. A male paramedic was holding her down.

"Are they gone?" she cried out.

"Who?" Kevin asked.

"When I opened the door someone knocked me to the ground. Are they still here?"

The paramedic released her arms immediately calling dispatch on his radio.

"I need police sent to this location for a female victim of a home invasion."

Home invasion? Naya began to sit up only to have Kevin restrain her, muttering something about not moving till the paramedics finished checking her out. A female paramedic knelt beside her, examining her eyes, listening to her heart. When she tried taking her blood pressure Naya pushed off the restraining hands.

"I'm fine," Naya insisted. Finally, she shouted, "Stop!"

The paramedic backed off as Kevin helped her sit up.

"Take slow, deep breaths till the dizziness passes," the woman advised.

How did she know that she was dizzy? She imagined how she must look: pale skin, unfocused eyes, shallow and rapid breathing. Taking her advice Naya felt better within seconds. The paramedic gave Kevin a nod and he helped Naya up to sit at the dining table. Close enough to make a run for the exit if the attacker was still in the house.

Before long the same officer that had responded to her first break-in, Charles Forgham, arrived at the front door. After a few words with one of the paramedics, he searched the house. She couldn't help noticing that although his gun was still holstered, he held his hand on it. He passed her without a word and climbed the stairs two at a time. She strained her neck trying to watch as he checked each room. Within seconds, he returned to the main floor. He moved quickly checking this floor, then she heard him go down to the basement. Back on the main floor, he passed her to go out to check the garage.

He returned to the foyer and sat in the chair beside her.

"The house is clear, Ms. Assad. Are you all right?"

"Yes, they just knocked me down when I opened the door."

"Can you describe them?"

"I just barely had enough time to see a blur push me down." She paused, thinking. "He wore a mask, you know, like a ski mask. It was dark, maybe black."

"You're sure it was a man?"

"That's the impression I had. The person was tall and had large shoulders. He wore a black leather jacket, like a motorcycle jacket. And jeans — dark, I think. Oh and he wore steel toe construction boots."

"Steel toe?" the cop looked up from his notepad.

"When I was on the ground and he stepped over me, I saw the green triangle on the boot. You know, the symbol to say it was certified."

Smiling, the officer continued writing.

"What's so funny?" she demanded.

"I thought you said that you didn't see anything," Charles said.

Her anger deflated, she calmed down and added with an apologetic shrug, "Guess I saw more than I thought."

"Ms. Assad?" the female paramedic interrupted. "We should probably take you to the hospital to check you out." At Naya's emphatic head shake, the woman added, "Then could you sign this form saying you declined transport, please?" A quick signature and the paramedics left.

"You don't look very comfortable," the officer said. "Maybe you'd like to move to the family room?" He glanced at Kevin, who took her arm to help her walk.

"Maybe the kitchen instead. I could use some water."

"I'll get it for you," Kevin offered.

"Sure, thanks," she said as the policeman helped her to the sofa, sitting next to her.

"Just relax and see if you remember anything else," he said.

Kevin arrived with a dripping glass of water, apparently his favourite type to fill.

"I guess you've decided to go back to working in your office again," Kevin said.

"What do you mean?" she asked after taking a sip of water.

"I see you that you moved your computer and papers off the kitchen table."

"What? No!" She shoved the glass of water back into Kevin's hands, spilling half of it on him and the carpet. She reached for Charles's shoulder and caught his bullet-proof vest instead. She used that to pull herself up, then hurried on rubbery legs to the kitchen. At the sight of her barren kitchen table, vertigo hit. She clutched the counter to steady herself. "It's gone. My computer. They took it."

"Ms. Assad, sit down," Charles said, taking her arm and guiding her to sit in a kitchen chair behind her. Distantly she wondered how he'd managed to get the chair from the table without her seeing. All she could focus on was the overwhelming thought of how could this happen? Again.

She could hear the officer on his radio reporting in. He was instructed to wait there for the detectives.

Once she'd recovered enough to walk, Kevin and Charles helped her back to the family room. This time Kevin found a bottle of brandy in the dining room and brought her a glass. One sip and the liquid warmed her throat. A second sip and a comforting heat enveloped her. Looking up at the men, the officer sitting on the opposite sofa and Kevin standing nearby still looking concerned and in pain.

"Sit down, please," Naya said to him, forcing a grin to assure him she was okay. "Kevin, I'm all right. Really. I just got upset because I'd only had the computer a few hours and now it's gone too."

"A few — few hours?" Kevin asked.

"Sometimes burglars will hit a place twice," Charles said. "The second time because they know the owners will have bought new stuff."

"Well, can't get any newer," Naya said. Looking at Kevin who was still standing and still looking like someone ate his cat, she snapped, "Can't you *please* sit down?" He sat next to her immediately. She didn't mean to be impatient, but damn it, she was the victim and having him stand around looking like he was, was really beginning to bug her.

"Speaking of the computer, I should phone my business partner and tell him about — this." Naya said. She pulled out her cell and keyed in the number. But the phone went directly to voice mail, the greeting saying he was on the phone. She didn't want to have him find out about the break-in through a message. "Hi, it's me. Could you give me a call at home when you get a chance, please? It's not urgent. I just wanted to see how, umm, that extra research project is going. Thanks." The men who were both staring at her quizzically, though Kevin's expression was tinged with distress.

"We're negotiating a new contract and I don't want him racing out of any meetings."

"High strung, is he?" Charles asked.

"Not usually," Naya said. Travis had to be the calmest person alive. In all the years that she'd known him she'd never seen him worry about anything. However, after everything she'd been going through recently, he'd changed. "Well, maybe a little."

Within an hour the detectives arrived. You would think in a city of this size there would be someone other than sleepy Sully to respond. Guess the hour of day didn't matter. This was his usual appearance. Naya got to meet another forensics person, a young girl, with black hair tied back in a high pony tail. She doubted that she could be much more than twelve.

The twelve-year-old took prints from around the entrance and moved to the kitchen, while Sleepy Sully yawned through several questions. Kevin stood by the family room entrance, watching with a look of pained concern.

The visit lasted only a few minutes due in part to the speed that the technician processed the crime scene. A place Naya used to call her kitchen.

Kevin saw everyone out, locked the door behind them and rushed back to Naya's side.

"Can I get you anything? Another brandy or something?"

"No, just sit with me." Naya settled back on the sofa. "Thank you for staying."

"Are you sure you're okay? I think I'd feel better if you went to the hospital to get checked out."

"I've had enough of doctors!" She took a calming breath. "Sorry about snapping."

"That's okay," Kevin said. After a moment he added, "I — I'm sure the police will find your things. Considering, it's a second break-in."

"You would think. But Detective Sleepy said the same thing as the constable. Thieves sometimes return to take the things you replaced. And, he told me the only reason he came was because it was a home invasion and I was knocked down. Damn, I should never have opened the door without looking first."

"I'm sorry," Kevin whispered.

"This isn't your fault. A security alarm isn't going to be that useful if you don't turn it on." When he didn't answer, she added, "I don't blame you. Please don't feel guilty. Besides, it looks like they were only after the computer. I didn't have it long enough to get attached to it."

"Do you have another computer here?" Kevin asked.

Her head snapped up and she glared at him sharply. Why would he ask that? Had she let it slip that she had Valerie's computer hidden here?

"I was thinking, uh, maybe we could uh, go on-line and check how many break-ins there've been in this area," he stuttered, his cheeks flushing.

Guess she'd unnerved him with the old evil-eye look. She really needed to learn to keep her emotions hidden. She smiled, in what she hoped was a relaxed way and said, "It's the only computer I own." She didn't bother reminding him about her cell phone, mainly because she wasn't about to waste time checking stupid stats.

"It was just a thought." He fiddled with the cuff of his shirt.

She tried to think of something to say to break the tension. She almost sighed loudly when her cell phone rang. Expecting it was Travis calling back, she checked the call display. She bolted upright. It was Rose.

"Would you excuse me, please?" She asked Kevin who nodded and left the room. She whispered, "Hello?"

"Hi, Naya?"

"Are you all right?"

"Yes, I don't have much time before that fool comes back. One day the ape's going to wonder why I keep asking for ice. Anyways, I just want to warn you to be careful. Everyone who's even remotely connected to our work is being watched."

"That might make sense. I've just had two break-ins in three days."

"Did they take much?"

"Just my computer and then my replacement computer."

"Do you keep any important info on it?"

"No, not a thing."

"Good girl. *No one* does these days." She muttered a curse. "My babysitter's back. Gotta go. Good luck."

"Wait..." But the line went dead. Hmm. What did she say? No one keeps things on their computer anymore. That was a pretty obvious thing to say to a fellow programmer. Obviously she was telling her that the files on Valerie's computer weren't the important ones. The current work was probably stored on her external network storage device. If Naya was lucky. If she wasn't lucky, then the files were backed up at SecurITe and that meant hacking into their system. Either way she needed to take Valerie's computer back to her condo.

And for that she needed Alice's spare key. She just hoped Kevin had it on him.

"Kevin?" But he didn't answer. He was probably in the kitchen and couldn't hear her. With her cane out of sight, she continued on her own to the kitchen, proud of herself for not losing her balance. She found Kevin opening the pantry cupboard in the corner. "Hi, Kevin."

Startled, he spun around paling suddenly. She was worried he was going to pass out.

"I'm sorry, Kevin, I didn't mean to startle you. You looking for something?"

"Yes," he puffed. "I was uh, looking for something to make for you to eat. I found some soup?" He pulled out a can of Country Vegetable Soup and showed it to her with a Cheshire cat grin as though he was doing a commercial.

"That's very thoughtful of you. But it's still too early for supper and I'm still full from lunch." Feeling suddenly awkward she took the can from him and returned it to the cupboard before shutting the door. "I'd like to ask you a favour. Could I borrow the key to Valerie's apartment, please?"

"I've got the key with me. I can drive you," he said eagerly.

"Thanks, but not tonight." Oh, no. She recognized that sad puppy pout. He had a crush on her. Not a complication she needed right now. And she didn't need the company at Valerie's place. He might be Alice's brother but she doubted the woman would have told anyone, including family, about the top secret project. Besides, she might need to hack in to someplace sensitive. Why make the poor guy an accomplice. "All this stress makes my MS symptoms, mostly the fatigue, worse. There's no telling when I'll be up to going out again." That was the truth, more or less.

"Uh, well, sure," he began. Reluctantly, he took the keys out of his pocket, removed a silver one and handed it to her. "But, but, if you want company, don't hesitate to call me. No matter what the time."

"I can't keep asking you to take time off from work," she said. "I could phone to let you know when I go and you could meet me there." Not something she planned to do. "If you're able to." She turned towards the kitchen doorway and was relieved to see that he got the hint.

"Are you sure I can't do anything for you before I leave?" he asked as he followed her to the door. "I could just wait while you have a rest. Better than being alone."

"Thanks but I feel pretty safe with the alarm on. As long as I actually keep it on. Kevin, I appreciate everything. Really."

"Okay, but keep in mind that, that I can come back any time, day or night."

"Thank you." As soon as he was gone, she locked the door and activated the system. With all the doors and windows alarmed, she did actually feel safe.

And thoroughly excited as she gripped the key in her hand. She slipped it into her jeans pocket on the way to the kitchen. She had barely poured a cup of coffee when the house phone startled her. She'd wipe up the coffee on the counter after she answered.

It was Travis.

"Sorry for the delay getting back to you," Travis said. "I was on the phone with Beckman, ironing out some extra work he wants us to do."

"Besides making sure his network is secure?"

"Now he wants us to check every employee's personal computer." Travis laughed. "I warned him that it's going to take more time and cost a lot more money. Money was no issue he said. Guess no one told him that maybe it was his employees' hard work that made him successful and he should trust them."

"I hope we can handle all that extra work."

"We should think about hiring an extra pair of hands," Travis said.

"Sure, we can talk about it. Travis, the reason I called was to tell you something," Naya paused. She hated giving bad news. "First, I'm all right. But I had another break-in."

"What! Since I left you this afternoon? How?"

"I was expecting someone and opened the door without looking. They knocked me down."

"Did you go to the hospital?"

"No, I'm fine. The paramedics were here and checked me out."

"You should have let them take you to the hospital," Travis scolded.

"I'm fine. Really," she said. "Another thing, Travis. The only thing they took was the new computer."

"That's just too weird. At least you didn't have time to get attached to it."

"That's what *I* said."

"You alone now?" Travis asked.

"Yes."

"With the alarm on?"

"Yes."

"There's no point in having an alarm if you're not going to use it."

"I know," Naya said with a loud impatient sigh. "Travis, I won't make the same mistake twice. Okay? Now, you said you were going to check some things out."

"I checked out Alice Vanderlund's background. She's quite a mystery woman. There's no trace of her prior to two years ago. I did a bit more digging and found out — let's not go into how — that before she used the name Alice, she used the name Celine Forest. That name lasted only six months. There've been a few other aliases. I eventually found out that her real name is Tracy Wall. And Tracy did have a brother."

"Are they in witness protection or something?"

"Umm, are you sitting down?"

"Yes," Naya said, after she did. Her skin prickled with the change in Travis's voice.

"She did have a brother named Adam." He hesitated then added. "Adam died when he was two weeks old."

"What?" Naya felt sick to her stomach. "Then who's Kevin?" How many times had she been alone with him and no one knew where she was.

Travis continued. "I tracked down some police records. Tracy Wall and her subsequent incarnations have had police reports about a stalker. She's been on the move since she was nineteen. Leaving town, changing her name. Starting over, just to have him show up at her door."

"My God." Her mind whirled in confusion. A single clear thought surfaced; luckily Travis had the security system installed. Then she remembered the way Kevin had looked at her. It wasn't a cute, innocent crush. With Alice gone he didn't seem to have any trouble transferring his affections to her. She took the cordless phone and went to the front door to peer out the window. She peeked through the blinds covering the long, narrow window beside the door but couldn't see anything. Barely eight o'clock and the overcast sky made it quite dark. A sure sign summer was ending. She moved to the window on the other side of the door that offered a better view of the street.

"Naya, do you think that maybe Alice found out that he'd found her and she and Valerie took off together?"

"If Valerie could easily leave her condo, maybe." Nothing moved outside. The street resembled a painting of shades of grey. Little pools of light illuminated dots of colour along the far side of the street. She was about to turn away when she noticed a car half in shadow. The half that was visible was oddly familiar. It was a dark sedan, from this distance she couldn't be sure of the make. It had a roof rack which didn't look quite right. Unbalanced somehow. Staring at it she started to make out more details. Half the bar on the driver's side was missing.

Kevin's car.

"Oh my God," she whispered needlessly. She flattened herself against the door further lowering her voice. "He's parked outside."

"I'm at work. Be there in a few minutes. I'll call from the driveway," Travis said. And hung up.

Ten minutes later she opened the garage door for him and he pulled in next to her BMW.

"I brought some company," Travis said once the garage door was safely closed. Mackay popped out from under a blanket in the back seat.

"Hi!" Mackay slid out the open window without bothering to open the door. "This is great. Real life spies and everything."

"Uh," Naya muttered as she stepped aside to let them in. Travis went in first as Mackay grabbed a backpack and a laptop case from the front seat then followed. Today his t-shirt depicted the slogan, 'Don't listen to an atom. They make up everything.' If she wasn't so scared, she might have laughed.

"Mackay was telling me that you'd asked him about tracking cell phones when they're off and he found out a way to do it. I thought it would be good if he came along. It was his idea to hide so that Kevin, or whatever his name is, doesn't know how many people are in here with you." As Mackay went ahead to the kitchen, Travis whispered, "Sorry for the cloak and dagger stuff but he insisted."

"That's okay." She reactivated the alarm, made sure all the curtains were closed tight. "The problem with thinking everyone's after you is, sometimes they are." She couldn't help smiling thinking about Elliot the conspiracy aficionado.

By the time they reached the kitchen Mackay already had his computer operational and was tapping the keys with rapid expertise.

"When you asked me about tracking cell phones, I wasn't thinking when I said they have to be on. I mean they do. The easiest thing would be to turn the phone on remotely." He stopped typing. "But that could kind of alert everyone in the area. And I doubt that's something we'd want in this case. Anyways another option is to send an intermittent pulse through the phone. Then I can triangulate its location."

"I wouldn't think it was that easy to do," Naya said as she joined him at the table. Travis remained standing, looking over his shoulder at the computer.

"It isn't for the average person," Mackay said. He gave her a lop-sided grin. "But I'm not average. Remember? Unfortunately this phone is really high tech secure. I haven't been able to hack it. Too bad you don't have its SIM card number or better yet the IMEI numbers."

"Hmm," Naya leaned back into the sofa. Could Valerie have kept a record in her computer? IMEI — International Mobile Equipment Identity number identified the phone itself and remained constant even if the SIM card was changed. It was a long shot, but...

"What if Valerie synced her phone with her computer?"

"Sure there'd be a record in there. Too bad you don't have her computer. Guess they grabbed it when they took your friend."

"Well, actually..." she said, heading to the pantry. She moved a couple of cereal boxes and the box of microwave popcorn, to a lower shelf. Stretching with a grunt, she pulled out the laptop. "I just happen to have her computer here." She laughed at his wide-eyed look. He looked like a child who was given a great birthday present as he came towards her, hands extended. He gingerly carried it back to the table shoving his computer out of the way and placed Valerie's down like some holy relic.

He tapped a non-rhythmic beat with his fingers on the table while it booted up. Travis was at the sink cleaning out the coffee maker to put on a fresh pot.

"When I went to Valerie's apartment," Naya said, "I discovered this laptop under her bed. I figured she stored it there for the night. I do that when I work in bed. Anyway, I checked through it in case there was something in her agenda. When I found the higher encrypted files, I didn't think it was safe to leave it there. Good thing I hid it."

"And that's when you had the first break-in," Mackay said.

"Not to mention the second break-in," Travis added.

"I got it," Mackay announced.

"That was fast," she said.

"This is a cutting edge processor but there were a few places that needed tweaking. I did have to download a few satellite programs otherwise I would have had it sooner." Without taking his eyes off the screen he held his hand out, "Do you have your cell? I'll download a recognition signal that'll help you once you get closer to the GPS signal." She handed it to him and he connected it to a USB port on Valerie's computer. Several keystrokes later he handed it back.

"Once you're close, it'll signal like this." Mackay showed her the readings on the screen.

"Thanks," she stared at the flashing zeroes on the screen. "Can't you pinpoint an exact location from here?"

"Still working on it. All I can tell you is it's lower east side. But I'll narrow it down soon."

"Okay great. Thanks. While you're working on it, I'm going back to Valerie's apartment to check things out. And I'll need to take the laptop." She pulled out her cell. "Relax and make yourselves at home. There's all kinds of snacks in the cupboard. I won't be long."

"You got any chips?" Mackay eagerly asked.

"Sure." Naya took out a bag of BBQ chips from the pantry. As she started to dial, she added. "There's beer and soft drinks in the fridge."

"Who're you phoning?" Travis asked.

"A cab," she said.

"That's a good one." Travis said, giving her a mechanical laugh. He abruptly cut off the laugh, took the phone from her hands and said, "Like I'm going to let you drive past this crazy stalker who'll follow you. I'm going with you. No discussion. No argument. That's final." He handed her back the phone. "Go get ready, I'll make some coffee to bring along."

Naya changed her mind about arguing and nodded. She was grateful to have a trusted friend at her side.

She got her backpack, put in a couple of energy bars and filled a water bottle from the tap. She slipped on a light jacket and runners and grabbed her fold-up cane. By the time she got back to the kitchen Travis was standing by the coffee pot, impatiently watching the drips.

"All ready," she said.

"What? That was fast?" He was completely crestfallen as his eyes darted back and forth between her and pot with its tiny coffee puddle at the bottom.

She patted his shoulder and said, "How about we stop by Tim's? I'll buy."

"If you're buying, can't say no. Try not to make a mess here, Mac. And answer your cell when we call."

"Yeah, yeah." Mackay closed the lid of Valerie's laptop and handed it to Naya. "I cloned the hard drive onto my computer."

"Thanks," Naya said packing everything into her backpack. "Come on, I'll show you how to use the alarm."

"You know," Mackay said following to the foyer, "I just thought of something."

"About the tracker?" Naya asked.

"No," Mackay said, "About your friend's boss. It seems strange that he didn't track her already — easy for him since it's his own company's phone."

"I haven't been able to figure out how he's involved," Naya said.

"Whatever's going on," Mackay said, "When you find her phone just make sure you don't turn it on. Cause that'll alert him for sure."

"Good thinking, thanks," Naya said as she slipped the laptop into her backpack and tested its weight. Not too heavy. She'd manage.

"Travis," Mackay added, "Make sure she hides under the blanket when you leave so crazy boy doesn't see her and follow you."

"Good idea," Travis said. Naya made sure he knew how to activate the alarm correctly, giving them a minute to go to the garage. She took the door remote from her car before she got into Travis's car.

"You know," Travis said, "Mac could be right about hiding. If he thinks you're still home he won't follow us."

"I agree too. But no way am I hiding under the blanket in the back seat. I'll just duck down in the front."

Travis used the remote to open the garage door, drove out then waited to ensure it closed all the way. He headed slowly down the street glancing at Kevin's car from the corner of his eye. The driver quickly turned his head away.

Once they passed him, Travis asked, "Does he have like a brush cut and a goatee?"

"Yes. Is he following?"

"Nope."

"Hope Mackay will be okay," she said. As soon as they rounded the corner, she pulled herself upright and clicked on her seatbelt.

"I'd worry more about Kevin," Travis said.

She nodded in agreement but continued to question the wisdom of leaving Mackay alone in the house with a maniac lurking outside.

❖ ❖ ❖

At Valerie's condo Naya double locked and chained the door. Not that she was expecting Kevin to have followed but who knew how many friends he had working with him.

Travis turned on the living room lights. She stopped near the door feeling strangely uncomfortable. The first time she'd been here, Naya had been hoping to find Valerie. Now that she knew her friend wasn't here, her skin prickled as though ants skittered over it. And she didn't know why.

"Are you okay?" Travis asked.

"Yes, I mean, I don't know. Something's not right. But I'm not sure..." She broke off, her voice dropping to a whisper as she pressed herself against the door. She stared down the hall that led to the bedroom. "I *know* I turned off all the lights before I left."

"Stay here," Travis whispered back. As he started to move away, Naya grabbed his arm. She slipped off the backpack and pulled out a mini crowbar. Travis's eyebrows lifted in surprise. He took the crowbar, shifting it in his hands as though testing its weight. He nodded to her and headed cautiously down the hall. A minute later with all the lights on he said, "It's okay. No one's here."

"I know I turned everything off," Naya said.

"I'm sure you did. Kevin's probably been here since." He handed her back the crowbar. "What other interesting things have you got in there?"

"Just stuff that might come in handy." Putting it away she added, "I bet you felt better searching the place with it."

He stepped aside, gesturing for her to proceed. "After you."

In the office, she asked, "Was this the light that was on?" When he nodded, she said, "Makes sense. Guess he was looking for the laptop."

"Or he was looking for clues to tell him where Alice went." Travis pulled out the desk chair for Naya to sit. "He doesn't sound like the type to give up easily on his ex-girlfriend."

She sat down and took Valerie's computer out of her backpack.

"She keeps her router behind the file cabinet under the window," Naya said. She stood and reached around the cabinet to turn on the external drive on the table under the window, sitting amidst the plants. Not that it was actually hidden, but it would be difficult to see the thin Network Access Server box, standing upright among the leafy plants unless you were actually looking for it.

She gave the file cabinet a tap before sitting down at the desk. "The top drawer's locked. Doesn't make sense why she'd lock it when she never leaves the apartment."

"Maybe she makes all her visitors go through a security clearance first," Travis suggested as he inspected the drawer.

"Funny," she said. "I wonder what's in there."

"Well, why don't we just look?" Travis said as he slid the top drawer open.

"How ..." Naya stared at him dumbfounded.

"A talent I picked up during my wayward youth, long before I met you and you set me on the straight and narrow." He put the lock pick back in the set and returned it to his jacket pocket. He smiled. "You never know when lock picking knowledge will come in handy."

"The drawer's barely a quarter full," Naya said, as she began to check the folders. "Here's one labelled emails and correspondence. Mostly between Valerie and the other team members. Oh and look. Even a bunch from good old Howard Dixon."

"Does he say anything useful?"

"Just co-ordinating data transfer between the team members. Strange that she printed everything out instead of keeping them on her computer. The rest seem to be research notes."

"Some weird stuff, too," Travis said. "She has something on digital cameras, smart cards, jewellery, watches."

Naya checked the folder contents briefly. "It looks like she was shopping on-line and printed out different products. Wait. Here's one on surgery. Different types of surgery..." She broke off pulling out one sheet. "Pacemakers? You don't suppose she has heart trouble?"

"I doubt it," Travis said. "Besides, if she admitted about her agoraphobia she would have told you about needing a pacemaker."

"Sure. You're right." She had to stay focussed. "Let's get to work."

Getting on the computer was simple, but she needed a password to access the network drive. She took a memory stick out of her backpack and easily got in.

The drive labelled HOME appeared to contain the same files that were on the computer.

"Guess she just used the network to store her backup files," Naya said.

"All the files the same?"

"I'm comparing files here with those on her hard drive." Naya took out another memory stick from her bag. She felt Travis go back to the file cabinet, as she immersed herself in a world of data comparisons and decryption. After a few minutes she said, "I thought I had something but then I found I was wrong."

"And you look happy, because..." Travis said.

"At first it does look like a backup. And I thought that since I'd already cracked the encryption on her computer this would be a piece of cake. But it wasn't. A little more digging and I found out that they were just fake files. Made to look like they're much bigger than they really are."

"Then it's not a real backup?" Travis asked. Naya nodded brightly. "And that's a good thing?"

"Sure. With her security know-how, why bother setting up decoy files?" When he continued to stare at her, she continued. "Think about it. If someone did try to hack her system, they'd waste a lot of time trying to decrypt files that didn't exist. In the meantime, her security protocols alert her to the breach. They then track down the intruder. Ingenious. I wish I'd thought of it."

"Sorry our trip here didn't pan out"

"No, you're missing the best part. She still needs to have a backup system, somewhere. I kept search until I found a hidden drive. Her backup's on SecurITe's server. The drive, labelled Z:// is hidden when you check out the available network drives."

Travis leaned on the desk to look at the screen. "What's on it?"

"That's the problem. I didn't bring anything powerful enough to get past that firewall."

"Maybe Valerie has something here?" Travis asked. They exchanged glances then silently each went through all the desk drawers, looking for memory sticks or even discs.

"Wait," Naya said looking at the file cabinet. "The stuff we found in that drawer didn't really need to be locked up, did it?"

Travis fully opened the drawer and groped around at the back of the drawer until he found a single memory stick. Naya slipped it into the USB port. Within seconds she gained access to SecurITe's network.

They found the files related to Valerie's project. Many were highly encrypted, but there were a few files she could open quickly. Most were memos about deadlines, though there wasn't enough information to tell them anything useful. She'd wasted enough time. About to exit from the server, she noticed an extra folder that had been greyed out.

"If these are all of Valerie's files, why wouldn't she be able to access this one?" Travis said.

"Probably an extra security feature. It may need a different password to access." She slipped in her own memory stick with the password cracking programs on it and her fingers began their expert dance on the keyboard.

A few minutes went by. Then a few more. And a couple more before she sat back in her chair and watched Travis as he checked out the books on the shelves.

"Guess I've been knocked off my self-appointed pedestal," Naya said. He gave her a questioning look. "Every time I hacked into Valerie's computer I very boldly thought, oh, she might be good, but I'm better. Now I know I was just kidding myself."

"Can't break the encryption?" He came to stand next to her and studied the screen.

"Maybe if I had a few days." She shook her head. "You want to give it a try?"

"Sure, you got any C-4 in your tool kit? It doesn't matter. We'll just wait for Mackay to pinpoint the location."

"I wonder..." Naya picked up her backpack.

"Don't tell me you do have explosives in there."

"I'd forgotten about this," she said as she searched through the pockets. She pulled out another memory stick. "I got this out of Alice's computer case when I searched her car at the impound lot."

This time it only took a few seconds and the greyed out folder darkened.

"Thank you, Alice," she said. The folder contained several files. Methodically opening each one in order, she discovered they contained lines of code. No title, no description to tell what they were for.

After several similar files, she opened one and almost whooped aloud. Travis however, did. It was the project proposal. Excited at the discovery, they leaned closer to the screen and read.

"The surveillance capabilities are more extensive than we thought," Naya said. "Not only can this program access any CCTV network, but it can also follow a target across different networks. For any cameras not linked to an external network, the program can access the records. I mean we're talking traffic cameras, gas stations, even private security cameras. All they need to do is tag their subject. They put a chip in their ID card, or insert it into their watch, jewellery. Anything that they'd always carry with them."

"What's that last line?" Travis said, taking the mouse to scroll back down. "Surgical implants? Wait a minute. Now the file on all types of surgical implants makes sense."

Naya joined him at the cabinet. "You really think that people would willingly let their company surgically implant chips into their bodies? Or maybe not willingly."

"One meeting with Elliot and you let your imagination get the better of you. Biometric ID chips is a growing fad, especially for high security places. Even subcutaneous implants. No need to worry about losing your ID card."

"Never mind pervasive. More like invasive," she said.

Naya's cell phone beeped. It was Mackay. She put it on speaker.

"I've got the GPS location, but it's going to take a bit of work to narrow it down some more. The best I can do at the moment is say it's in the 1900 block."

"There are commercially available programs that can do better," Travis said.

"Commercial programs can't hack into high security programs."

"You sure you'll be able to pinpoint the signal?" Naya asked more calmly, though inside she felt herself screaming with frustration.

"Wait there and as soon as I have it, I'll call you."

"No, the lower east side is about a half hour away," Naya said. "We'll head over there now. Just call when you get it."

"Okay," Mackay hung up.

"You sure you want to go?" Travis asked.

"There's nothing here that's going to help us find her. Mackay's signal will lead us right to her. I'd like to be in the area when he does."

CHAPTER TEN

After a quick detour to pick up two large, black coffees, Naya and Travis drove to the lower east side in silence. She knew Travis had to be exhausted. Between an all-nighter preparing for a meeting, presenting their proposal, then working on finalizing the contract for the new client, he'd been awake close to forty hours. He should be at home relaxing with a beer, not driving into the shady part of town where success was measured by how early you got parole.

She hoped that the caffeine was helping to revive him the way it was her. She felt guilty that she had a definite advantage. A few months after her MS attack and she was finally getting used to the constant exhaustion. In order to function each day she'd had to learn how to push through the fatigue. When she had trouble getting up in the morning, she'd promise herself a nap later and that somehow helped her out of bed.

She studied Travis's profile in the strobe effect of the passing street lights. After years of friendship she knew his moods perfectly. Beneath his exhaustion lay a mixture of emotions. She recognized concern, not for Valerie, but for her. She saw determination. And loyalty. He wouldn't give up. For that she was grateful.

She tried to be patient and wait for Mackay's update with an exact location. She lasted barely five minutes and had to phone to see how he was doing. Nothing yet. She waited. Sipped her coffee. Tried to be patient. Failed. And pulled out her cell again until Travis intervened.

"Naya, you're distracting him. Let the guy work."

"Okay, you're right." She put her phone in her pocket and fought the urge to call. He was right, she was breaking his concentration and slowing him down. She did have to give Mackay credit for answering each time she called. Normally he would have shut his phone off to avoid being nagged.

They reached the lower east side of town in twenty minutes thanks to little traffic and few red lights. Most houses were either boarded up, or so run-down they couldn't possibly be occupied. There were a few 'For Sale' signs here and there but she suspected that many of the residents had just walked away. Several houses were occupied and she wondered about the tenacity of those people.

After ten minutes of aimlessly driving around the neighbourhood, Travis cursed and pulled over.

"This is ridiculous," he said. "And don't even think of saying we can go door to door."

"That won't be necessary," she said, as she pointed out the front window. "We just need to follow the power." When he nodded, she knew that he understood. One house had cables running from the side of the house up to the main power lines overhead — using the traditional squatter's energy supply. If they hadn't stopped she might not have seen it.

"Whoever is in there, isn't supposed to be," Travis said.

"Feel like going for a walk?"

Travis parked around the corner from the house. Naya held onto her cane with one hand and took Travis's arm with the other. She hoped that they gave off an aura of an ordinary couple out for a walk at ten o'clock at night. In a neighbourhood where it looked like Jason or Freddie was ready to jump out of one of the boarded up houses and slice and dice them into bits.

Naya hoped to get a glimpse inside as they walked past the house. The tightly drawn curtains across the large picture window negated any chance of a peek.

They continued past the house and then its neighbour — a boarded up two-storey — to pause out of sight around the side. Seeing the scattered remains of a wood fence that once separated the backyards of each property, Naya's elation returned. A sad sight for someone interested in real estate. A welcoming sight for someone interested in skulking around in the dark.

They left the tattle-tale street lights and cut through the neighbour's backyard. Naya held on tight to Travis's arm, each step a struggle to keep her balance on the uneven ground and shards of patio stones. She imagined a happier time when these backyards hosted BBQ parties and friendly beer fests. Now the only revellers were the rats — one of which skittered over her foot. She stifled a gasp and kept her balance thanks to Travis. Even he grimaced at the rodent. They reached the edge of the house.

Naya took a step forward only to be yanked back. After a brief silent argument of sharp and forceful hand signals, she reluctantly agreed to wait while Travis did a quick reconnoitre. He rushed forward, passing quickly through the light cast by a street lamp and stopped, his back against the other house. She could see him take a deep breath then move closer to the back door. He stayed for several minutes. Then he crab-walked back to her side.

"I couldn't see a thing, but I heard voices," he whispered.

"We have to get a look inside. Find out if Valerie or Alice is in there," she said.

"The windows are covered with foil. I couldn't find any gap to look through."

"We have to do *something*," Naya said, searching for stray light escaping from the windows which could potentially offer a microscopic view in. She shifted her weight from foot to foot wondering how far she could get before Travis caught her.

Before she could decide one way or another, the back door opened. Travis yanked her back into the dark shadows as two men came out. Quietly shutting the door, they took long easy strides away from the house and stopped at the fence remains. They lit cigarettes and exhaled slowly as they looked up at the stars in silence, their backs to the house. She hadn't noticed that the clouds had cleared. Other than the street lights there was little light pollution to dilute the night sky. The stars were brilliant, the Milky Way dramatically clear. She and Valerie used to lie on their backs for hours watching the stars that appeared close enough to touch. No time for childhood memories now she berated herself. Once she freed Valerie they could reminisce for as long as they wanted about anything they wanted.

She started for an intact section of fence not far from the men, only to have Travis hold her arm emphatically, shaking his head 'no.' She tried to pull her arm free then realized he was right. How the hell was she supposed to sneak around in the shadows with a cane, a limp and the occasional loss of balance?

Reluctantly she nodded and waited in the shadows while Travis duck-walked to the fence. Frustrated that the men's voices were too low to hear a thing, she had to fight her desire to crawl on hands and knees behind Travis. Without warning, a commotion erupted in the house. It sounded like furniture being thrown about then the back door crashed open and a woman bellowed at the men.

"Get the fuck back in here and get these fucking women under fucking control!"

Like a tightly choreographed dance, the men dropped their cigarettes, spun and dashed back to the house.

Naya pressed into the shadows feeling the siding, hard and cold on her back. She ignored the sharp something poking her left shoulder blade and remained motionless. Once the door slammed shut, she relaxed and moved away from the hook in the wall.

Her relief was short lived as she watched in silent horror as Travis crept up to the house stopping at the four steps leading up to the backdoor. She could see his outline in the few stray beams of light that escaped from around the warped wooden door. Then her heart caught in her throat as he stood, climbed the few steps and pressed his ear against the door. He didn't really need to take the risk because she could hear the yelling from where she was. Most of the voices were muffled and unintelligible, but the occasional female screech rose above the rest leaving no doubt who it was.

"You brought them here, you make them work!" There were a series of garbled, not very manly sounding protests.

Then she heard a hauntingly familiar voice cry out, "We can't do anymore. Please let us go home!"

It was Valerie!

Even from this distance the distorted voice had the same tone, same inflection as her friend's. Naya felt a surge of strength and confidence as she stepped into the light prepared to join Travis. Without warning, he bolted off the steps and landed in a crouch near the house a fraction of a second before the back door swung open to a chorus of yells and a few curses she'd never heard before.

Naya rushed to the safety of the shadows. Her toe caught on something. She pitched forward before she had time to raise her hands to break her fall. Even with the wind knocked out of her, she realized that she was still bathed in the bright light of a street lamp. She rolled into her dark sanctuary just as one of the men trudged past her. She held her breath, remained motionless and clamped her eyes shut when his half gallop of a walk flung gravel into her face.

She heard the woman scream out the door, "And don't forget the fucking anchovies this time!" Slam!

He was on a pizza run. Maybe they were smart enough not to draw attention to themselves by having delivery cars visit a supposedly abandoned house. Somehow she believed the real reason was that no one would deliver to this neighbourhood at night.

She didn't move until she heard his boot thuds on the sidewalk fade away. She wiped the dirt and tears from her eyes with her sleeve.

She yelped when someone touched her arm.

"It's me," Travis said, helping her up. "That was close."

"What..."

"Not here. We better get back to the car."

She took a step and her right leg collapsed under her as Travis managed to catch her. She sucked in deep mouthfuls of air trying to control the stabbing pain in her knee. It felt exactly like an injury she'd got during a marathon three years ago when a runner fell across her path. She'd tripped over him, twisting her knee. She'd finished the last kilometre in agony. Getting to the car a mere block away shouldn't be a problem.

His arm around her waist, Travis half supported, half carried her. With the doors safely locked she managed tiny sips from her water bottle. Then she wet a Kleenex and tried to clean the gravel and dirt through the rip in her jeans. Her knee was badly skinned. She'd live.

"It was hard to make out everything," Travis said, breathless. He took a drink from his coffee cup, wiped his mouth with the back of his hand all the while staring at the house, scanning all around and checking the rear view mirror. He added, "Whatever's going on, that woman's in charge. The two men had brought two women to do some work and apparently they weren't living up to her expectations. I think the people three blocks away could hear that she was pissed."

"I heard another woman's voice."

"They kept insisting they were doing their best, but I couldn't make out everything. I did hear them say that they'd finish if there was one more, or they needed a third person, something like that. Then the boss woman wanted pizza."

"I heard Valerie's voice."

Travis stopped scanning the area to look at her. "You can't be sure. I found the voices muffled. You were by the next house."

"I know her voice."

"Naya," Travis began.

"Okay," Naya said. No point in arguing when she couldn't win. "You're probably right. But we do know that there are two girls being held against their will. We can't leave them there." She pulled out her cell phone from her jacket's pocket. "Time to call in the professionals."

"We don't know what's going on."

"We know it's not good, whatever it is," she said, dialling Sergeant Philadelphia Ashantre, from missing persons.

"Yes, Ms. Assad, I remember you." Ashantre sighed. "How can I help you — now?"

Naya had to pause. Being dismissed before she'd even spoken was not a good sign. She had to make the detective listen. If Naya mentioned hearing Valerie's voice, there was no doubt that her only answer would be a very loud and distinct hang up.

"My friend and I were driving around in the lower east side and ran across some men holding at least one girl hostage. We heard her begging to be let go."

"Ms. Assad, I don't have time for any games, role playing or otherwise."

Naya bit back a reflex response to the stereotyping. Naturally all computer people were nerds and only lived to play video games. She continued as though the sergeant hadn't spoken.

"We were driving in this neighbourhood when we noticed one house was stealing power from the hydro lines. When we checked it out, we heard voices inside arguing and one voice crying to go home. What if I'm right and you ignore me and then someone gets hurt? Or worse."

She imagined hearing the debate in Ashantre's mind. Then Naya heard a sigh that was full of resignation, exasperation and a hint of long suffering tolerance.

"What's the address?"

❖ ❖ ❖

Despite the detective's opinion of her, the police arrived quickly. It gave her hope. Travis and Naya waited a safe distance from the squatter house as they watched the tactical team prepare to move in.

After all the nail biting preparations, the actual entry of the team was anticlimactic. One second everyone was crouched in the shadows, invisible even to those who knew they were there. Next second — one officer knocked the door in with a single punch of a battering ram. He stepped aside to let the others charge in. He tossed the battering ram on the grass and followed his friends joining in the shouts of, "Police! Down on the ground."

And just like that the house was secured.

Naya felt a little cheated at the swiftness and ease of the assault. She was also relieved that no shots were fired. That meant Valerie was still safe.

Even while police tape was being strung up around the house, a small crowd of neighbours had gathered. All were in their pyjamas, several wore robes, but she suspected more to protect them from the night chill than for the sake of modesty. There was an elderly couple: the husband held a miniature white poodle, the wife a black one. There was a young woman carrying a sleeping toddler, while the woman standing next to her breast fed an infant. Naya wasn't sure how smart it was to bring babies out to a watch a police raid. She supposed it was better than leaving the babies alone in the house. There were five teenage boys, fully dressed and looking like they'd been partying hard. She couldn't figure out where everyone had come from since many of the houses looked deserted. Nothing like a little police raid in the middle of the night to start a neighbourhood block party.

She nudged Travis and together they pushed through the spectators and finally got to the yellow police tape. Naya had hoped to see the house occupants. She scanned the sea of cops hoping to find Philadelphia Ashantre. Kind of tough, considering they'd never met.

Finally, Naya called to one of the officers monitoring the crowd. The officer eyed her critically for several seconds.

"I spoke to Sergeant Ashantre earlier," Naya said. She lowered her voice further trying not to be overheard by the crowd. "I'm the one who phoned her about this."

"Wait here," he said, giving her a last head to toe disapproving look.

She gritted her teeth really getting angry now. She was about to ask him what the hell was his problem? Hadn't he ever seen anyone with a cane before? Then, for the first time tonight she checked her clothes. Her jeans were torn on both knees while the rest of her clothes were filthy. She probably even had dirt on her face. She touched her hair and was glad that she didn't have a mirror. The cop probably thought she was just another drug addict informant. Whatever, she decided, putting her vanity aside. As long he got the detective for her.

The officer made a bee-line to a tall black woman wearing jeans and a windbreaker with POLICE printed in large bold white lettering on the back. She made eye contact with Naya. She could see that the woman was beautiful, her skin a smooth chocolate cream. Her hair was cut close to the scalp. Even with the loose windbreaker, it was obvious that she was in great shape. Statuesque was the word that came to mind. Naya had heard the expression before but had never met anyone who could be described that way. All of her running friends could be described as fit with lean muscles. Never statuesque.

With the floodlights the Sergeant's look of annoyance was obvious. She said a few words to the officer who then went into the house as Ashantre strode toward her and Travis.

"Ms. Assad?" She motioned for Naya to cross the yellow police tape. She scowled at Travis. "Who's this?"

"Travis Bloom. Naya's friend," he said.

Naya asked, "Are Valerie and Alice okay?"

"Excuse me?"

"I heard Valerie's voice inside. Is she hurt?"

"Ms. Assad, Mr. Bloom. Come with me." She led the way entering through the front door.

Excited and a little nervous, Naya held onto Travis's arm as they climbed the two rickety steps to the front door. Barely inside, they stopped short and stared at the sight. Several tables crammed so close together there didn't seem to be room to walk between them. And on the tables were row upon row of plants.

"It's a grow-op?" Travis said.

That explained the covered windows, the stolen electricity from the power lines and the stifling humidity inside the house.

"Are Valerie and Alice here?" Naya asked.

The officer gave her a strange, close mouthed smirk before walking ahead. They followed her to the kitchen. A stack of pizza boxes towered in one corner. Empty fast food bags overflowed from the garbage can as though they too were trying to escape the stench of rotting food. On their knees, hands cuffed behind their backs, were the two men and their female boss. And behind them sat two other women. Naya stepped forward expecting to find Valerie also in handcuffs.

One was a skinny girl, the other was a heavy set woman with burgundy hair naturally born from a bottle. Her eyes were red and she sniffled trying to wipe her red nose on her shoulder. She gave Naya an unfocused glance before giving her full attention to her nose. Even with her hands cuffed behind her back the track marks were clearly visible on both arms. Although she wasn't speaking, her mouth was moving constantly and rapidly.

Naya felt sick to her stomach. Her eyes began to water. She clamped her mouth tight against the howl that was building in her throat.

"I take it from your expression neither of these women are your friends," she said.

Afraid to start bawling if she spoke, Naya kept her lips clamped tight and shook her head.

"Ms. Assad it's unwise to play cops and robbers. The real world is a dangerous place. You could have been shot." She nodded towards the stack of hand guns, semi-automatics and a shot gun on the kitchen table. "It's obvious why you were in this neighbourhood. Go home, Ms. Assad. You look like you need a rest."

"But..." Naya wanted to explain.

"The only reason I don't arrest you," she said then glared at Travis, "Or you, for public nuisance and generally being a pain is because you did help us shut down this grow-op. We knew it was somewhere in this area — we just didn't have the manpower to search. Thank you for your help. Go home."

Tight-lipped and stiff-legged Naya leaned heavily on Travis's arm. Once they were back in the car he put the water bottle into her hands and guided it to her mouth. She drank mechanically. Finally she found her voice.

"I'm sorry. I really thought she was there." Naya continued to watch the house, feeling as though she'd reached the end of the road but didn't know how to turn around. Then she remembered. "Wait, Mac said her cell phone was in this area. It has to be close by." She reached for the door handle and pushed it open. Travis grabbed her arm, pulling her back inside.

"Are you planning to search house to house? We'll go back to your place. You rest and we'll wait for Mackay to fine tune the GPS. No more guesswork."

Ready to argue that the police raid could have spooked the kidnappers forcing them to move their prisoners, the beep of her cell interrupted.

It was Mackay. She put him on speaker-phone. He sounded as though he was simply giving a weather report.

"You're at the wrong location."

CHAPTER ELEVEN

The soft rock station strained to fill the silence. They were too tired, too embarrassed and too frustrated for conversation. Naya was grateful that Travis hadn't complained the entire trip about why Mackay hadn't figured out earlier that the GPS had a built-in signal offset. He should have investigated why he hadn't been able to narrow down the signal in the first place. If he had, then the offset would have been immediately obvious.

There was no point in complaining about what should have been done. Just like she didn't dwell on the fact that they — she — had made a complete idiot of herself and was now on the police's most unwanted list.

Driving through the industrial park filled with large, silent buildings, she shuddered at the surreal feeling of being on a post-apocalyptic movie set. The only thing missing were zombies strolling across the road.

They drove past colossal, white fuel storage tanks. She couldn't help but notice the largest one with a staircase spiralling up to the top had streaks of rust running down its side. She imagined a deafening crack followed by a fiery explosion engulfing the zombies. Shuddering, she tried to get her mind to drift to something other than the walking dead as they continued to drive.

When they arrived at the warehouse district, she shut off the radio to better concentrate on finding unit 8842. The numbers didn't seem to be in any kind of logical order. After searching forever, but in reality was a few painful minutes, they spotted it. Travis parked his Mustang around the side of the neighbouring building, backing in for a quick escape. He took the keys out of the ignition.

"I'll leave these under the seat," he said, "just in case."

She took out her phone and checked the reading. It read 539, but without the benefit of distance units, she had no idea how close they were. Even with the modified program Mackay had emailed her, its workings were still a mystery. Mackay had been in too much of a hurry to get back to making more modifications, to explain anything but the basics. He'd assured her that the display would flash when she was right on top of the other cell phone.

She forced herself to trust that they were at the right location this time. She glanced at Travis and could see the determined look in his eyes and the hard set of his mouth in the dim light. She knew he was thinking the same thing.

She put the phone in her jacket pocket and slipped on the backpack. He went ahead to check the building, signalled with a thumbs up. Cane in hand she followed to the main door.

They tried the smaller door next to the large garage entrance, not surprised to find it locked.

"Do you think you can pick it?" Naya whispered.

"I think so," Travis said after checking out the lock. He traced his fingers along the edge of the door frame. "Do you have a flashlight?"

"Yes," Naya said. Slipping her pack off, she took out a mini flashlight and handed it to him.

"What's this?" He studied the device in his hand. "How do you turn it on?"

"Here," Naya said pointing to a button on the side. "This is a level, if you need to see if something's, well, level. Pull the cap off at this end and you have screwdriver heads."

"And there's a flashlight too?" He pushed the button and an intense narrow beam came on. "Whoa. That's bright. And no stray light."

"That'll teach you to make fun of my gadgets." Naya smiled.

He examined the entire perimeter of the door, spending a lot of time at the top edge. He gave Naya a sour look. "It's what I was afraid of. There's an alarm."

"Can't we disarm it?"

"I'm not sure I can. Wait here while I take a look around for another way in."

"Maybe it's better to stick together," she said.

"You're right." Travis nodded. Together they searched the perimeter of the building. Their bad luck didn't look like it was about to end anytime soon. All the windows had bars and there were no other doors. Before they became completely deflated, Naya spotted a window with a missing bar.

"I might be able to squeeze through if we get the window open," she said. After Travis ensured that it wasn't alarmed, she took the crowbar out of her pack. "You're taller. Want to try?" The window was tightly shut with no space to let them get anything in to pry it open.

"This is too big. What else you got in there?"

"You can use the screw driver head in the end of the flashlight. It fits in near the light and you can see what you're doing." She took the flashlight, opened the end and pulled out the flat head bit. "Try this."

"Nope still too big. What else you got?"

"A couple of granola bars and a bottle of water. We can break the window and get at the latch that way."

"But then we'd risk alerting the night guard or something."

Naya rested a shoulder against the building thinking. Finally she asked, "How about your lock pick set? You must have something thin enough to fit."

He studied the set, selected a long, thin tool. She watched him scrape at the bottom of the window, trying to get at the latch. The window popped open.

"Okay," he said, slipping the now bent device back into his case. "I'll give you a boost." He cupped his hands for her to step up.

She lifted her strong, right leg and pulled herself to the window bars. A very snug fit — but she refused to give up. Just like when she was a kid sneaking into the fenced school yard. Her friends easily climbed it, but for some reason, as adventurous as she was, she could never cross over the top. Instead she'd squeezed through the small gap in the gate. Holding on to that memory, she pretended she was that same six-year-old pushing through a narrow gap.

Success. Travis held onto her legs to keep her from dropping onto her head. She reached the floor in a handstand and was able to lower her feet without too much of a thud. A quick scan confirmed she was alone in the dim light. There were crates piled two and three high everywhere hiding her from view.

Unfortunately the view was also hidden from her. She stood, rubbing her aching ribs. There'd be bruises in the morning.

She listened carefully for any footsteps or sound to betray the presence of someone else in the building but the distant bass hum of fans masked any chance of hearing. On the other hand the fans would also cover any accidental noise she made.

She was about ask for her cane only to watch it float through the window. She could hear Travis's footsteps jog away obviously to the front door. He didn't exactly have to rush — not like she had a chance of beating him there.

She kept to the wall, partly for added support, mostly to remain in the shadows. It felt like a much longer distance inside than it had been outside as she finally reached the door. She was relieved to find that the boxes were piled high at the door. That meant she wouldn't have to work on the alarm out in the open.

She opened the panel. Damn. The alarm wasn't even on. Maybe they took a page from her book — install an alarm and don't use it. Or maybe it meant there wasn't anything, or anyone, of value here.

She let Travis in then closed the door gently. The unavoidable click of the latch engaging made Naya's heart thud. Both froze and listened for running footsteps. The fans continued their song undisturbed.

Declining his offer to carry the backpack for her, she put it on. She'd feel naked without all her tools close at hand. She checked the GPS reading. It still read 539.

"Maybe we need to be closer inside," Travis whispered. He led the way through the high wall of crates which ran along the perimeter of the building. The rest of the floor was a wide open expanse with a few scattered crates. In the middle of the building was a metal staircase leading up to a smaller second level mezzanine.

Travis would be able to scamper across the floor ducking behind boxes for cover. How was she going to do the same? She just had to reach the small stack of crates near the staircase that offered a hiding place.

As though reading her mind Travis pointed at the boxes then held out his arm. She took a deep breath hoping the exhaustion she felt lingering just out of range wouldn't decide to make its presence known and steal the strength from her legs. Together they walked quickly across the open floor to their sanctuary. She gave him a proud grin, surprised at how fast she'd been able to move. She was getting better. Tougher. Stronger.

"Okay," Naya whispered, "Ready for the stairs?"

"I am," Travis whispered, giving her a look that meant she wasn't going anywhere.

"I am too," she said lifting her chin stubbornly then marched to the stairs. As soon as she put her hand on the railing, a new light shone from the upper level. Travis lifted her by the waist and carried her to a stack of crates beneath the mezzanine invisible from anyone above.

They ducked down and listened to a mixture of angry male voices. With the echo through the warehouse they couldn't make out a single word. A door slammed. Heavy boots clanged down the staircase.

Travis and Naya pressed themselves against the wooden box clinging to the shadows as the entire staircase and mezzanine above them shook. They chanced a look to see if he was coming in their direction. A large, black man with shoulders that seemed too wide to go through a door unless he turned sideways, pounded across the clearing. Incredibly, his footsteps drowned out the sound of the ceiling fans. Only when they heard the door slam shut did they resume breathing.

"Who needs an alarm with someone that big around," Naya whispered.

"What's the reading now?"

She checked the display. "It says thirty-one." She looked up at the floor of the mezzanine. "Valerie must be upstairs."

"Yes, I think so too."

"Let's go," she said and started to stand up. But Travis yanked her back into shadow.

"Are you crazy?" he whispered as loudly as he dared. "I have a chance to hide or I can try to outrun them. I'm sorry, I'd never dream of telling you that you can't do everything you used to. But you *know* you can't do this." When she opened her mouth to speak, he interrupted with, "Right?"

"Right," she answered unhappily. Of course he was right but she didn't have to like it.

"Besides, if something does happen to me you'd be able to go for help," he said and gave her a quick kiss on the forehead.

At the bottom of the stairs, he paused to look back at her with an expression that made her shiver. Why did it have to look like he was saying goodbye? He climbed taking the steps three at a time. His sneakers silent on the metal steps.

Travis reached the top safely. Her heart pounded when he disappeared from sight. All she could do was crouch down and wait like a pathetic invalid.

She strained to listen for any sounds other than the whir of the building fans. Before she had time to sigh with relief, a cacophony of shouts, grunts and scuffling reverberated on the metal floor above her.

Bang!

"Travis!" Was that a gunshot?

She stood. Headed for the stairs. Within seconds reason took over and she returned to her hiding place. She listened hoping to hear her friend's voice. Nothing.

If he were still alive she should hear him explaining, negotiating to be let go. Only the building fans answered her silent plea.

She sat on the floor. Leaned against the crate. She should have had some guts. She should have come alone. She should never have involved Travis. She should have gone up the stairs herself. She should have visited Valerie at home.

She shouldn't have gotten sick.

Naya pulled out her cell and called Sergeant Ashantre. Damn! It went straight to voice mail. Even though she'd only been involved in the raid because of Naya's call, she might be at the grow-op and too busy to answer. Or, her heart ached at the thought. The detective was screening her calls. She left a message.

"This is Naya Assad again. Please don't hang up. We're in the warehouse district, off of Division Street, in Unit 8842. We tracked Valerie's cell phone's GPS. Travis has been shot — I, I don't know how badly he's hurt. I'm going to try to see if I can help him. I know I screwed up at the grow-op. Please, we need your help now. Please."

She shoved the phone back into her jacket. Made sure the backpack was secure. Took a firm hold of her cane. And crossed the short expanse to the staircase. Looking up at the metal stairs she felt a touch of vertigo. It didn't look stable. But that humongous man had clomped down this very staircase not that long ago. It *was* stable she assured herself.

With her cane in her right hand and the other on the railing, she began her climb. She dug deep inside, searched for every ounce of energy she could scavenge. She found a rhythm and her legs moved quickly.

She reached the top in less than a minute, panting hard, ribs burning. A cramp in her side threatened to double her over. She breathed deeply, worked through the pain and scanned the area. A wave of relief flooded over her when she didn't find a body lying anywhere. And she didn't see a pool of blood on the floor. It meant that Travis was still alive. He had to be.

The mezzanine was perhaps fifteen feet wide. There were three doors, two of which were open. Plus a fourth to the far right, open to reveal a bathroom. Room number three must be where Travis and hopefully Valerie and Alice were being held.

She took a step forward and cringed when her cane reverberated on the metal floor sounding like a gong. She folded it up, shoved it into her backpack. As long as she concentrated her balance should hold out.

With fatigue whispering in her ear she reached the middle room, closest to the stairs without incident. She pulled out her penlight and scanned inside. Nothing except for a couple of empty metal shelving units. Probably used to be a storage room. Now it was just another place that dust could call home.

She headed left to the other open door. A dust encrusted office. Then, her beam of light caught two purses on the desk. A quick inspection through the first, produced a wallet with ID for Alice Vanderlund. Her hands trembled as she opened the second purse and found a wallet.

Valerie's.

Naya's eyes welled up. She never really doubted that she'd find Valerie. But to actually hold physical evidence in her hands, validated her theories to the police. Sergeant Ashantre would have to admit that she had been right all along. If she ever phoned back.

She put the wallet away and pulled out Valerie's cell phone. She heeded Mackay's warning not to turn it on and alert Howard Dixon that the game had changed. But why hadn't Dixon traced the phone here himself? At this point she didn't care about the whys. She planned to get everyone out then worry about answers later.

What if — Naya's blood chilled at the new thought — the phone was all that was left of Valerie. Naya shoved that thought away. Guards wouldn't be watching a couple of purses. She put Valerie's cell into her jacket pocket.

Naya took out her own cell to call Mackay and fill him in on what was happening. He didn't answer. Damn him for being on another plane of existence whenever he was working on the computer. Despite the anger inside she managed a calm, if desperate message.

"We think we found Valerie and Alice, but Travis has been caught. I heard a gun shot but — but I don't know how he is. The police might be coming but I kind've doubt it. I'm going to see if I can help him. Try to send help. Or come yourself. I'm shutting off the ringer. Text me."

Though it was middle of the night she took a chance that Taylor might still be awake. She frequently worked strange hours. When it went straight to voice mail. She listened to Taylor's brief outgoing message,

"It's me — talk."

131

Naya took a moment to calm herself before speaking. "I don't have much time to explain but Travis and I may have found Valerie. We're in the warehouse district, unit 8842. Mackay's at my place but he's not answering his phone. I've — Travis is missing and he — he may have been shot. When you get this message please send the police. I've screwed up so much with them that they won't listen to me anymore. I'm going in." She hung up.

Going in? How melodramatic. She had to at least try to save him and — well — everybody. And how the hell was she planning to do that? All alone? Once upon another life she was pretty good at self-defence. No chance in hand to hand combat now. She couldn't compete physically so she'd have to outsmart them instead. All she had to do was somehow get the bad guys out of the room. Then she could release everyone.

A loud noise on the main floor? Nice idea, the only problem was that if she climbed down she wouldn't have the strength or the time to get back up and free the prisoners. She could throw something heavy from up here. She pushed the metal desk. It didn't budge. Even if it did, the deafening scrapping noise on the metal mezzanine floor would alert people in the next town before she wrestled it close to the railing. The chair was light. Too light to be heard over the fans.

A fine rescue. Couldn't have been better thought out.

With all the missing computers maybe Valerie was working on her own desktop. Naya quickly checked her phone. Yes! There was a Wi-Fi network here. The signal was weak, with no external access, but it was available.

Which meant Naya might be able to hack her way in. Much easier considering she had Valerie's laptop. She sat on the floor behind the desk concealed from view of the doorway and pulled out the computer.

She easily accessed the desktop. She checked out a few files and found a lot of programming. The code was beautiful. Had great finesse. Very neat and succinct.

And total gibberish.

Included were frequent notations in the comment lines; "waiting for third portion." Had to be a stall tactic.

If only Naya could be sure it was safe to send Valerie a message. She'd tell her that help was close. Such as it was.

She knew the police weren't coming. Realistically at this time of night Taylor wouldn't be picking up her message until morning. She could call 911. If the police blindly barged in the kidnappers might kill their hostages. If Naya explained the situation then she ran the risk of a background check of her previous calls. They already thought she was a crackpot. She'd be dismissed, signing Valerie and Alice's death warrants. And Travis's.

Frustrated, she leaned her head back against the wall with a thud. She'd never felt this damned helpless. So useless. Maybe Doctor Gregory and her flogging a dead horse analogy had been right. The old Naya was gone. She had to accept it. The old Naya would have made the police believe her. She'd have gone in with fists ready and a rescue army behind her. This new Naya was an impotent shadow of her former self. Remaining on the floor with her back against the wall, she stared up at the ceiling. In the stray light coming in from the outside, she saw it.

An air vent.

She smiled. Maybe she'd watched too many movies. That air vent offered a better alternative to breaking down the door and tripping into everyone with her cane.

She repacked the computer. With the flashlight in her mouth, she reached to lift a chair up onto the desk. But after a second thought, she decided there was no way she wanted to try to climb into the vent with a flashlight shoved in her mouth.

A quick look outside the office confirmed no one was nearby. She shut the door and flipped on the light switch. She'd have to move the desk under the vent. She grabbed hold of the edge and yanked.

"Oh, my God," she gasped. The desk was heavy. She took a firmer hold and pulled. It moved a short distance. Another pull. Another short distance. Bracing herself, she called on every strand of muscle to give it one more yank. The desk slid across the tiled floor with an ear piercing screech. She was afraid to stop pulling even after the stumble. Keeping her balance long enough to line it up under the vent before falling backwards to land on her butt.

Scrambling to her feet she rushed to open the door a crack. Still clear. She shut it again and leaned against it panting and sweating. She rubbed her backside. What was another bruise? She noticed there was thick yellow wax build-up that outlined where the desk's feet had sat for years. No wonder it wouldn't move. She frowned at a paperclip caught under a thick layer of floor wax. Whoever owned this building needed to hire a new cleaning crew.

Trembling with excitement, nerves and fatigue, she lifted the wooden desk chair up on the desk. Good thing the ceiling wasn't that high. With a little extra effort she managed to climb up on the desk. Not too elegantly she managed to step onto the chair holding the chair back for balance. Planting her feet firmly she straightened and reached for the vent with both arms. Slipped her fingers through the vent holes. She examined the screen. Only three screws held it in place. Keeping one hand on the screen to steady herself she pulled out the combo flashlight from her pocket. Afraid to breath she released her hold on the screen and selected a flat head screwdriver bit.

Damn, the screws were rusted in. Next time she went skulking around she'd make sure she packed some WD-40. For now she had to settle for elbow grease and a lot of determination. She let each screw fall to the floor confident the tiny *ping* couldn't be heard outside. Pushing on the screen to keep it in place she removed the final screw. When she tried to remove it, the screen didn't budge. In fact she needed to pry it out of its home with the screwdriver. The screen dropped abruptly. She gasped, caught it and kept her balance. Clutching the screen tightly to her body, she giggled with relief.

She climbed down, leaned the screen against the desk and sat on the floor cross-legged. Her mouth felt like cardboard and she drank greedily from her water bottle. This was the last kilometre of the race. Time to dig deep. Collect all her reserve strength. And push on.

Already warm, she didn't need the jacket. She took the cell phones out, slipped one into each back pocket of her jeans then folded up the windbreaker and stuffed it in her bag next to the computer.

She climbed back up on the chair. Found her centre of gravity. Lifted the backpack over her head. The chair wobbled. She kept her balance by sheer resolve. She lifted the bag again and tossed it into the vent. It rolled just out of reach of the opening. No going back now.

Naya took hold of either side of the large vent. Sucked in a breath. Pulled herself up.

She got a quick glimpse inside the vent. Then dropped back to the chair. She kept one hand on the vent opening to steady herself.

Not as easy as she'd imagined. She may have been dutifully doing all her exercises but she hadn't been doing any push-ups. Definitely no chin-ups. She wasn't coming this far to be stopped by weak muscles. Travis was in room three, possibly bleeding to death. Valerie could also be in there. And Alice.

She was all they had.

Naya took a firm grip. Pulled herself up. Muscles screamed and trembled. She dropped back on the chair. Rubbed her hands together.

Eased the burning in her palms. Ignored the pain in her shoulders. Took a determined hold of the vent. A few preparatory breaths. A last deep one. She heaved herself up. As far as her chest. Her body begged her to stop. With a grunt she leaned forward. Kicked with her legs to give her momentum to lift another few inches. One more Herculean pull and she was in.

She rolled onto her side, gasping, wanting to cry out from the pain of muscles that felt like they'd been torn apart and set on fire. Imagining how loud her screams would echo in the metal vent she settled for a sad, tiny whimper. Several minutes passed before she felt strong enough to just sit up.

She struggled to ignore the dizziness that begged her to close her eyes for a second. There was no time to fall for *that* old trick. Nap time was not on the agenda. She took a sip of water, then another and soon the light-headedness faded. She put away the water bottle and pulled out the flashlight to inspect her path.

Luckily it was spacious enough to crawl on hands and knees. No commando crawl required. She put the backpack on. And started moving.

The movies always portrayed these things as being so easy with the heroine skittering along unimpeded. She barely broke a sweat and her hair and makeup remained unblemished. Naya stopped crawling and reviewed her new mantra, "It looked a lot easier in the movies." How pathetic was that? Her life used to be the stuff movies were made of. Now... She dared any fictitious character to deal with the obstacles she'd endured. The anger spurred her on.

At first her progress was easy. Then her right knee, injured at the grow-op house, began to ache. She ignored it and kept going despite now crawling with a limp. Only fair considering she walked with one.

She reached the vent for room two. This opening was bigger than the one she'd come through. She hadn't thought of that when she'd first inspected the much larger room. Though to be fair she couldn't have imagined that she'd be crawling over it. The screen itself was over half her height. She pushed on it with all her might. Seemed solid. But would it hold her full weight? How embarrassing to be this close only to crash through the ceiling and then join her friends as a fellow prisoner not a saviour. She might even make that list of the world's dumbest criminals, although technically she wasn't a criminal. Or she'd win the infamous Darwin Award: given to people whose major contribution is dying before they can procreate and pollute the gene pool with their "stupid trait" that killed them in the first place.

She checked the distance she'd come. Not that far to go back. And do what? Call the police again? Hope they'd come? Phone someone else? Hope they'd answer. Without knowing what was going on inside the third room could she really afford to waste time?

No other choice.

She knelt close to the edge of the opening. Braced her hands on the walls. Stretched as far across as possible until she reached the other side. She lowered her body in a slow, cautious movement. And lay on the vent distributing her weight evenly. No telltale cracking sounds. She slid across, propelling herself forward by pushing her feet along the walls.

Clear. She collapsed on her stomach. Her whimpering muscles listened to the growing feeling of urgency inside her and calmed enough to let her get up on her hands and knees. The next vent was a lot farther thanks to the larger middle room. She continued slowly, steadily, trying to pace herself and conserve her energy.

She remembered an incident during physiotherapy at the rehab centre. Under Mike, her physiotherapist's watchful eye, Naya had practised using the walker. Each day she'd do warm up exercises then walk back and forth in the gym for an hour. She'd been so excited the first time she succeeded in crossing the entire length without stopping. Mike had timed her on the next trip in the hopes of demonstrating how fast she was progressing. A despicable six minutes to traverse a span that should have taken thirty seconds.

Naya's competitive spirit was rekindled in a way that she doubted her therapist had intended. Later that night, she'd snuck back to the gym in her wheelchair. She set the timer on her watch and headed out across the floor using a walker. Every few steps she checked the time and her smile grew wider. No problem breaking this morning's record.

Her smile vanished when her toe caught. She lurched forward. The speed that she fell surprised her. Although not as shocking as the speed with which the walker was jettisoned towards the opposite wall.

She lay on the ground stunned. Eventually she pushed herself up on her elbows. She tried to stand. With nothing to hold onto, she failed. With each attempt she'd almost get her feet under her, but her leg muscles wouldn't hold her weight. With each failed attempt she grew more tired until she collapsed on her stomach. She struggled to catch her breath and not cry. She hadn't thought things through. As usual. If she'd kept to the edge of the gym, she could have used the wall to help her stand. She wouldn't be in the middle of the gym.

Stranded.

She rolled onto her back and stared up at the ceiling. Interesting. The lights were encased in metal cages. Was the administration afraid that a deranged patient was going to throw their walker, cane or prosthetic leg at the lights and break them? She lifted her head and for the first time noticed that there were basketball nets. Of course, this gym doubled as — well — a gym.

A few more minutes of drifting thoughts, she zeroed in on a single, uber important one. No way was she going to be found lying here in the morning doing trapped turtle impressions. She turned over. Pushed herself up on hands and knees. Slowly. Steadily. She crawled. Until she reached the finish line. Her walker.

Today, she reached another goal. The vent for the third room.

She peeked through the screen and her heart pounded with excitement when she found Valerie seated at a computer. There was also a petite girl with short brown hair sitting next to her. That had to be Alice. Naya also saw a "guard" snoring on the sofa, a magazine on his chest. And there, barely in her line of sight she stifled a cry of relief when she spotted Travis sitting on the floor in the far corner. He was holding a bloody towel to his forehead. But he was alive.

Against the wall, opposite the door were two narrow army cots, the sheets and blankets rumpled. Travis's arrival had obviously woken them. And as she watched, Alice had gradually slumped forward to rest her head on the table.

From her vantage point Naya could see that her friend was playing Spider Solitaire — difficult level of four suits. She moved as quietly as possible to pull out the laptop and sent Valerie a broadcast message.

Val — it's Naya — I'm here to get you out.

She looked through the opening in time to see her friend yank her hands away from the keyboard as though burnt. Valerie spun around to make sure the guard was asleep, then nudged Alice awake. Valerie held a finger to her own lips then pointed at the screen. They glanced at each other, then at the sleeping guard, then at the door.

Where? Valerie typed.

Don't look. In the vent above you. Naya answered.

What do we do?

Naya paused. A plan would have been nice. Still not thinking things through. But in the past she'd always managed to come up with something.

Can you get rid of guard? Naya typed.

Sure.

She watched as Valerie and Alice glanced at the snoring man. Then Alice reached around the desktop and yanked out a cable. From her vantage point Naya wasn't sure what she'd done but then she noticed the screen was dark. Both women took deep breaths in unison.

"Damn!" Valerie yelled.

The man sputtered awake and fell off the sofa, arms waving as he fought to get to his feet. It would have been comical under other circumstances.

"What?" He spun around, arms out from his side, ready to take on any surprises. He turned to the women. "What happened?"

"Remember I told you that if we work too fast we'd burn out the screen?" Valerie asked him, her tone sounding like she was talking to a child. The guard slowly nodded. "Yes, well, the cable that connects the screen to the computer has overheated."

"Can't you wait till, uh, I dunno, it cools down?" he asked, moving closer to squint at the computer, his head titled.

"It's completely fried. We can't do anything until we get a new cable," Valerie said, nodding to Alice who removed a random cable.

Alice stood up to hand him the cable apparently not intimidated by the fact that she only came up to his chest. She smiled and asked in a voice that any man would do anything for.

"Would you mind going to a computer store and getting us another one of these, please?"

"Uh, I dunno," he stared at the cable in his hand as though trying to understand it. When he turned his attention to the women he had the same expression. "Uh, I dunno."

"Oh don't worry about us," Valerie added, using a gentle maternal tone. After all, she never went in for that sexy stuff. "We'll try and do some figuring out on paper and when you get back we'll be ready to go."

"It's such a shame because we were close to figuring out the third part too," Alice said, her voice sounding forlorn.

"Yes, it's such a shame," Valerie added, shaking her head.

"Uh, I guess so." He started for the door. Even from this distance Naya could see an extra neuron fire. "But it's the middle of the night. All the stores are closed."

"There's that 24 hour place on Alexander," Valerie said.

"Is that close to here?" Alice asked innocently. "We don't know where we are and well, I really hope it's not too far from here."

"Uh, no, uh," he stuttered. Finally he said, "No, it's not far. Do you need anything before I go? Like the uh, the ladies?"

"No, we're fine," Alice said.

"Do you want me to lock that guy up somewhere else?"

"No!" both women snapped. Giving a nervous giggle, Valerie added, "I'm sure we can keep him under control."

"Sure," the guard said. He unlocked the door with the key from his pocket and left. When they heard the sound of the lock turning, both women rushed to the air vent.

"Naya?" Valerie whispered.

"I'm here," she whispered back. As soon as she spoke Travis's head snapped up and he scrambled to his feet.

"Naya?" he forced himself to whisper, "are you out of your mind? You were supposed to go for help."

"Do you want to argue or do you want to get out?" Naya asked. Not expecting an answer, she packed up the computer, slipped the backpack on and said, "I'll try to find something to open the door with. Don't go anywhere."

"Funny," all three answered.

She crawled back much faster with the anticipation of an actual rescue spurring her on. Back in the office she made a quick search of the desk for spare key. Nothing but cobwebs, mouse droppings and something that may have been a sandwich once. Wrinkling her nose in disgust at the fossilized meal she closed the drawer. She went out to the mezzanine planning to use the crowbar to force the door open. As she got closer, she laughed. On a hook by the door hung a key. Funny, this didn't look like Mayberry.

She unlocked the door and pulled it open.

"Anyone order a rescue?" she said with a flourish.

Valerie rushed to give her a big hug.

"I can't believe you found us," Valerie cried into Naya's shoulder.

Naya said as they stepped apart, "I'm just glad you're okay." She turned to Travis still holding the bloody towel to his head. "Are you shot?" Naya inspected the wound. It had a straight edge, not a round hole.

"No. When I got up here that white guy came out of the bathroom. As soon as he saw me, he fired but missed. I was too busy ducking and he had time to tackle me. My head hit the edge of something. It's stopped bleeding now." He tossed the towel away. "See? I'm fine."

"Valerie," Naya said, "I was really worried."

"I know I should have phoned you at seven o'clock when I got outside but I didn't want to break my concentration. And then those men grabbed us."

"You were kidnapped at seven?" Naya said. She'd missed saving them by only five minutes? If she hadn't wasted time selfishly thinking about herself she would have got there in time to stop the kidnapping. No time for feeling guilty now. They still weren't in the clear.

"I can't believe you found us!" Valerie hugged Naya again.

"And I can't believe that guy actually fell for it," Alice said. "You just saw firsthand why we call him Einstein."

"Good thing Mr. T wasn't here," Valerie said, wiping tears from her eyes. "He'd never have fallen for this."

"Mr. T?" Naya said. "Oh, the big black guy I saw leaving."

"Look, we better get out of here before either of them comes back," Travis interrupted.

"Do you want to take both computers?" Naya asked, noticing the laptop on the floor.

"Leave 'em. Nothing of value on either of them," Valerie said.

"They took the laptop from my car," Alice said, "but it doesn't even work and I was taking it to be recycled. There's no information on it."

"I've got your case," Naya said. At the questioning look, she added, "It's a long story."

"Which we can listen to later," Travis said, waving both hands to the door like an airport rampy trying to guide in an airplane.

Holding Valerie's hand Naya led the way out of the room directing Travis to the office to pick up the two purses. As he ran to retrieve them the three women stepped out of their prison. Valerie froze. She gaped around the mezzanine, then up at the high ceiling. Immediately she began to tremble. Her hand was suddenly clammy. Her breath came in short gasps. Without warning, she ran back into the room. She pressed herself into the far corner.

"I can't. Something bad'll happen. I can't go out there." Valerie kept shaking her head 'no', her eyes wide and unblinking as she repeated the phrases over and over.

"Valerie! What're you doing?" Naya followed. "We've got to go!" She reached for her hand. Valerie cried out and pulled away.

"What the hell's wrong with her?" Travis yelled running back. He shoved both purses into Alice's hands then grabbed Valerie's arm. That just made her scream louder.

"Stop it!" Naya scolded him pushing his hand away. "She's agoraphobic. She can't help herself."

"And this big warehouse doesn't help," Alice said.

"How the hell did she get in here then?" Travis said, making another try for her arm but Naya slapped his hand away.

"Are you kidding? Didn't you see the size of those guys?" Alice said. "They just picked her up and carried her."

"Wait," Naya paused, trying to think of something other than trying to carry her out kicking and crying. "How did she get to the bathroom?"

"She focussed on the wall, her hands flat against it. Then with me beside her, she sidestepped there."

"Okay, Valerie," Naya began, "how about a blind fold?" She got her jacket out of the backpack. "Just imagine yourself inside a nice safe, small room." Her friend sniffled and nodded. She reached for Naya's hand with a shaky one and stood. "Just stay close to me and imagine that we're both in your apartment. Okay?"

"I...I'll try." Valerie sniffed again and after a momentary panic, she let Naya cover her head with the windbreaker.

"Just keep your eyes closed and we'll walk slowly," Naya said.

Holding onto her, in part to steady herself and in part to provide emotional support for her friend, Naya led the way out of the room. There was a strong resistance at the doorway, but she could feel her friend taking in a few deep breaths. This time the repeating phrases were calm and more positive.

"I can do it. Nothing's going to happen. It's safe." Valerie stepped through the door. Then she took a single step. Followed by another. Then another. And they made it to the staircase. Now it was Naya's turn to hesitate. If she lost her footing she'd take both of them down.

"I think it's better if you let Travis and Alice guide you."

"No!" Valerie protested.

"I need both hands to hold the railing." She didn't need to explain further. Immediately, Valerie reached out. Travis and Alice each took an arm and guided her down the stairs.

Naya followed, sliding her hands down the cold steel railing, moving as quickly as she dared. They others reached the bottom while she was still three quarters of the way down. They stopped to wait for her.

"Travis get them out to the car," she called, "I'm right behind you." She saw them hesitate briefly, then Travis and Alice glanced at Valerie. They looked up at Naya only three steps from the bottom and with an apologetic shake of their heads, led Valerie out.

When she stepped away from the support of the railing she lost her balance and fell landing on the left knee. Great, she was running out of new places to bruise.

Panting and lightheaded she sat on the bottom step. She slipped off her backpack. Unfolded her cane.

She put the pack on again. Grasped the railing with both hands and pulled herself to her feet.

Ignoring the pounding headache she limped towards the exit. Relieved to be able to hold onto the boxes for added support she now tottered along at a much faster pace. The door was within reach. A surge of energy coursed through her at the sure taste of freedom.

She reached to push the door. It swung open. She got ready to scold Travis for deserting the others to come back for her.

Instead Naya came face to chest with the guard, Einstein. Behind him stood a very irate looking Mr. T.

CHAPTER TWELVE

Naya froze mid-step trying not to look like a cat caught in the middle of eating the family parakeet.

"How'd you get in?" Mr. T growled as he shoved Einstein aside.

Einstein peered over Mr. T's shoulder at her. His eyes flicked towards the second floor then back at her. She could actually see him try to process the situation, the mental exercise an obviously painful process as he slowly blinked and opened his mouth about to speak. He swallowed hard then squinted at Mr. T as though his partner was the town's executioner and chose to remain silent.

"Through this door." She pointed, hoping her terror didn't taint her sweet, innocent demeanour.

"You even left the door open, you moron!" he snapped at Einstein.

Einstein shrank in size under the reproachful glare. Apparently he hadn't told his partner about capturing an intruder. Otherwise the very large, extremely angry man would have locked her up without a word. Bad for Einstein. Good for her. She played up her role of invalid, making sure she didn't ham it up too much.

"Thank goodness I found someone," she said with a loud dramatic sigh. She paused to judge his reaction. His face suggested he didn't think of her as a threat. In that case she could rely on the artful science of babble to get herself out of trouble.

"I'm looking for number 8-8-2-4. And it seems like I've been wandering around all evening trying to find it. It's a storage unit. I'm meeting my cousin there and we're getting together to go through our grandfather's things. He was really a nice old man, but a really serious hoarder. We were going to sort through things in the afternoon but my cousin's going out of town and we have..."

"Okay, okay," Mr. T interrupted, waving both hands to cut her off. "This is 8-8-4-2. Twenty-four is several buildings to the left."

"Thank you very much," she said, as she headed for the door trying not to rush, wishing she could. She struggled to push the heavy door open and did risk a glance over her shoulder when she heard Mr. T's scolding voice.

"Those women are always messing with you. You can't burn out the screen by working too fast. And *this* is a printer cable!"

The door slammed shut cutting off Einstein's protests. Once outside she limped as fast as she could to the car. After only a few steps, headlights blinded her. No! More accomplices had arrived! The car skidded to a stop beside her.

Travis!

As she opened the car door the two men burst out of the warehouse. She froze at the sight of a gun in Mr. T's hand. A frantic call from Travis and she dove head first into the front seat. Travis hit the gas pedal. But her feet still dangled outside the car. She screamed in agony when the door slammed across her calves. Travis held onto the waist of her jeans and drove. The car lurched from side to side. With no strength left to pull herself to safety, Naya desperately clung to the seatbelt strap.

As she lost her grip new hands dragged her all the way into the car. She heard the car door shut. Hands helped her sit up. It was Alice reaching forward from the back seat. Beside her Valerie huddled in a ball with the jacket clutched tightly around her head.

Straightening herself up, Naya clicked her seatbelt on. Alice sat back and put on her own belt. Travis made a sharp corner. Naya checked over her shoulder in time to see a car four-wheel skid into view in pursuit.

"They're following us!" Naya yelled.

"I know!" he yelled back. He was hunched over the steering wheel and frequently glanced in the rear view mirror. "Alice, did you call 911?"

"Yes, they're still on the line."

"Tell them they're armed," Naya shouted.

"They're armed?" Alice cried out in panic. "You mean they have guns?" Into the phone she screamed. "They've got guns. Hurry. Oh my God, they're getting closer!"

"Not if I can help it," Travis called out and careened around another corner.

"Valerie," Naya called, "Are you okay?"

"Sure. Fine. Don't worry." Her voice came out muffled and a little high pitched. Finished talking, she pulled the jacket tighter around her head and curled into a smaller ball.

The car zoomed around another corner, slamming the passengers to one side. It straightened and jerked the passengers upright again.

Travis called out, "Someone look for a sign to the main road. Anything to get out of this maze!"

Naya fought nausea as she tried to look between the blur of dark buildings searching for anything that was different. At this speed she hoped that there'd be enough time to change course if she did spot something. Finally she saw bright lights on the left.

"I think I saw something," Naya told Travis. "To the left. I'm not sure."

"It's better than racing around here blind." He hit the brakes and spun the steering wheel. Too fast. The car fish-tailed and slammed into the corner of the building.

Naya cried out when the door dented in towards her. Her voice blending in discord with the screams from the back seat. Unfazed, Travis continued driving. She looked out the rear window in time to see the chase car zip past. She heard the squeal of tires. This should put some distance between them. Give them a chance to find an exit. They turned and she saw street lights.

"Go left!"

This time the car hit the building on the driver's side. Again, Travis kept going. Naya checked behind. No sign of pursuit. They had a chance now. She faced the front and everyone in the car screamed as Travis hit the brakes. The car screeched to a stop inches from a barricade of metal drums. They'd reached a dead end.

Travis cursed. Put the car in reverse. Backed out at high speed. He spun around. Slammed the gear into drive and kept going.

"Where did you see the lights?" Travis asked.

"It was in this direction," Naya said. "But I'm not sure anymore. Alice, how long before the police get here?"

"They've arrived at warehouse 8842. Where are we?"

"If I knew that we'd be out of here." Travis snapped, as all four tires screeched around a corner.

"Can't they lock onto your GPS?" Naya asked.

"I'll ask," Alice said. "Lock on to my phone. Use the GPS signal. What?" To Naya she said, "They say it's not working?"

"I'll call from my phone," Naya said, reaching into her back pocket. It was empty. She tried the other pocket for Valerie's. Nothing. Maybe she left them in her jacket.

"Alice check my jacket pockets." While the other girl searched the pockets and Valerie whimpered, Naya searched the floor of the car hoping they'd fallen out when she jumped into the car. Nothing. She looked up at Alice who shook her head, no.

"Oh, God," Naya said. "I lost them. I'm sorry. Travis, how about your phone?"

"Busy now." Barely blinking he stared straight ahead as he gripped the wheel with both hands.

Alice paused listening and then called out, "She says to look for any signs, billboards — anything to figure out where we are?"

The long, desperate silence deepened. Travis concentrated on not hitting anything. Naya and Alice scanned the dark. Valerie huddled under the jacket and tried not to whimper.

In a blink they drove past a building with a brightly lit sign.

"We just passed Dovercraft Industries," Naya yelled, as though she needed the operator to hear her. Alice repeated the location into the phone.

"She says to stay in the area."

"I'll try," Travis said. He circled one building three times. Then he skidded to pass the pursuers in the opposite direction. Seeing their confused looks made everyone in the car give a victory hoot.

"What's going on?" Valerie called out.

"Travis doubled back and lost them," Naya told her.

"You should have seen their faces," Alice added. "It's a shame I'm too terrified to enjoy this."

"Mr. T scared me, but Einstein was always entertaining," Valerie called out.

Naya was glad to see that Valerie had stopped whimpering and was actually engaged in what was going on around her. A bit strange with the jacket still clutched securely around her head.

The temporary light mood vanished when the pursuit car materialized from behind a building to settle into a very close chase position. Naya could see their faces clearly, then gasped at the sight of a gun in Einstein's hand.

"Travis," Naya cried out, "I think he's going to shoot."

At that instant Einstein stuck his arm out of the window and fired. Everyone screamed and ducked.

"They're shooting at us," Alice screeched into the phone.

Naya split her attention between staring at the gun waving out the window and Travis clutching the steering wheel driving like some stock car racer. They passed Dovercraft Industries for a second time.

Finally something working in their favour. Now, all they had to do was stay in the area, elude the two men, avoid crashing and wait for the police to save the day.

Travis sped around the building, then immediately around a second building. He shut off the lights and screeched to a stop behind a third building. The ploy worked.

The other car never slowed. They waited and listened for the approaching sound of screeching tires. She could imagine Mr. T grinding his teeth, maybe swearing at Einstein, punching a fist into the steering wheel. Whatever it took to break his concentration was good.

"Maybe I should risk trying to get out of here?" Travis said.

"We're safe here," Naya said shaking her head emphatically.

"911 says the police are minutes away," Alice said. "They say don't..." She broke off in a high pitched gasp. There, between the buildings were bright headlights betraying them.

"Make sure your seatbelts are tight," Travis said as he revved the engine.

"Travis," Naya warned him when she saw the intense determination on his face. "You're not going to ..."

"Everyone hold on!" Travis released the brakes and accelerated towards the headlights. The lights came straight at them. Alice wrapped her arms around Valerie's shoulders. Naya braced for the head-on crash.

The other car swerved missing them by a paint layer. Naya could've sworn she saw Einstein grab the steering wheel. The other car smashed into a building creating a crater in the steel plate wall. Travis skidded to a stop to avoid crashing into a stack of drums.

Before everyone had time to feel relief, the other car reversed out of the building. With no bumper and accordion hood, the car resumed its chase with renewed intensity.

Travis's driving skills were magical. He passed three warehouses at top speed. Made a sharp left. Only to have Mr. T practically tailgate them around the corner. Travis repeated the tactic. Except this time he went right after only one building. It worked. The kidnappers missed the turn.

Was it possible that they'd finally given up? She watched the road behind them. No cars. No lights.

"Travis, turn the head lights back on," Naya said.

"I can see fine," he said.

"Travis, at least slow down."

"Okay." He took his foot off the gas. Immediately Naya released the breath she didn't realize she was holding.

The chase car appeared suddenly in front of them. Naya and Alice screamed. Valerie cried out, "What is it?"

Travis hit the brakes. They lurched forward as seatbelts yanked them back. The car fish-tailed. Skidded. And stopped with a gentle kiss on the other car's front bumper.

Occupants of both vehicles gawked at each other through the front windshield. Naya knew that both sets had seen death coming. If they hadn't slowed down...

"Travis!"

He'd hit his head on the steering wheel when he'd slammed on the brakes. His head lolled forward on his chest.

"Travis," Naya repeated, touching his shoulder. "We need to get moving." She watched the other men get out, Einstein aiming the gun at them. "Travis, get up!" He groaned and started to move. Too late. Mr. T marched around to Naya's door calling through the open window.

"You two in the back, get out, or someone gets hurt." He tried to open the door, but it was too damaged from the first collision. He went around the car and opened the driver's door. He unclipped Travis's seatbelt, yanked him out of the car by his collar and threw him to the ground. He pushed the seat forward and ordered in a throaty growl, "Get out of the back. Now!"

"No," Naya pushed the seat back. To Alice she said, "Don't get out."

"If you ladies don't come with me now, her boyfriend gets it." Mr. T nodded to Einstein who stepped forward aiming the gun, somewhat hesitatingly. Travis was still groggy and lay on the ground, his arms and legs moving slightly.

Mr. T pushed the chair forward again.

"Naya, it's okay," Valerie called out from under the jacket. "We'll go with you. Please don't hurt anyone."

"No," Naya yelled and pushed the seat back. "You're not going anywhere with them."

"Lady," Mr. T snapped. "I don't plan to do this all night. Your boyfriend's dead if you don't stop bugging me."

Naya couldn't let them hurt Travis. She couldn't let them take the women. And she couldn't think of what to do. Their only chance was to waste more time and hope that the police arrived soon. Before she could even start a babbling argument, the joyous sound of sirens echoed in the distance.

Mr. T heard it too. He shoved the seat forward. Without missing a beat Naya pushed it back.

"We gotta go," Einstein called out. He shoved the gun in his belt and rushed back to their car getting into the driver's seat.

"Wait, you idiot." Mr. T started back, looking as though he planned to pull his partner out of the driver's seat. Partway to the car Mr. T paused, listening. The sirens were closing in. He prudently jumped into the passenger seat.

They were getting away. And with them the answers. How could her friend live knowing the architect of their ordeal was still out there? That they could be kidnapped again? Valerie would probably hide deeper inside her home. She might shun all personal human contact. And Alice — years spent hiding from a stalker. How would she cope with this new constant threat?

No way was Naya going to stand by and let both these women become prisoners in their own lives.

"Make sure your seatbelts are tight!" She called out as she slid into the driver's seat fighting to get over the gear shift.

"Are you crazy?" Valerie shouted.

In the rear view mirror Naya saw her friend yank the jacket from her head to gape at her. She allowed herself a tiny smile. How well her friend knew her.

Naya started up the engine. Clicked on her seatbelt. Einstein backed up and started to turn, his car now perpendicular to theirs.

"Hold on!" She hit the gas. Released the clutch.

The impact slammed both cars into a building. The Mustang's airbag exploded. Naya felt like she was hurtling through space with stars materializing around her. The distant roar of sirens sounded odd. Like voices screaming. Wailing. Insisting on being heard.

Naya forced herself to see past the stars. To focus on the sound of sirens knowing that help was close. Her panic subsided when she saw Travis's face through the field of stars. Eventually the points of light faded.

"Are you all right?" she asked.

"Me? What the hell were you doing ramming their car like that? You could have been killed."

"Sorry about your car," she said, shaking her head. Trying to hear him through all the racket around her. Within moments she realized the noise was from inside her own head. The thundering roar subsided and she could now distinguish the sound of crying behind her. She remembered.

"Valerie! Alice!" Naya tried to check on them but Travis held her still.

"The ambulance is on its way," Travis said. "Don't move till they check you out."

"I'm fine. I'm not hurt. Where are they?"

"We're here," Valerie said.

Naya patted his hand saying, "I'm okay. The airbag just stunned me."

He hesitated but finally helped her out of the car. Her legs felt like overcooked spaghetti. Eventually she managed to stand. Naya saw the damage, amazed that anyone survived. The heavy front end of the Mustang appeared to be relatively undamaged. The same couldn't be said for the other vehicle. The front tire was lying sideways under the car. The entire side was pushed in turning the fan-fold damaged hood into a piece of abstract art.

She hadn't intended to hit the car so hard. She really hoped Einstein and Mr. T were okay. She exhaled with relief when she spotted them. Unharmed, they were leaning on the hood of a squad car getting patted down and handcuffed.

Alice joined Travis and Naya to inspect the damage. A policeman came over to them.

"Everyone okay?" he asked, looking into the back of the car. "Are you hurt?"

"I'm just fine," Valerie answered, her voice muffled by the jacket on her head. The officer questioned the others with a shake of his head.

"She's agoraphobic," Naya explained but the puzzled look on the cop's face just deepened. "She has panic attacks in open spaces."

The cop nodded and said, "She needs to get out of the car. Think you can help her to my cruiser?"

By the time they moved Valerie to the squad car more police had arrived, lights flashing, sirens blaring. Einstein and Mr. T were put into the back of two different cars.

They recounted details of their adventure as the officer scribbled madly in his notebook. Finally after looking like he was getting dizzy from hearing the story from three points of view, Naya took pity on him.

"I'd suggest you give Sergeant Philadelphia Ashantre a call. She's familiar with me."

The officer wrote down the name. "The ambulance is almost here," he said. To Travis he said, "you definitely need to have that cut — cuts looked at. You may need stitches."

"I will," Travis said. "When can we get out of here?"

"Once you're checked out," the officer said and moved away to speak with the other police there.

Naya said, "I think that was cop lingo for 'after we check out your story.'"

"You don't mean they might arrest us?" Alice asked, her voice tiny.

"No," Naya said, "of course not."

Naya watched the officer that had been taking their statement talking on the cell phone. She assumed he was talking to Ashantre, especially with the way he kept looking at them and nodding. The paramedics checked everyone out. They cleaned the cuts on Travis's forehead and used suture tape. No sign of a concussion. Naya had always told him he had a hard head. She checked out as well. Just a few bruises here and there. In fact, a lot of bruises everywhere. Her knee felt much better when they cleaned and bandaged it up.

After everyone signed waivers and promised to visit their family doctors, the paramedics left the scene. With the Mustang damaged, their constable, Naya liked to think of him as their own personal constable, drove them to Naya's home.

On the way, using Travis's cell, Naya tried phoning Mackay again. Still no answer. Damn that man. She didn't bother leaving a message this time. Sure the cyber world was a wonderful place to lose yourself in. But people managed to keep part of their brain aware of reality.

She was tired. She was dirty. She was in pain. And she planned to give Mackay the longest lecture on reliability as soon as she saw him.

CHAPTER THIRTEEN

The drive to Naya's home was subdued and, if the word on some other plane of existence could be used, relaxed. Naya reclined in the back of the squad car with jacket-for-a-hat Valerie sandwiched between her and Alice. She kept her calm by firmly holding her hands with the occasional reminder to visualize a small space. Travis dozed in the front seat.

"We're almost there," Naya announced when her house came into view. She bolted upright startling Valerie into a quivering ball again. "There's a car in my driveway!"

"Is it Kevin?" Travis came fully awake and signalled the policeman to stop.

"No," Naya sighed as she got closer. "It's okay. It's Taylor's car," To Valerie she said, "I'm sorry I scared you. I just let my imagination get to me."

"It's okay," Valerie said as she squeezed the circulation out of Naya's hand.

To think that a little over a week ago she'd been thinking about how boring she'd let her life become. Now she couldn't wait to wrap herself in monotony again.

The cruiser pulled into her driveway just as a faint glow from the east paled the sky. As they got out of the car, Naya wished that she'd thought to grab the garage remote from Travis's car. It might have taken a lot less muscle to drag Valerie out of the back seat. As soon as the engine was cut and even before the door was opened, Valerie clutched at the seatbelts. At the metal grating that separated the back seat from the front. All the while repeating, "I'm sorry."

"Valerie," Naya coaxed. "It's just a few steps to the front door. Then you'll be safe inside." Nothing worked. They were left with only one option. Plain, old fashioned, brute force.

Naya leaned on Alice's arm for added balance and rushed ahead to unlock the door. She stepped aside to let Travis and the cop carry a mannequin-stiff Valerie past. The officer gave a polite nod and left. She reached to deactivate the alarm before the blaring sirens made Valerie's phobia worse.

It was already off. Damn, why hadn't Mackay turned it back on after Taylor arrived? Shutting and locking the door she ignored the irritation — for now.

"Valerie," Naya said, touching her shoulder gently hoping not to make her jump but failing. "You're safe now. You can take the jacket off your head."

Valerie responded by reluctantly peeking out from under her security blanket. Looking around the smaller entrance she heaved a sigh of relief and took the jacket completely off. She spoke in a small, vulnerable voice. "I'm really sorry for all the trouble I'm causing. It's just, well, the car chase..."

"Come on," Naya said, as she took her hand. "I'm sure after we eat something and get some rest we'll all feel better." Other than tightening her grip and a slight faltering, Valerie entered the spacious foyer.

"We're home," Naya called. She passed Valerie's hand to Alice, saying, "Go ahead to the kitchen." She checked the family room thinking they might be asleep. No one there. She hadn't expected them to come running to greet her though she did expect one of them to at least answer.

She practically stomped to the kitchen. They were probably both absorbed by the cloned data from Valerie's computer. She really hoped Valerie wouldn't be too upset about the breach in security. And she wondered how angry Dixon would be when he found out.

"We should call our boss," Alice said over her shoulder to Naya. "He'll be happy to hear we're back and..." She broke off, jerking to a sudden stop. "Victor?"

Travis also looked surprise. She pushed past them to see who Victor was and what the hell he'd said to get Mackay to let him in. She stopped mid-step, her stomach somersaulting. Kevin was standing behind Mackay who was seated at the kitchen table, his mouth pinched tight. He stared at them with wide, unblinking eyes. In the chair next to him sat a very sombre Taylor. She kept her head bowed and only occasionally glanced at Naya from the corner of her eyes.

Alice's calm demeanour confused her. Not a normal reaction for someone coming face to face with their stalker.

Before Naya could utter a word Travis leapt in front of the three women, his arms extended in a protective gesture. Naya peered around him, her mouth falling open at the sight of a gun in the man's hand.

"Kevin, what're you doing?" Naya asked. If she'd taken a moment to think, she'd never have spoken out loud because now he aimed the gun at her.

"This is Victor Brewerton." Alice's voice came out as a trembling whisper.

"Victor from accounting?" Valerie asked. Calmly she added, "Did Howard send you? You don't need the gun, these people just rescued us."

"What?" Naya cut in, asking Alice, "You mean, he's not your stalker?"

"My what?" Alice said.

"At first I thought he was your brother," Naya said. "When I went to your place he was already there."

"You were in my home?" Alice asked him, her demeanour transforming from one of confusion to that of dark understanding.

"We spent the whole day together," Victor said playfully. "She was naively helping me search your computer for the program."

"You're the one behind all this?" Alice said. "Why?"

Victor shrugged. "I got tired of seeing huge pay cheques going out to people like you that 'worked' from home for a few hours a day." He framed the words with quotation marks. "No one checking to see that you were actually 'working.'"

"Weren't you worried someone might come by Alice's place and expose your plan?" Valerie said.

"Who's going to come by when she's not home?" Victor answered like it should be obvious. "Enough wasting time," Victor said, then punctuated each word with a wave of the gun. "I want the program. Now!"

"I thought we were friends." Alice sounded hurt. "You were always nice to me. Bringing me donuts and coffee."

"I just wanted information," Victor interrupted. "But after I wasted all kinds of money on donuts you wouldn't even drop a hint about what you were working on. Luckily, Jenny from Research and Development only needed a couple of cups of coffee before she let a gold mine slip out. She told me enough for me to figure the program you were writing was worth millions to the right buyer."

"How could you kidnap us?" Valerie demanded.

"Trust me, that wasn't part of the plan," Victor said, shaking his head in a way that made you feel sorry for him. Almost. "It was those two fools I hired to keep an eye on you. When you — " he pointed at

Alice with his gun, "went out, I went in to search your computer for copies of the program. No luck. Since you practically camped out at Valerie's apartment, I figured the main program had to be there. I had them keep an eye on her place.

"I had to sell my brand new Lexus to keep paying them and buy that third hand rust bucket to drive. But finally after two months, they called to report that both of you were outside."

"And that's when you told them to kidnap us," Alice said, her voice level despite the underlying tone of fear.

"No! My original instructions were as soon as you left the apartment to go in and grab any computers they could find. When one of them phoned to tell me that you were both on the street, I said, great, go and get 'em now. Meaning the computers. I didn't realize what those idiots had done till they called from the warehouse." He broke off, rubbing his forehead and shaking his head wearily.

"You make it sound like it was, oops they made a mistake," Valerie said, trembling with anger. "Do you have any idea what it's like being forced into a car at gunpoint?"

He waved his gun towards Valerie. "This is all your fault you know. Two months and you never, ever stepped out of your apartment. Or answered your door."

"I never answer the door unless I'm expecting someone," Valerie said, managing to sound condescending.

"If you'd both just acted like normal people and co-operated, it would've been over sooner," Kevin shouted.

"If the kidnapping was a mistake," Naya asked quickly, hoping to calm him down, "why didn't you just let them go?"

"When they could identify the men who wouldn't hesitate to identify me?" He snorted then continued. "Once I had the program and got out of the country, I was going to tell them to let you go. But it didn't work out that way, did it?" His anger began to escalate again. "They grabbed a computer with nothing on it. I went to the apartment myself. The moron forgot to lock the door behind him and that's how you –" he pointed at Naya with the gun, "got in. I checked out your ID and left. I should've kept searching but I didn't want another complication if you woke up. Imagine my surprise when you showed up at Alice's door the next day. They kept talking about needing to figure out the third part of the program written by someone else, I figured it could be you."

"But I didn't know what they were working on," Naya said. "You knew that."

"The way I figured it, if you didn't have the whole program yourself, at least you were trying to find it. Either way, I stuck close."

For the first time she noticed his fluid speech pattern.

"What happened to your stutter?"

"My what?"

Now she realized that his stutter wasn't due to some childhood trauma. The hesitations were a result of him trying to come up with a fake story quickly. In other words, he sucked at imagination. He pulled a key from his shirt pocket.

"I took this from your keychain at the apartment," he said. "But I've tried it on every damn storage unit in the basement several times. What the hell's it for?"

Naya squinted at it not wanting to move closer to see. It did look familiar. She remembered double checking her keys at the time. Among her house and car keys, were a few old, forgotten ones that she kept meaning to remove. They'd become invisible. This tiny key hadn't been used since last year. No wonder she hadn't missed it.

"That's for my garden shed," she said blandly.

"Damn!" he tossed it onto the table.

"You actually tried to force them to rewrite the program from scratch?" Naya said, hoping to delay him long enough for her to figure out how to stop him.

"I knew that I better have insurance. In case I didn't find the right computer." Victor shook his head, his voice whiny. "I kept asking for progress reports but..."

"Did you really believe we'd rewrite a program in a few days that's taken over two years?" Valerie asked, sounding like she was talking to a fool. "Did you really think we'd give it our best try?"

"Doesn't matter now. It's all right here." He closed the laptop and slapped it against Mackay's chest. "Let's go."

"What?" Mackay's voice cracked. Wide-eyed, Taylor looked at Victor then pleadingly at Naya. Rather than repeat himself, Victor aimed the gun at Mackay's face. He stood slowly not breaking eye contact with the muzzle, hugging the computer tightly to his chest. He was even paler than Taylor.

Naya put her hand on Travis's shoulder and whispered, "Trust me, okay?" He gave her a tiny nod. No way could she let this nut take

Mackay anywhere. She stepped out from behind Travis and stared Victor straight in the eye. He stopped and aimed at her.

"What're you doing?" Victor asked.

"Kevin — I mean Victor," she said, sounding like her feelings had been hurt. "I trusted you and you ordered your goons to attack me."

"I never meant for that to happen."

"You phoned me to say you were coming over to trick me into shutting off the alarm."

"No!" Victor said, sounding defensive. "They were supposed to wait till I got you out of the house, *then* break in. I would never hurt you."

"Do I look unhurt?" She took another step forward. Her clothes were torn, dirty and bloody. Victor lowered his eyes but the weapon remained steady. Another step. "Do any of us look unhurt?" She watched as Victor took in Travis's appearance. Bandaged head. Blood soaked shirt. The gun aim wavered.

She remembered his face after the home invasion. It had been guilt and remorse. She had to believe that he was greedy, not ruthless.

"After all the time I spent with you," Naya said, her voice gentle. "I know you're not violent." She extended a hand. "Why not give me the gun?" He returned his aim, just as she knew he would. She could hear Travis and the others gasp behind her. She just hoped no one did anything dumb. At least not until after she did.

"I promise that once I'm away I'll let him go," Victor said.

"Just put down the gun and we can forget about all this," Naya said. She suddenly stumbled forward. Eyes rolled up in her head. She reached for the counter. Her legs collapsed.

Predictably, Victor reached forward to catch her. She swung her cane. Knocked the gun out of his hand. She swung again targeting his knee. His leg buckled. Travis tackled him. Within seconds he had him pinned on the floor. Taylor grabbed Mackay by the arm and pulled him out of the way cramming both of them into the corner.

Victor struggled and groaned and kicked his legs, almost getting free. Before Naya could think what to do, Alice sat on his legs. Valerie held down his arms.

Slapping him in the head, Valerie added, "And that's for locking us up without a proper shower."

"What kind of stupid are you anyway?" Alice added.

"It doesn't seem like he thought things through," Valerie said.

"I did so," Victor insisted, his voice coming in between short gasps as Travis shifted his weight to keep him down. "If you'd ever answered your door..."

"Are you serious?" Valerie asked. "What? Were you expecting it would be on my coffee table waiting to be stolen?" She laughed. "You really thought it would be that easy?"

"Yeah, it should've been," Victor said. Even with Travis's crushing weight he still managed to sound cocky. "Next time..."

"There won't be a next time." The new voice startled everyone and they looked up.

Howard Dixon stood at the kitchen entrance surrounded by a small army of uniformed police.

"Howard," Alice and Valerie chimed happily.

"I suspected it might be Brewerton," Dixon said. "Thought I recognized your voice when you phoned me and claimed to be a relative. Guess you didn't bother checking if she had any family."

Dixon motioned to two officers and they moved in to arrest Victor. Travis got up reluctantly. Taylor sat back at the table and leaned forward to rest her cheek on her hand. Mackay collapsed into the other chair still hugging the computer like a shield. The police patted Victor down, handcuffed him and pulled him to his feet. Taking his gun into evidence, they started to leave. He paused in front of Dixon to give him a glare most likely intended to show defiance. It came off as hollow bravado. The police led him out of the kitchen and the house.

Valerie stood with her hands on hips, similar to Rose's stance at the motel. Naya began to wonder who really was in charge.

"You're a little late for the rescue," Valerie huffed.

"Rescue?" Naya interrupted. "He knew where you were all along and never bothered to get you out?"

"They know I always take excellent care of my people," Dixon said.

"Such good care that you let that nutcase kidnap them," Naya said.

"We were monitoring the entire situation, making sure nothing got out of control," Dixon said.

"Why didn't you end all this sooner. Especially at the warehouse?" Naya demanded.

"We needed to find out who else was involved," Dixon said. "As I said, we had the warehouse bugged to make sure nothing went wrong. Of course no one could have predicted that you two would show up. Unfortunately, by the time surveillance realized what was happening and moved in, you'd already left the warehouse."

"We were almost killed trying to escape," Travis spoke up. His stance was more of a street fighter getting ready to pound someone into the dirt.

"We tried. But lost you in among the warehouses. As soon as we heard what was happening here, I called the police."

"Are you saying my house is bugged?" Naya snapped. Bad enough when she thought she was being watched by a psychotic lunatic, but now to discover that she'd been spied on by a high powered security expert. The latter creeped her out even more.

"It was the only way to make sure you didn't — how should I put this? — get into too much trouble," Dixon said. "Sorry about the delay moving in. I wanted to hear him give all the details."

"I want all the bugs out of my house!"

"I've got a team waiting to move in whenever you want," he paused. "Which obviously is immediately." Dixon nodded to a man wearing a grey three piece suit. Naya thought he was about to salute before he left, but didn't.

"I knew you were a real firecracker when you walked into my office," Dixon said to Naya. "All bent over and limping like some invalid. Good acting."

"In case you didn't notice, I *am* an invalid," Naya snapped. She wasn't sure if she was angry because of his smugness or because he'd reminded her that she was disabled.

"Young lady, you may walk with a limp, which you can really exaggerate at times to lull people into a false sense of trust. But, you're certainly no invalid."

Naya blushed. She hadn't thought her ploys had been that transparent. Apparently he was the one that was the good actor.

"What about Rose? Why were you hiding her at the motel?"

"How..." Dixon broke off smiling. "Once again you amaze me."

"And the other two that worked on the project, Bill Chang and Kirk Stroud? I guess they weren't on holidays either?"

"No and neither were the other three." Dixon paused noticing Naya's look of surprise. Laughing he added, "Aha! We managed to keep a few secrets from you. After these two ladies disappeared I had all previous team members picked up for safety. Unfortunately, Rose's husband missed getting the message we left for him and panicked. That's when you showed up."

"Yes, you always seem to show up at the strangest times." A woman spoke from behind Dixon. He turned and smiled widely as she came into the kitchen.

Sergeant Philadelphia Ashantre.

"Hello, Ms. Assad." She was still wearing her police jacket from the raid.

"Uh, hi," was all Naya could say. She had promised herself to say 'I told you so' if she ever saw the detective again. Rather than be petty, she asked instead, "What are you doing here?"

"When I heard a call come in to this address on the radio, I decided to check the situation out." Ashantre nodded towards Dixon. "Had I known he was involved I would have believed you. We've had dealings in the past. You definitely have the right to tell me, 'I told you so.'"

"Thanks," Naya said, not sure how to handle this new surprise. "You know Mr. Dixon?"

"Better than he thinks," she said with a wink at him. To Naya, "I'm glad that you're safe. All of you. Have a good night."

"But..." Naya tried to stop her, but the detective was gone. She glanced at her friends then back at Dixon.

"It's time I get going. Give you a chance to rest." Before leaving, he added, "I guess I do need to make a short stop at R&D to have a word with Jenny about her big mouth and her future work prospects."

Naya wondered about all this cloak and dagger stuff and how it would make a great TV movie. Ah, don't be ridiculous she chided herself.

This was definitely big screen stuff.

CHAPTER FOURTEEN

After Ashantre and Dixon had left, Travis exhaled slowly then took Naya in his arms and hugged her with such emotional intensity that it surprised her. Last night felt like a dream. More like a nightmare. But everyone, especially Travis, was finally safe.

Releasing the hug, she gave him a tiny smile, then they turned their attention to Mackay and Taylor.

"Are you all right?" She asked. Taylor nodded, her mouth in a tight line.

"Mac? Mac!" Travis shook him by the shoulder. He still had the laptop clutched to his chest. "Snap out of it."

"Huh?" Mackay drifted out of his dream-like stupor, then cried, "I thought I was going to die!"

"How did that man get in?" Naya asked.

"I'm sorry," Taylor said. "I didn't get your message 'til a little while ago. I called the police and told them where you were. Then I came over to check on Mac. Yeah, I figured he was asleep and that's why he wasn't answering your calls. Yeah and as soon as I unlocked the door, that Victor guy came up from behind me and pushed me in. I didn't want to deactivate the alarm, honestly. But, but, he had a gun."

"I'm the one who's sorry," Naya said. "I should have realized that he'd still be watching the house and warned you about him."

"I'm just glad everything worked out okay," Travis said.

Naya said to Alice, "We thought Victor was your ex-boyfriend and he was stalking you."

"Why would you think that?" Alice said.

"Travis was a bit suspicious of him and checked out a few things," Naya began.

"When I found out that your brother died as an infant..." Travis began

"I, I never had a brother," Alice said, eyes darting around like trapped prey looking for an escape.

He quickly added, "I checked into your background just to figure out how that guy fit into things. I'm sorry..."

"No, I'm sorry. I've been guarding my identity for so long it's become instinct," Alice said. She closed her eyes as though in pain and said, "I left my entire life behind. Every time he'd find me, I'd have to start all over again. Howard understands how hard it's been."

"You mean you told Howard but not me?" Valerie asked, sounding hurt.

"I had to. My fake identity wouldn't hold up to a security check."

"Is he due to find you again?" Naya asked.

"Just before we were kidnapped Howard came to me with some news. Devlin did track me down again. But before he could do anything he died in a freak accident."

"Devlin?" Naya said. "Why is that name familiar? Oh, wait, I remember the news report last week. He was drunk and fell off a hotel balcony."

"I feel bad for him, of course," Alice said, "But it means I'm finally free."

"I guess you'll be going home," Valerie said, disappointment obvious in her tone.

"This is my home now," Alice said. "But I can't wait to actually see my family. To tell them it's finally over."

"Yes, everything's over," Naya said.

"It's been a long night," Travis said. "We should get some rest."

"How about something to eat first?" Naya said.

"Can we order pizza?" Mackay asked, though still cradling the laptop, he looked quite happy.

❖ ❖ ❖

Everyone lounged in the family room, celebrating the end of their adventure. They'd finished off pizza and multiple beers. Now comfortable conversation was accompanied by cheeses, grapes and a lot of wine. Mackay had beamed with joy when offered Root Beer and BBQ chips. As a result they unanimously voted him the designated driver.

The sun had been up for while and as Travis opened the curtains, he recoiled like a vampire about to burst into flames. Giggles and snickers accompanied gasps of pain as people tried to open their eyes in the bright glare. It was going to be a beautiful day. Too bad they were probably going to sleep through it. For now they settled down and continued the quiet party.

Naya sat between Alice and Valerie on one sofa, while Travis and Mackay shared the other. Taylor sat cross-legged on the floor near the TV.

"You know," Naya said, "First chance we have I'd like to get some equipment and sweep the place to make sure that Dixon's exterminators didn't forget any insects." Everyone groaned. "Sorry — I wasn't trying to be funny."

"Good," Travis said, "'cause you failed."

"Don't worry," Taylor said, "I already checked out the house. Inside and out."

"Seriously, you just happened to be carrying a detector in your bag?" Naya asked.

"Is that any stranger than carrying a crowbar?" Travis added.

"Okay, fine," Naya said with feigned insult. Becoming serious, she told Valerie. "I'm afraid I have a small confession." She retrieved her backpack from beside the sofa, pulled out the laptop and handed it to her friend. "I believe this is yours."

"My computer?"

"Victor was right about my knowing where the program was. Your computer helped me find you...I, uh, I hope your boss won't be too mad," Naya said.

"No. Well, maybe. Let's not tell him." Valerie laughed.

As everyone continued chatting, Naya noticed Taylor sitting apart from the rest looking more solemn than usual. She joined her on the floor.

"How's your grandmother doing?"

"She's still in a coma. I've been going there to read to her. The nurses told me that her pulse and blood pressure are lower when I'm there. That's where I was tonight — when I got your message."

"Would it be okay if I visited her sometimes?"

"Yeah?"

"The sound of a different voice might help," Naya said.

"I think she'd like that," Taylor said. Despite the faint smile, she still appeared to be disturbed.

At first Naya couldn't think why. "I told you it wasn't your fault that Victor got in."

"Yeah, I know," Taylor said quietly. Keeping an eye on the others, she leaned close and whispered. "It's weird that Devlin died when Alice works for an ex-Ranger who is used to solving problems the old fashioned way."

"You don't mean that Dixon..."

Taylor's only response was a shrug.

Dixon's words echoed in Naya's head. 'They know I always take excellent care of my people.'

She glanced at Valerie. Her friend had always been a good judge of character. She would never work for a man capable of such a thing.

He obviously took the security of his company seriously. How mad would he be that she'd not only hacked Valerie's computer but his company's network as well? His background checks on her and her people would tell him they'd frequently handled sensitive work. That should count for something.

At least that's what she hoped.

❖ ❖ ❖

The impromptu party ended after another couple of hours as exhaustion finally beat down the adrenaline rush. Taylor leaned heavily on Mackay, while Alice and Travis linked arms and hummed an off-key version of Ninety-nine Bottles of Beer on the Wall as they did a jig to the front door. In the foyer, Valerie realized that she was more than reluctant to face the vast expanse of nature again so soon. Naya was thrilled when she had eagerly accepted the invitation to stay for a few days.

But all too soon the visit ended and Travis arrived to drive her home.

They parked in front of Valerie's building without incident. Travis shut off the engine and announced to his passengers in the back seat, "We're here."

"Ow," Naya said, as Valerie clutched her arm with a vice-like grip. "This could take a while." Everyone gasped when someone knocked on the window.

"Rose!" Naya exclaimed and rolled down the window.

"Hi ladies, and gentleman," Rose said, her newly dyed red hair moved in the breeze like flickering flames. "I thought you might need some help getting Valerie inside. I heard jackets work well." She held a jean jacket up and added, "Would you like me to put it on your head, or have you progressed to doing it yourself?"

A few minutes later, Valerie smoothed her hair and handed Rose the jacket back with a giggle.

"Anyone heard from Alice?" Rose asked. "I couldn't get in touch with her."

"She's visiting her family," Valerie said. "She did conveniently forget to take her cell phone along."

"I'm glad for her," Rose said nodding. "Both of you must have been so frightened in that warehouse."

"Not at first," Valerie said. "We knew Howard would find us. But by Friday we had no idea what was going on. All we could do was continue to stall for time." Valerie laughed, adding "That Einstein was like a child. He'd believe anything we told him. And Mr. T was always yelling at him for being gullible. When you showed up," she told Travis, "we thought, aha! The troops are on their way! Then when you showed up," she said to Naya, "we were really confused."

"I just can't believe you're not mad at Dixon," Travis said. "He knew where you were all along and didn't do anything"

"Everything worked out," Valerie said nonchalantly.

Rose huffed and said, "She and Alice are a lot more forgiving than I am. Howard tends to get carried away. When you said they were missing, I figured he'd want to monitor, investigate and gather evidence in order to figure out who was behind *everything*. I only cared about getting them back. I knew Howard would be picking me up soon to hide me, but after meeting you, I knew you'd never give up looking for them. Though I never thought you were tenacious enough to track me down at the motel."

"So that's why you talked openly about the project," Naya said.

"I only talked about a past project for a non-related company. No security breach there."

"No, I guess not," Naya agreed. "At least I did get Howard's secretary to talk all by myself."

"Not really," Rose said sheepishly. "I phoned Mussette and told her that you'd probably be dropping by the office and to help how she could."

"Oh," Naya said. "Guess I won't quit my job to become a P.I."

❖ ❖ ❖

Later, at home, Naya phoned her parents to break the news to them about her diagnosis. She spent a long time telling them about the many tests she'd undergone at the hospital. Told them about her therapy at the rehabilitation centre. They asked a lot of questions, some of which she didn't have answers for but they didn't seem to care. Eventually she realized that they weren't really asking questions to get information, as much as they simply wanted to hear her voice.

When she hung up Naya felt very calm. They'd be taking the next flight back home to see her. She was honestly looking forward to it.

Afterwards, she settled on the sofa. With the news on in the background, she flipped through a new book. A thank you gift from Valerie. It was a collection of short stories dealing with personal triumph. With what she'd gone through these last few months she had more than enough material to fill an entire book all on her own. She picked a story at random when the announcer switched to local news and caught her attention.

"And a little bit of James Bond type intrigue has come to town. Sources report that the computer security company, SecurITe's head of accounting Victor Brewerton has been arrested and charged with industrial espionage. Considered a flight risk, Brewerton has been remanded without bail until his hearing next Tuesday. However sources close to SecurITe hint that a plea agreement may be reached before that."

Naya shut off the TV. It was a good bet that Dixon was behind the plea bargain. He'd do anything to avoid a trial that could reveal more secrets than he'd want to share.

She looked outside the window. The sun was low in the sky and would be setting in another hour. It was getting dark much earlier now. A sure sign that fall was coming. A beautiful evening for a walk.

Yes, outside. Where her neighbours could see her. She got her cane, laced up her runners and grabbed her cell and keys.

She savoured the feel of the light breeze on her face. The high stratus clouds promised a colourful sunset. She reached the corner still feeling energetic. She decided to continue around the block.

An intense rush of pride filled her when she rounded the corner and her house came back into view. The sense of accomplishment was amazing when she realized that she wasn't relying on the cane as much. The best part? She felt ready to go around again.

This was exactly how she'd felt when she'd first started running and made it around the block without stopping. Her goal now — to get to the point where she didn't need the cane at all. Once she got her walking speed up, maybe she'd try jogging.

Could a marathon be far behind?

THE END

THE FIRST STEP

At the 30K mark Naya glanced at her watch. A new personal best.

Her feet pounded in a comfortable rhythm along Sussex Drive. The breeze blowing from across the Ottawa River seemed strangely warm. She passed the Rideau Centre Shopping Mall. Her familiar stride that could fly across any type of terrain, unexpectedly transformed into an off-beat slog through water. Maybe it wouldn't be her best time but she would make it to that finish line. She always completed a race.

Until now.

She woke up three days later in the hospital. Paralyzed. Terrified at first but by the end of the day she could move her arms. Over the next several days she improved and planned for her next marathon, while the doctors continued with their tests.

Then Dr. Montgomery had tried his best, gentle fatherly tone to soften his words.

"You have multiple sclerosis."

Left alone and in peace, she knew that she could figure out how to deal with this and push on.

Unfortunately, that was difficult to do with so many of her running friends dropping by to visit. Before she'd got the final diagnosis, she had honestly answered that she'd injured her back when she'd fallen. And since she'd been more tired than usual before the race, she assumed that she had over trained — something she'd been guilty of in the past.

But after she learned the truth a week later, she chose to stick to her original story. On top of everything else that she had to contend with now, she refused to deal with pity.

❖ ❖ ❖

After two weeks Dr. Montgomery pronounced her strong enough to start physiotherapy. Sitting up in a stretcher, she gave the nurses at the desk a polite smile as they stiffly waved goodbye. She knew that they'd miss her as much as she'd miss them. She'd snuck a peek at one of their notes in her file. A single emotional outburst hadn't warranted her being labeled a "difficult patient". She wanted to see how pleasant any one of them would be in her place.

Her heart pounded against her chest in anticipation as the ambulance drove the short distance to the Ottawa Hospital Rehabilitation Centre. Some of the country's greatest athletes went there to recover from serious injuries. She looked forward to healing alongside the best.

A few minutes later she was in the rehab centre's elevator. When the doors opened on the third floor she was greeted with a sobering reminder that it wasn't just athletes recovering here. Close to the elevator was an elderly woman stooped over a walker. She shuffled an inch at a time with two nurses on either side of her ready to steady her. At the far side of the wide reception area was an elderly man also using a walker. He walked with a military straight back at a pace slightly faster than a shuffle and was gaining on the woman. Naya smiled, imaging that he had romantic notions of a walk together in the garden — despite the nurse chaperones.

There was another forty-something man that passed by at a speed just shy of trotting, pushing the walker ahead with a finger then catching up to it. At first she thought he might be staff, but without a hospital ID tag he could be a patient. Now that was an inspiring sight and something to aim for.

The attendants zig-zagged her past the old woman barely slowing at the nursing station to hand over her files. Halfway down the hall they turned into a spacious room with large windows and bright sunshine streaming in. On top of one of two neatly made beds, a sleeping woman in her sixties sat propped up with several pillows. She wore a bright red track suit. As the stretcher glided in silently, the woman's eyes snapped open and she gave Naya a denture perfect grin.

"Hello. You must be my new roommate. I'm Helen," she said. Her strong voice a definite contrast to the frail looking body. She sat up and said, with a wink, "Excuse me for not getting up."

Naya suppressed the slight queasy sensation when she noticed the empty left pant leg. Recovering, she returned the smile and said, "Only if you excuse me. I'm Naya." The attendants transferred her onto her bed, adjusting it so she could sit up comfortably.

"I see you've noticed that I misplaced by leg," Helen said.

"I'm sorry..."

"Don't be. I'm lucky to keep the better looking one." She laughed. "Oh, here comes my limousine." She nodded at the nurse pushing in a wheelchair. "I'm off to try my replacement. So, Jennifer, you think this one will fit better?"

"Third time's the charm, Helen," the nurse said. To Naya she added, "your nurse is Grace. She's busy at the moment but will get here as soon as she can." To the attendants, she said, "Just put her things near the cupboard."

The nurse gave Naya a goodbye nod then pushed the chair towards the door. All the while Helen was calling over her shoulder, "Welcome to the third floor! We'll crack open a few beers when I get back to celebrate your arrival and hopefully my new leg."

After only a couple of minutes with her, Naya suspected that there might actually be beer hidden somewhere.

She leaned back on the pillows and sighed with happiness. She couldn't wait for some intense therapy. Hearing a noise at the door her head snapped up. Back at the hospital this would be the time when the nurses swarmed in with their needles and pills and "squeeze my fingers, dear" tests. Though still weak compared to her left hand, her right hand could now tighten until their fingertips turned purple. Woohoo! It had only taken two weeks.

A pleasant looking nurse, with dark skin and sparkling grey eyes walked in.

"Hi, Naya," she said, extending a hand. "I'm Grace."

"Hi." She shook the nurse's hand.

"Let's get you unpacked and settled in, then I'll fill you in on your therapy schedule. Hope you're ready to work hard."

"Definitely."

"You're going to love your roommate, Helen," Grace picked up the backpack and put it on the bed next to Naya.

"Oh we've met," Naya said unzipping the bag.

"She's so delightful to have around. Quite something. Oh, by the way," Grace said as she started unpacking, "we suspect she has beer hidden in here somewhere, but damned if we can find it. I'm not asking you to tattle on her. All I ask is that you be discreet. Alcohol is against the rules."

"Uh, okay," Naya said, holding back a giggle and looking forward to a beer.

❖ ❖ ❖

The next morning the occupational therapist, Amanda, a Chinese woman with short jet blue-black hair came to see her. The therapist did a quick physical assessment of her mobility and strength. Of course, the only reason it was quick was because she couldn't stand and the two pound weight clutched in both hands put up a good fight. Naya liked the woman's enthusiasm and happily anticipated starting therapy tomorrow. They'd help her learn how to do simple tasks with limited mobility, such as cooking.

After lunch, Naya waited in itchy anticipation for the porter to come and take her to physiotherapy. That was the place where she'd improve her strength. When the porter, Mario, showed up with a wheelchair she stared at it like it was some monster waiting to swallow her up. If she sat in it she might never get out again. After seeing the expression on her face he parked the chair in the hall and came back to her.

"I know, it's not very nice to look at," Mario said. "And I don't blame you for not wanting to use it. I'll tell you what. How about if I just sling you over my shoulder and carry you down to therapy?"

She didn't believe he was serious, until he started to pick her up. All she could picture was her head bobbing against his back while he marched down the hall. The chair looked a hell of a lot more dignified.

Pulling away, she hastily said, "I think the chair's the best way to get to therapy. But, I don't plan to use it for too long."

"That's the spirit," he said as he wheeled the chair back and helped her into it.

Trying to maintain some independence, she wheeled herself to the elevator. He walked beside her, chatting, though she barely heard him. She had to concentrate on pushing through the burning pain in her shoulders and back. Muscles screamed for her to stop but she ignored them. With a huge sigh of relief she got into the elevator, happy to be able to rest briefly.

When she tried to move out of the elevator, the muscles protested. But she wasn't giving in. Whether she walked, or rolled, it was still exercise and she was determined to get to the appointment on her own.

Closing in on the reception area her excitement really kicked in. It gave her the boost of energy she needed. Oh. She caught a glimpse of

Mario's hand on the chair's handle. Pride was one thing but she was exhausted and foolishly hadn't thought about saving strength for the session itself. She pretended not to notice his help and continued to go through the motions of pushing.

There were about fifteen people waiting, several in manual wheelchairs like hers, some electric chairs, some walkers and canes and a few with no assistive devices at all. Mario patted her on the shoulder gave a friendly, "good job" and left her to wait with the others for 1:00 pm. Five minutes later the flurry of activity was amazing. Several patients moved into the treatment rooms around the corner on their own. A few therapists came out to greet others. Within seconds the room was clear. Except for her. She continued waiting for another minute then realized that she hadn't checked in. She rolled to the receptionist's counter and identified herself. Assured that her therapist was coming, she waited. But by 1:20 she went back to the secretary.

"Is there any hope, here?" Naya asked, not able to control the impatience in her voice.

"Sorry, I didn't see that you were still out here. I'll page Tiffany."

Five minutes later, a full twenty-five minutes late, the therapist came up behind her.

"Hi, Naya. Follow me."

Without a glance to make sure she could actually follow, the therapist sauntered on ahead. Guess that young woman with bleach blonde hair tied in a side pony tail was Tiffany. She gave the wheels a push and discovered that her muscles had seized up. After a lot of grunting she got the chair moving into the treatment room.

There were two rows of low, wooden beds. Half were filled with patients doing a variety of exercises, some similar to her pre and post-run stretches. Tiffany pointed at a bed then disappeared through a 'Staff Only' door. To say Naya was a little pissed was an understatement. First Tiffany didn't apologize for being late, then she didn't even make sure she could actually get out of the wheelchair without help.

She remained in the chair — her little form of protest. As the minutes ticked by, Naya kept reminding herself that this was the first session and there was probably something to finish preparing and completing, such as, who knew, paperwork? She had to give her the benefit of the doubt. As the minutes ticked by, patience became a memory. Eventually Tiffany returned — munching on a cupcake. Seriously?

With barely fifteen minutes of her one hour session remaining, Tiffany explained that she was going to assess Naya's strength and mobility. She asked her to lift one knee. It didn't move. Then the other. It barely twitched. Lift an arm. Then the other.

"Okay, good." She tossed the cupcake paper into a nearby garbage can, licked her fingers, wiped them on her jeans. "That gives me an idea of where to start. Rest up and tomorrow we'll really get to work." With that, she disappeared back into the office.

Naya just sat there feeling dumb and awkward. Tiffany could have got more information if she'd read the medical reports. Taking a deep breath, she braced herself for the painful ride to the waiting room. Spotting Mario waiting for her she was relieved when he met her halfway.

"Looks like you worked up quite a sweat. How about I drive home?" he said, cheerfully.

"No problem, thanks." Trying to look on the bright side, she had to admit that she did feel like she'd had a full workout. There were many reasons why Tiffany may have been late. After all, this was only the first day. Occupational therapy's assessment had also been brief this morning.

Tomorrow the real work would start.

The next morning she finished her session in occupational therapy, then ensured she got a lot of rest before physio, careful not to waste excessive energy because of ego. She arrived in the waiting room thinking positive thoughts even after Tiffany arrived late, but only ten minutes this time. Last night Naya had met another patient with MS who was in worse condition than herself and her therapy included swimming. Naya suggested it to the therapist.

"No, no," Tiffany said, waving a hand as though she were shooing a fly, "that wouldn't be good for you because it would just sap your strength."

Considering how little energy she did have, Naya accepted the explanation and lay down on the exercise bed.

With Tiffany supporting her legs, Naya began with some simple stretching. After approximately fifteen minutes, Tiffany helped her sit up and Naya expected to start on harder exercises.

"Good work," Tiffany said. "We'll really get started tomorrow. Make sure you rest up."

Naya glanced at the clock. By the time she looked back Tiffany had vanished into that mysterious 'Staff Only' room. Naya was eager to get to work on recovering her strength. But at this rate, she'd be in that damn chair forever.

Frustrated, she reached for the wheelchair barely brushing the armrest with her fingertips. Oh no! She'd forgotten to lock the brakes! When it moved away in nightmarish slow motion, she began to fall. Out of nowhere hands grabbed her in time.

He helped her sit on the edge of the treatment table and sat next to her.

Breathless, she managed to say, "Thank you. You saved my dignity."

"No need to get embarrassed. Hey, people here fall down all the time. And sometimes the occasional patient falls too, but we usually catch them on the first bounce."

"Thanks for getting me before I bounced."

"How's it going with your therapy?"

"I just started. I usually do everything full tilt, but now I guess I have to accept going slow."

"Where you heading now?"

"Guess back to my room."

He blinked at her. Checked his wrist watch, then the wall clock. "It's only 1:25. You have thirty-five minutes left." Then he blushed and Naya thought it was sweet of him to worry about her feelings. "Sorry, guess you're not up to it."

"Honestly, I can't wait to really get started. But Tiffany said I'd done enough for today. Guess I have to learn to pace myself."

"Really?" He patted her on the shoulder and said, "Wait right here." Then he disappeared through the 'Staff Only' door, slamming it shut behind him.

She thought she heard muffled voices arguing inside and wished she was in the wheelchair to move closer to eavesdrop. Before she had time to finish the thought, the door opened and he came out, holding a file folder. He gave her a wide, though slightly tense, smile.

"My name's Mike." He handed her the file and she had enough time to see that it was hers before he picked her up, put her into the wheelchair and pushed her towards a door at the back of the treatment area. "I heard you're a marathon runner. Which means you know about hard work. As long as you work hard and do your best to keep up, we'll get along just fine."

"Uh, what about..." Naya started to ask about Tiffany.

"This is what you'll be aiming for," he announced as he pushed her into a large gym. People were walking, some between balance bars, some with walkers, some canes. It was great to see so many people at different stages of recovery. She had hope again. She had confidence.

She had a real therapist.

❖ ❖ ❖

For the next two weeks she worked hard. Amanda, in occupational therapy, demonstrated alternate ways to do everyday tasks; washing herself, cooking, cleaning, doing dishes. She explained some simple and cheap modifications for the house, such as removing the cupboard doors under the kitchen sink to be able to slide closer to the sink with the wheelchair. Naya listened politely, but the chair was temporary.

One morning, the occupational therapist student, Mireille, met her at the door.

"Today you're going to start a little project. So come on this way."

Naya rolled the wheelchair with ease now that her arms had regained most, if not all of their strength. She followed into a room with several tables with plants, pots and potting soil, as well as another table with some coloured strips of straws and partly constructed baskets.

"How about over here?" Mireille said gesturing at the straw. "You could try making a basket. There are various shapes and sizes."

"Really?" Naya began. Giggling she added, "I thought that was like an urban legend or something. Do people actually do that?"

"You can make a lid? If you want?" Mireille added hesitantly, her smile wavering.

"You know, now that I think about it, it actually sounds like fun," Naya began feeling bad about making Mireille nervous. This was the student's first work term and she'd only been at university a few months. She was a still a kid and if she really wanted to make baskets, then Naya could make some.

The therapist arrived greeting them both.

"There you are," Amanda said. "I was expecting you would have gone straight into the wood working area. So, Naya, does that sound like something you'd like?"

"Uh." She didn't want to hurt Mireille's feelings. But she really did prefer the idea of working with tools.

"I leave it up to you," Amanda said. Then looking at Mireille, she added, "What do you think? Would you be comfortable showing Naya how to do wood working?"

When Mireille's face brightened at the suggestion, Naya jumped in and said, "That sounds like fun."

"Good," Amanda said. "Mireille, go ahead and tell Tony that we'll be coming in soon." With a delighted nod she hurried on ahead. Amanda came around to push the wheelchair saying, "Basket weaving is something we suggest to people with dexterity issues, although you'd be surprised at how many people want to make baskets."

"Thanks. I didn't want to hurt Mireille's feelings, so I would have endured it."

"That's nice of you. But she needs to learn how to read patient's needs too."

They reached a large room. One technician was taking a wheelchair motor apart. Another was making height adjustments on a walker for a patient, an older man Naya had seen before. There were a couple of large wooden work tables with vices.

"You'll come here once a week," Amanda said, "It'll give you a bit of variety. Now, you just need to decide what you'd like to make."

There were many to choose from, but Naya opted to make a bird house. She just hoped she'd be home soon to put it up in her backyard by herself.

❖ ❖ ❖

At the end of each day she was so exhausted. Every muscle burned and practically screamed when she moved. And she'd never felt so good. After supper she'd go outside in her wheelchair to explore the walking paths, even commune with a few squirrels. But after the intense activity of the day, those nightly sojourns were always cut short. Which left her with a lot of free time in the evenings.

After a lot more nagging and finally being forced to resort to the undignified tactic of whining, she finally got Travis to agree to bring in her laptop. Always one step ahead of her, he'd removed all work related files citing intellectual property and security. Well, that was one way to make sure she got rest.

She usually left the on-line advertising and contacts to Travis, choosing not to get lost in the time-wasting social media sites herself. But she was so painfully bored now that she succumbed and signed up for Facebook. She'd never been happier to break one of her own rules.

She found her childhood best friend, Valerie Peters. They hadn't seen each other since they were fifteen when Valerie's parents had to move out of the country for her mother's work. They kept in touch with long emails, the occasional phone calls, but then high school filled their time and they lost touch.

Within minutes of making contact on-line they were talking on the phone.

"It's so great to hear your voice. It sounds so wonderfully familiar," Naya said.

"Yours too. I see that you work in computers now. What happened to your love affair with acting?"

"Well, once I finished high school, the grease paint was out and computers got into my blood instead. I'm part owner of a computer security company. How about you? I thought you were determined to go into graphic design?"

"I discovered I loved designing computer programs more. I'm freelance now. Keeps me busy. Hey, if you're looking to subcontract..."

"I know where to go." Naya laughed then added, "I can't believe we've lived in the same city for the last several years. I can't wait to see you."

"Oh," Valerie's voice cracked, then she added, "I'm really sorry, but, I've got this thing about hospitals, and well..."

"Don't worry. The phone is almost as good."

They talked late into the evening, catching up on what they've been doing, but mostly reliving their greatest childhood escapades. They spoke every night. At first, Naya didn't want to intrude too much on her friend's time, but if she didn't phone, Valerie would send a text reminding her to call.

❖ ❖ ❖

Several days later, Naya arrived for physio and spotted Mike in the middle of the gym standing next to a walker with wheels. As she rolled herself closer he gave her a serious look that really got her worried. He was always so cheerful.

"Hi," she said, cautiously. "What's up?"

He moved closer, dragging the walker behind him. Setting it in front of her wheel chair, he said, "I think it's time to get out of that chair. Don't you?"

Was he serious?

He held onto the walker as she put her wheelchair brakes on then moved the foot rests out of the way. Taking a deep breath she stood up. Her legs held her up.

"Come on, it's just like walking between the bars. Use the walker for balance."

She wanted to say how she'd managed to fool him. That her arms had held her up with brute force. Well, he'd find out soon enough as she concentrated and took a tentative step forward. She had to keep gripping the brakes to stop the walker from rolling too far ahead. Another step. A couple more. She was actually using the walker only for balance. This was definitely not an arm exercise. The frown vanished and her face brightened. He came around behind her and unlocked the wheelchair.

"Let's go for a little walk," he said. "And don't worry, I'll be close behind you with the wheelchair if you need to sit."

She continued slowly, deliberately, one step at a time. After a dozen steps her legs began to tremble. Will power managed three more steps before her knees buckled. She'd expected to hit the ground but Mike quickly slipped the chair close and grabbed her arm to guide her in. Just those few steps had changed her attitude towards life and all that she'd taken for granted.

She had a sense of freedom from a prison she'd always expected to leave, but hadn't truly believed she would. Till now.

❖ ❖ ❖

Helen sat on the edge of her bed with one leg dangling, the other on the bed. Naya tried to remember which one was prosthetic. Eventually Helen glared at the dangling left leg and commanded, "Move." Its only response was a slight twitch. She looked at Naya, shaking her head with an exasperated sigh. "She just won't co-operate."

"I thought the physiotherapist said you need to be patient."

"Look who's calling the kettle purple," Helen retorted and pointed at Naya seated on the floor.

"First of all, the expression is black. Calling the kettle black," Naya said, as she tried to pull herself back up onto the bed, only to lose her grip and thud to the ground again. "Second, I was not being impatient. I was exercising." From the knowing smirk Helen gave her, she knew that the other woman didn't believe her for a second. Sure, she could tell her roommate that she was exercising her legs when she got off the bed and tried to 'walk' to the cupboard to hang up her sweater. Though her legs were getting stronger, balance was another thing. It was amazing how fast the floor had come up to catch her.

"Well, young lady," Helen said, with her most condescending voice ever, "First, I've never owned a black kettle and second," she stretched to reach for the button clipped to her pillow to call the nurse, "The fact you were able to stand for half a second in physio yesterday is great. How about you give yourself another couple of hours."

A retort of any kind would have been nice, if she wasn't still sitting on the floor. So, she concentrated on getting herself up before the nurse arrived. By sheer will, stubbornness and fear of yet another scolding for not calling for assistance before getting out of bed, she was back up panting heavily and sweating by the time the nurse arrived.

Grace noted Naya's dishevelled appearance, then put her hands on her hips.

"Can you at least wait to see if you really need help before you call me," she said. "There are other patients that actually need me." And she spun on her heels to leave.

"Grace, if it's not too much trouble," Helen asked, "would you please close the door?" When the nurse turned slowly, her face stern, Helen and Naya gave her an innocent smile. Silently, the nurse pulled the door gently shut behind her, but Naya could see that she'd wanted, more than anything, to slam it.

"You know we're testing her patience," Naya said, feeling bad.

"I thought she'd never leave," Helen said. Then slowly got off the bed, making sure her new leg was steady, she grabbed her cane and hobbled over to the radiator under the window. Reaching underneath she pulled out two bottles of beer and carrying both in one hand, joined Naya on her bed. "You look like you can use a drink."

"Thanks," she said, as she twisted off the cap and took a sip. "Certainly hits the spot."

"Did you hear the latest gossip?"

"You mean about Kathleen and Rob?"

"Ah," Helen waved a dismissive hand. "That's this morning's story. No, I'm talking about Wayne. He's been suspended."

"Why?" Wayne was one of the newest nurses hired only last month. Every patient loved him. Not only was he cute as hell but he was one of the most attentive nurses and it never hurt when he took blood samples.

"Apparently some drugs are missing. And I don't mean aspirin," Helen said taking another tiny sip.

Had to be the narcotics then, Naya thought. She remembered the first time she'd heard the announcement over the PA system requesting the Narcotics Key and had to actually question someone that she'd heard right. Medications like morphine were strictly controlled. One nurse was always in charge of the key to the cabinet and whenever someone needed to get a dose it required two signatures. The nurse in charge of the key and the one taking the dose. As a new employee he wouldn't have had access to the key or the cabinet. So, why suspect him?

About to ask Helen, she noticed her roommate taking small, measured drinks of beer. Usually a few large gulps and it would be gone.

"You really are upset," Naya said, "You've barely touched your beer."

"No, uh, yes, of course I'm unhappy about Wayne. But my supplier has to go away for a week. Work. Unfortunately that means that I have to make my last few bottles last."

"Or maybe not," Naya said with a wink. She pulled out her cell from the top drawer of the night table and dialled.

"Hi, Travis. How's it going?"

❖ ❖ ❖

The next morning Travis arrived clutching his backpack to his chest.

Naya laughed. "You think you could look any guiltier?" After he shut the door, she pointed to the radiator in the corner closest to Helen's bed. "There's a shelf inside."

Reaching underneath, he said, "Amazing what you can do with duct tape." After four bottles were carefully placed and the capped empties stowed in his backpack, he stood up. "Where's your fellow bootlegger?"

"Down in physio," Naya said.

"When you called last night I really thought it was some kind of practical joke. How did you manage to keep the beer hidden?"

"Not me, it's all Helen," Naya said with a laugh. "Most of the nurses know she has beer here but haven't been able to find it. Honestly, I doubt they're looking that hard."

"I just hope you don't get caught..." He let his voice trail off as he gave her a mock shudder.

"Don't worry. We'll never give up your name no matter how much meatloaf they force us to eat."

"Anything new to report?" he asked after a small chuckle.

"Yes, it's terrible," Naya started, fighting not to get angry, "Wayne, the new nurse who started last month, has been suspended. There were some missing drugs and because he had the key on him he's become the main suspect and it looks like he's going to be charged and..." She broke off when she noticed Travis was waving at her.

"I meant anything new about you. Your progress."

"Oh, sure. I'm doing fine. Muscles remember what they're supposed to do. But about Wayne, the whole thing is completely unfair. He's the nicest, most honest guy. And it's all because the nurse in charge of the key that night says the lanyard had been cut, which means it wasn't accidently lost. For some reason, she says it has to be Wayne just because he found the key and returned it to her."

"If he's innocent the police investigation will prove it."

"You can't really believe that? She's got thirty years, he's barely been here a month. Scapegoat is the word that comes to mind."

"The police will get to the truth." He checked his watch, "Hey, I don't want to make you late." He brought the wheelchair close for her.

"I just don't like injustice," Naya said as Travis pushed her down the hall.

"You just have to accept things and make the best out of what you can." He gave her a good bye pat on the shoulder before getting into the elevator. She wasn't sure if Travis was talking about her or Wayne.

"Not if you can do something about it," she told the closed doors. She had to do something besides whine about the injustice. She'd start by talking to the staff about what they suspected. Listen to the general gossip.

She spotted Mario a few paces ahead, the porter that had once threatened to sling her over his shoulder and take her to therapy when she'd first arrived. She hurried to catch up.

"Hey, hello there, speedy," Mario gave her with a big, warm smile. "Haven't seen you for a while."

"They've been keeping me busy on the first floor. I just came up to get a patient's running shoes. You look great."

"Thanks. Mario, I know you're in a hurry, I just wanted to ask you. Guess you've heard about Wayne?"

"I know his family well. Watched him grow up. All he ever wanted to do was help people. There's no way..." He paused in the hall so suddenly, that Naya had to roll back to him. "We all know he'd never do anything like this."

"But if he hasn't been charged, how can the hospital suspend him?"

"Guess they think where there's smoke."

"Do you think he did it?" she asked.

"Wayne wouldn't cross against a red light at three in the morning on a deserted island. Don't give me that look. You know what I mean." He shook his head. "I'm sure things'll work out. Get going before you're late."

He hurried down the hall. Why was everyone worried about her schedule and not Wayne's innocence?

During her session in occupational therapy she managed to listen in and join the few conversations about the missing drugs and how there was no chance that Wayne was guilty.

Not that she doubted Wayne's innocence for a second, but she'd feel pretty foolish if she was fighting to clear someone who'd been caught on surveillance video stealing the drugs. A direct question to one of the security guards who was doing her patrol answered that question easily. The cameras had been down in their wing. Convenient for the thief. This also made it sound like an inside job. Didn't look good for Wayne.

She talked to as many people as she could, from nurses to orderlies to cleaning staff. In the end she found two people that didn't quite sit right with her. Naya put one of the nurses at the top of the list, until she thought it through. This nurse wasn't liked by many of the patients, mostly because of her attitude. She never once hid the fact that she really wanted to be outside enjoying the beautiful summer weather rather than being trapped inside dealing with needy patients. Unfortunately, just because she was a big jerk it didn't make her a thief.

She decided to give Valerie a quick call before dinner to fill her in on what's been going on.

"And what does your suspect radar tell you?" Valerie asked.

"Not much. The ones I thought could have done it were off that night."

"They were probably lying."

"No, I didn't ask them directly. Last night, when the night nurse was doing her rounds, I snuck onto her computer and printed out a copy of the schedule." She laughed. "I almost freaked when I heard the nurse coming back. She wears these shoes that squeak like crazy when she walks. For the record, I want to mention how hard it is to make a stealthy escape in a wheelchair."

"You should have been a spy," Valerie added with a chuckle.

"Missed my calling. Anyway, I've been working through the list of people on duty that night, talking to each of them to see if they saw anything."

"How about the one who accused him?"

"Abigail? She's really strict and scares the hell out of me, but she's been a nurse for thirty years and has a spotless record."

"Did you actually check?" Valerie asked.

"No, it's just what I've heard. I have limited internet access here."

"I can look into her background for you. Also any other names on your list."

Naya considered saying no. It didn't seem right to pry into people's private lives like that. But if she didn't do it and Wayne went to prison, where would the morality be then?

"Okay. Check Abigail first. I'll refine my list to people who would have been in the area. Or if they were on break. Or if they give me a creepy feeling."

"That's my girl. Scientific to the end."

After a stimulating evening talking to more staff as well as several patients, she got into bed feeling a bit like Sherlock Holmes. She rolled over on her side, hugging her pillow, trying to get comfortable. Trying to sleep. Trying to think of new questions to ask in the morning.

❖ ❖ ❖

The bird house project in occupational therapy was really beginning to take shape. Painting would be next. She just had to decide on the colour. Amanda had been right that wood working would break up her schedule. Of course, that didn't mean the regular sessions were boring.

It had been a few days since she'd taken those first few steps in the gym. Walking great distances was still out so she still had to use the wheelchair to get around. But that meant that now Amanda could show her how to do things standing up.

The student, Mireille, met her in the kitchen.

"Sorry but Amanda's delayed at a staff meeting, so I'm going to give you a hand today."

"Great. What's on the menu?"

Mireille read her notes. "Amanda wants you to get a can of soup from the pantry then heat it and bring it to the table."

"Sounds straightforward enough," Naya said as she used the walker to get to the cupboard and picked vegetable soup. She put the can in the walker's basket and went to the stove. Everything was within reach of the stove to minimize steps, which she appreciated. Once the soup was heated, she poured a bowl, placed it on the walker seat. After two steps, the bowl began to slide. Fortunately, Mireille caught it in time.

"Maybe try putting it in the basket," Mireille suggested and moved it as she spoke. Of course neither of them realized that the bottom was not flat until the bowl started to tip.

"I got it!" Naya announced and reached around the walker to get at the basket. Unfortunately, she forgot about her balance. She also forgot the walker's brakes weren't on. Mireille did her best to catch her, but the young girl's strength was no match for Naya's much taller frame, or for her rapid acceleration towards the floor.

Both gasped, "Oh no!" Mireille hit the floor first. Naya landed on top. The soup bowl bounced along the floor, spreading its colourful contents.

"I thought you therapists are supposed to catch patients on the first bounce," Naya said.

"But," Mireille gasped.

Naya rolled off of her. They both sat up as Mireille finished saying, "I'm still waiting for you to bounce." Their uncontrollable laughter ended any hope of either of them getting up.

"What's going on here?" They looked up to see Amanda frowning down at them, arms crossed. The laughter ended.

"I made soup," Naya said, indicating the floor. "More of an abstract soup art."

She shook her head then with Mireille's help, got Naya to her feet and helped her to sit at the kitchen table. Amanda pointed at the mop and bucket and a chastised student cleaned the floor.

After the slip hazard was removed, Amanda said, "Let's start with something a bit easier. Like toast."

The next day, kitchen duty started out fine. Naya made toast, with ham in it this time and a cup of coffee. While Mireille mopped the floor, Naya repeatedly apologized, promising to do better next time.

"Now you know why," Amanda paused, giving a long dramatic sigh, "our dishes are plastic." She grinned.

By the time lunch arrived Naya had had enough of sandwiches and decided to phone Valerie instead. She had narrowed her list of suspects to three. However, after Valerie finished her report on head nurse Abigail, Naya didn't need to give her the other names.

Abigail was working days this week, which meant no need to suffer waiting until the evening shift to talk to her. Barely saying "good bye" to Valerie and certainly breaking wheelchair speed limits down the hall to get to the nursing station, Naya stopped at the corner. Taking slow, deep breaths to calm down, she rolled towards Abigail.

"Good morning." When the nurse looked up from the computer and scrutinized her with an expression that could freeze lava, Naya faltered. Her initial plan to drop by for a casual chat then steer the conversation to the missing drugs and Wayne was obviously naive. The intensifying glare meant that she had three seconds to find another tactic.

"I was wondering if you would be able to ask the doctor to prescribe something to help me sleep?" The speed that she'd come up with that impressed her. She always did work better under pressure.

"I'll talk to him when we go over the patient files." She returned her attention to the computer.

"I've been having trouble sleeping the last while."

"Obviously."

"Yes, umm," Naya wondered if she should just bring her findings to the police and let them investigate. But if she was wrong, then she'd stir up trouble for another innocent person. She had another idea, glad that she really did work best under duress.

"Usually when I can't sleep, I go for a little spin around the ward. Too bad I can't leave the floor. It would be nice to go outside when the weather's pleasant."

"Patients aren't allowed to leave the floor during the night," she said without even looking up.

"Right." Naya took a deep breath. "Usually the halls are pretty deserted at night. But I did run into a young man last week. Can't really remember when exactly." That got the nurse's attention. She didn't look up but she had stopped typing. "Maybe you've seen him? Tall, slim, dark curly hair?" The truth was she hadn't ever seen him and hoped this description did match the Facebook photo Valerie had found. And it was a guess that he'd been here at all.

Slowly Abigail pulled her attention away from the screen and made eye contact. Her expression was stone cold. Her voice however, was full of emotion.

"He's my son." Swallowing hard, she continued. "He always stops by Tuesday and Thursday after he gets off shift at the gas station and we have breakfast together."

"It's nice that you're close." Might as well jump in all the way. "How's rehab going? He mentioned it had been tough but he's managed to stay away from any cocaine. Even marijuana, for, I forgot how long he said."

"He's been clean two months." Abigail let out a long, desperate sigh. "That boy. He makes me so tired sometimes. He's been in trouble practically from the time he could walk. Cute things back then. The drug problems started when he was fourteen. He's 28 and still acts like a teen. Never takes any responsibility. Sometimes I wish I could just walk away from everything..." She broke off looking guilty.

At this moment Naya didn't see a scary nurse who ruled her slaves without mercy, but a desperate mother whose son constantly tested her love and returned only grief. Valerie had managed to look at his criminal record which started when he was fifteen. Naya had prudently not asked how her friend had accessed sealed juvenile records.

"I have a friend with a teenage daughter that's put her through hell," Naya said. "Her daughter's the type that's always drawn to people who choose to live on the edge. Constantly shoplifting, stealing from students, blackout drunk twice a week. The hardest, most painful thing my friend ever did was turn her daughter in. She believes it saved her life. Now her daughter's getting the help that she needs. And her future, well, now she has a future."

Naya paused to study Abigail's expression. Was she thinking about the story? Applying it to her own situation?

"I really need to get back to work," Abigail said tightly.

Or maybe she was just hoping Naya would shut the hell up and go away? Before she did leave, she had one more question.

"There's something I've been wondering about for a while. When I first arrived here, everyone was very, well..."

"Everyone was sympathetic? Promised you things would be okay? Told you not to worry? Let me guess, was I too mean to you? Always scolding you when you didn't move fast enough, but everyone else was 'oh let me help you, dear'? When I was around didn't you actually put more effort in and push yourself harder? If I'd babied you like everyone else, you wouldn't be walking practically the full length of the gym without stopping to rest. Is that what you would have preferred?"

Naya gawked at her. She had no idea that Abigail was keeping track of her successes in the gym. And yes, it was true that sometimes the nurse made her so angry that Naya pushed herself harder just to prove the woman wrong. But any real credit went to Mike and his patient, gentle and no-nonsense approach. Did Abigail see Mike as weak because he didn't yell and berate his patients?

Naya had her mouth open to tell the woman just that, when she took a closer look at her. It could be that tough love was all she'd ever known and it had become so ingrained in her that she used it on everyone. Instead, she changed her answer.

"I guess you had my best interests at heart after all. Thank you. You know, when I think about it, you are always trying to help, in your own way. When you push your staff, there's usually a reason. Keep them from goofing off too much, making sure every patient is taken care of. You really do care about people or you wouldn't have stayed in nursing for thirty years. You wouldn't stand by and watch someone get hurt."

"No."

"So what about Wayne?"

"What do you mean? I can't help him if he's stupid."

"You don't really believe that he stole your keys. Or the drugs. Do you? But you do know, or suspect who did. Don't you?"

"I think you should go rest up so you'll have energy for physio this afternoon. I have work to do." This time Abigail just glared at her, unblinking, making Naya feel like a tiny rabbit with a wolf staring at her.

Having angered the head nurse enough for one day, she nodded and wheeled herself away from the desk, only to pause around the corner. Abigail was just sitting there. Staring into nothingness. A shame that the simple approach hadn't worked. She had no choice but take what she knew to the police. If they believed that Abigail had conspired with her son, then it was simple karma for refusing to help an innocent man.

Finally Abigail moved in ultra-slow motion to pick up the phone and dial.

"Zach? It's mom. I have some questions to ask you and you better not lie, because you know I can tell when you do."

Naya grinned all the way back to her room. Abigail's tough love was finally being used where it was really needed.

Wayne was back to work later that week. No one even suspected that Naya had anything to do with clearing his name.

And she liked it that way.

❖ ❖ ❖

Naya looked forward to her daily chats with Valerie. She enjoyed the trips down memory lane, but loved to fill her in on daily happenings. They laughed about her frequent mishaps in occupational therapy. She told her about the good and the bad. And always her friend listened with interest and encouragement.

"I'm so glad to hear that Wayne's been cleared," Valerie said. Barely missing a beat asked, "What did you spill in the kitchen today?"

"Nothing. I finally figured out I was pushing the walker too fast and things just didn't hold on. Once I slowed down, Mireille put the mop away for good."

"Moving too fast, eh, guess your physio is helping."

"Yes, Mike's been terrific. He really encourages me. Especially when we do aqua-therapy."

"I thought you said it would drain your strength so you didn't want to do it," Valerie said.

"No, that's what Tiffany said and at first I did believe her. I realized afterwards that she didn't want to do pool therapy because it would mean she'd have to come back from lunch on time. Mike and I started at once a week, now up to twice. After the first few sessions, I was so exhausted that I slept through dinner. And you know me, I'd really have to be tired to miss a meal." Naya laughed. "But now I can feel my stamina increase."

"I'm so proud that you're able to walk the full length of the gym now. Just don't do any more turtle impressions."

"Cute," Naya managed to say through the laughter.

Though Mike and Amanda were responsible for helping her physically recover, she knew that Valerie kept her going. If it hadn't been for her best friend's support, she doubted she'd have lasted the full three months.

❖ ❖ ❖

One week before getting discharged from the rehab centre, the occupational therapist accompanied Naya to her house to do a home assessment. Naya waited in the family room for Amanda to finish the inspection.

"You have a beautiful home," she said as she joined Naya on the sofa. "So bright and airy."

"Thank you, the large windows were a major factor for me." Naya didn't mention the other reasons that she first fell in love with the house; the sweeping spiral staircase and the three spacious bedrooms upstairs. All of which were now out of reach for her.

"Well, I think with a few small additions you'll be comfortable when you get back home next week." Amanda barely glanced at her notes. "You can have a chair lift installed to get to the second floor. If price is a problem the MS society can help out. I can suggest the names of a few companies that can install grab bars in the bathtub if you'd like." She handed her a sheet of paper. "I've listed a few things that aren't really essential, but you might find useful."

"Okay," Naya said, nodding but thinking that the walker was enough of a reminder of what her once perfect life had been. She'd get Travis to find someone to put in a shower on this floor. That would solve the problem of stairs. But because Amanda had always been so good to her, trying to help her adapt to a new way of doing things, she added pleasantly, "You've got some great ideas. Thanks."

After they returned to the rehab centre Naya settled in for the last week, surprised at how quickly the time went. Before she knew it, she was saying good bye to Mike, Amanda and the rest of the staff. Even Abigail who'd been imperceptibly nicer since the incident with the missing drugs.

Bidding her roommate good bye had started out fine until Helen burst into tears giving her a surprisingly strong bear hug. Barely holding back tears of her own she'd watched her ex-partner in crime head out to physiotherapy.

Travis would be here soon to drive her home. Naya sat on the edge of the bed to admire the view outside the window. The deep blue sky, with the occasional white smudge in the distance, was so reminiscent of the morning that she'd left for the marathon. The day that she'd lost herself. Though it had been difficult, she'd taken the first step to find herself again, here.

But home was where the long journey would truly begin.

ACKNOWLEDGEMENTS

A special thank you to my critique group, *Lyngarde*, made up of Leslie Brown, Hildegarde Henderson, Valerie Kirkwood, Lynne MacLean, Cathy McBride, John Park and Andrea Schlecht. Although there are others who come and go, we've been together for years and you've become dear and trusted friends. And I haven't forgotten our newest member, Jim Davies. A special thought goes to Sansoucy Kathenor who always answered the phone when I called in a panic because a character refused to co-operate with a major plot line — you are missed.

To Barbara Fradkin, a long-time friend and fellow writer, thanks for your encouragement.

I'd like to also dedicate this book to Steve Skaff, my brother and best friend. And my parents Carimé and George, who made me the independent person I am.

I enjoyed working with my wonderfully calm editor Marjolaine Lafrenière, whose creative suggestions made my job so much easier. And my copy editors Evelyn Cimesa and L. P. Vallée and their great eye for detail.

Also thank you to Caroline Fréchette for answering all of my questions at weird times, day or night. Every writer dreams of the perfect cover and I'm eternally grateful to her for creating exactly what I imagined along with Dana Fradkin, the wonderful actor who brought it to life.

A special heartfelt thanks to my daughter Sarah who unwittingly made a great writing suggestion and now wants to legally change her name to "long suffering editor". And to my husband, David, who was always there to give me that extra push. Where would this book be without both of you?

Lastly, I'd like to acknowledge all the strangers in coffee shops and on the street who inadvertently made it into the world of my mind and eventually onto the page. Sorry for staring at you creepily, but it was all for a good cause.

AUTHOR'S NOTE

They say, write what you know. Does that mean if you haven't been on an alien space ship or lived in a post-apocalyptic society that you shouldn't write Science Fiction? What if you're not a thief or serial killer or a little old lady with a bonnet chasing some nefarious type around town? Can you write a mystery? That would make our fictional universe rather limited, and could make the art of writing sort of boring. So, I've always written about things I've never experienced.

That notion changed a few years ago after I was diagnosed with multiple sclerosis. I took a whole day to indulge in self-pity, then I picked up my life just where I'd left it. With time I did have to make minor adjustments to accommodate my changing mobility and continued doing the things I enjoyed, including travel.

However, when we planned our trip to Hawaii, I realized it wouldn't be as straightforward as travelling by car or train. So I contacted the MS Society here in Ottawa and they helped with all those pesky details that you don't think about, as well as putting me in touch with the MS Society in Hawaii. Since then I've flown to various destinations including Great Britain, San Francisco and Nevada to tour the Grand Canyon. I wasn't about to let a diagnosis slow me down or limit me.

That's when I began thinking that there might be something in that ancient bit of wisdom: write what you know. And so "Journey of a Thousand Steps" was born.

Some readers may assume that Naya is me. The only real similarity is I understand her physical and emotional feelings. I have tried running in the past, but I always hit the wall after a block, so I got a 10-speed and biked everywhere instead. As for being a computer genius, I frequently cry for help when I click on something and my computer's reaction is unexpected. Fortunately, now when I use my PVR to record a TV show, the flashbacks of the horror of trying to program my VCR — a time I like to call the dark ages — are now minimal.

One other similarity is that both Naya and I spent time at the Ottawa Hospital Rehabilitation Centre. In my case people were very helpful and nice. So please don't go looking for an airhead therapist named Tiffany, or a harsh nurse named Abigail. As for Helen — well, she's based on a friend who lost a leg to diabetes.

I would like to believe that if someone close is kidnapped, I'd risk everything to rescue them. Or... maybe just mortgage the house and hire an excellent private investigator.

Do you enjoy books set in Ottawa?
Check out this other Renaissance title!

The King in Darkness
Supernatural Suspense

Adam Godwinson, former priest, isn't sure what he believes in anymore. These days he deals in used books at a small store in Ottawa. But an old text, written in an unfamiliar language, is about to change that forever. Adam now finds himself the target of a powerful conspiracy. These shadowy figures, wielding abilities he can't understand, want to cleanse society of its sins – even if that means destroying it. Adam will have to figure out what he believes in to have a chance to save himself and the rest of the world.

http://renaissancebookpress.com/2015/04/22/the-king-in-darkness-evan-may/

If you enjoyed this book, you should check out this other Renaissance title!

The Admirer
Historical/Mystery/Romance

This city will ruin you. Just like it ruined your mother.

Rose Fraser has been given the opportunity of a lifetime: the chance to go to London as a debutante for the London season, as Viscountess Latimer's personal protégé. She is nervous yet excited at the idea. However, her excitement soon fades away when she starts receiving threats in the form of intricately folded, anonymous notes. Nerves turn to fear as the notes escalate. Feeling trapped, unable to go to the police, she turns to the only person she thinks can help her: her most serious suitor, private investigator James Grey. But will he uncover the truth before things take a turn for the worse?

http://renaissancebookpress.com/2013/10/26/theadmireraureliaosborne/

34372691R10112

Made in the USA
San Bernardino, CA
27 May 2016